Village of Secrets

Rowena was writhing on the rug, her skirt above her waist, her bare belly rising and falling as she breathed heavily. Laura's view was perfect. She couldn't believe what she was watching; what she had been invited to join in with. The French dominatrix Odile took Rory's cock in her rubber-gloved hands and expertly caressed him. Now Rowena was desperate, touching herself, waiting for the male presence inside her.

Laura was rubbing herself, too, unable to stop her excitement. She placed her fingers inside the split-crotch Edwardian knickers and knew that her release wouldn't be long in coming.

Village of Secrets

MERCEDES KELLY

BLACK
lace

Black Lace novels are sexual fantasies.
In real life, make sure you practise safe sex.

First published in 1999 by
Black Lace
Thames Wharf Studios,
Rainville Road, London W6 9HT

Typeset by SetSystems Ltd, Saffron Walden, Essex
Printed and bound by Mackays of Chatham PLC

ISBN 0 352 33344 8

Prologue:

A Funeral in the Village

*T*he little Cornish granite church was full of local people. Men's unaccompanied voices were raised in harmony, singing the old Cornish hymns. As the mourners filed out they spoke to Laura of her grandmother. She was moved to tears by the sympathy she received.

'You do resemble your mother, my cheel,' said an old man with a stick. 'Beauty she were.'

'You have grown away,' said another.

'Your grandmother was a wonderful woman, dear of her,' said another man.

'She will be sadly missed.'

Laura was the only family mourner apart from her Aunt Celia and Uncle John. At least she had good old Ethan there, and Anna, another Porthzelah friend.

Laura's parents had died in a mysterious and unexplained car crash at Doom Rock Point, near Newquay, when Laura was three. She had been brought up by Aunt Celia, her father's sister, in Devon, but had frequently returned for long visits to her beloved grandparents in Porthzelah. They buried her grandmother in the cemetery overlooking the sea, next to the graves of her husband and Laura's parents.

Laura had not thought about a wake.

Her gay friend, Ethan, took Laura back to his cottage to have a drink and some cake. Celia and John had already set off for Devon. The roads were icy and they wanted to get back before dark.

'Have a whisky, darl'. It was a lovely funeral.'

'Is it all right if I stay for Christmas? You are sure?'

'Of course it's all right. You know I love your company. We can curl up on the sofa and play Scrabble.'

Ethan's ginger cat stretched itself by the fire. Laura leant forward to stroke it.

'I could stay at the house. I'll go up the hill and have a good look at it tomorrow, if I can just stay here tonight.'

'Whatever makes you happy, darl'. You look gorgeous in black, did you know?'

'I have lots of black, Ethan. But I've never had to wear it to a funeral before.' She only vaguely remembered her parents' funeral. She had been a very small child and her grandparents had kept her from the sadness as much as they could. Her parents had lived with her in a police flat in the town, and her grandparents had been babysitting the night of the accident. All she did remember was the next morning: the dreadful wailing of her grandmother, like an animal caught in a metal trap.

'How's the glamorous work of magazines, then, Laura?'

'Fine, thanks. You know I'm freelancing now? Well, I've just had an idea accepted by *Health and You* magazine: a whole issue on sex.'

'Oh well, just ask me anything you don't already know,' said Ethan.

'Thanks, I will,' Laura laughed. 'It will mean proper money. Enough for me to take time off in Porthzelah for the whole summer, I hope. Shall we follow the carol singers on Christmas Eve? I always used to.'

'That would be lovely,' said Ethan.

Next day, Laura wandered up the hill to her grand-mother's house – her house now.

She lit the pilot light on the Rayburn and turned it up high. She opened curtains and windows and let in the fresh air. The house was smaller than she remembered. The attic room looked out over the town. A few boats bobbed at moorings in the harbour. She heard a voice in the far distance. Sounds travelled far up the bowl of the village. The sun shone bravely but the east wind was cold. She noticed that land was being cleared further up the hill.

She sat on the doorstep in the sunshine and drank a cup of coffee.

It was a large garden compared with most of the properties in Porthzelah. Her grandfather had been a keen gardener all his life. He had even grown their own vegetables, but the plot was overgrown now. She could sell the house and buy something bigger than her small flat in London. She daydreamed about it. But the idea of never being able to stay in Porthzelah again moved her to tears. And the spirit of her grandmother lived on in the fabric of the house. She couldn't sell.

She spent the next day, Christmas Eve, cleaning the house, washing down the white paintwork and tiles in the kitchen. Her grandmother had spent a long time in hospital before she died and the house had been neglected. She examined the wooden window frames and saw that they all needed attention. She made up a clean bed in her old room, the place she had slept as a child. There was no view of the sea here, but she could not yet bring herself to sleep in her grandmother's bed.

She ate with Ethan. They had a fish pie made from megrim sole and cod and prawns – a Christmas fishy treat before the overindulgence of turkey and ham.

'What are you up to, Ethan?' Laura asked over a Scrabble board and a bottle of red wine in the shabby comfort of Ethan's rented cottage.

'What do you mean, hon?'

'Well, you can't just give up teaching. What will you do?'

Ethan had been moaning about his teaching job for years and now he had decided to throw in the towel.

'I don't know yet. But life is too short to waste in a job you hate.'

'True, sweetie, but you can't do nothing. What will you live on?'

'I could do supply teaching. I could get a seasonal job as a barman or waiter, like most of the other unemployable men here.'

'You'd go barmy, doing that.'

'Yes, I suppose I would. I could be a smuggler, a pirate with a black eye patch and a bandana.' He giggled into his glass. 'Did you know that there is a smuggling ring here in town?'

'What? Are you serious? I haven't seen anything in the paper.'

'No, you wouldn't. But someone got locked up recently for selling stolen goods or something. One of the local fishermen. I'm sure he was part of an illegal ring of smugglers. There are lots of funny people here, I'd have you know. People aren't always what they seem.'

'Ethan, this doesn't sound very likely. Who was it? When? Perhaps I should do a story about it.'

'Can't remember, darling. Pour us another drink.' He placed all seven of his letters down to make his favourite word – gorgeous – and Laura threw up her hands in pretend horror.

'That's twelve thousand pounds you owe me,' said Ethan, grinning inanely.

After the game they went out into the cold night and found the carol singers. They were gathered, about seventy of them, in a courtyard near the harbour. Their resonant voices rang through the dark night. Heads appeared at windows and people called out 'Thank you!' and 'Happy Christmas!' Laura knew some of the hymns and carols from her childhood, but she did not recognise some of the more elaborate part songs. Late into the night the singers moved through the village, bringing joy and a feeling of peace with them. They made a point of singing under the windows of the old and infirm. When Laura went home at midnight, she was filled with a sort of happiness. She felt safe in the small narrow bed with tartan blankets tucked around her and a satin eiderdown that kept slipping off.

It had been like coming home.

Chapter One
The Sex Issue

EXTRA LARGE SEPTEMBER ISSUE WITH A TEN PAGE
PULL-OUT-AND-KEEP MANUAL ON SEX!
EVERYTHING YOU WANT TO KNOW BUT DIDN'T
DARE ASK. MAKING LOVE. TENDERNESS AND
UNDERSTANDING BETWEEN SEXUAL PARTNERS.
NORMAL AND ABNORMAL SEXUAL DEMANDS.

*B*ack in London, after a chilly Christmas, Laura was
back in the throes of work. It was as if Cornwall
did not exist. *Health and You* had decided to go ahead
with her idea for a special issue straight away, and it
fell to Laura to hire the photographer, cast the models
for the cover and inside spreads, and art-direct the
shots. She went through the head-sheets and model
books of the glamour agencies to choose a girl who
wouldn't mind appearing naked. It was difficult to
imagine them without make-up. A natural beauty was
what she needed. Most of the girls looked too raunchy.
Their tits were too big, their lips too pouting. Ideally,
she needed a couple: a good-looking couple who were
having a relationship, so they would look natural
together. Large breasts were out – they photograph

7

badly in certain positions. Small tits were more aesthetically desirable.

She narrowed the field down to three girls and called their agents to get them in to see her. The man was more difficult. She needed a good-looking man of normal height, normal inclinations and abnormal exhibitionism. Or anyway, someone who wouldn't mind showing his all to several thousand readers. The Z-cards, head-sheets and flyers of models littered her desk and floor. People wandered in and out of the small space she had been given in the open-plan office murmuring approval or otherwise of her choices. Eventually, Laura chose three men and organised their interviews for the same day as she saw the three girls. The girls were to come with no make-up.

There were to be at least six pictures: man and woman naked full-frontal, man and woman kissing, man and woman embracing, man and woman in various sexual congress positions.

The first girl would only 'do it' with her boyfriend. She showed Laura a photograph – he was a shaven-headed lout with earrings, a pierced nose and a tattooed neck. The second girl was much thinner than she looked in her portfolio photographs. Her eyes glowed with an unnatural brightness and she sniffed and scratched her arms.

The third girl, Stella, was blonde, slender and pretty, a twenty-year-old Swedish type with long straight hair, smallish breasts and long legs. She didn't object to appearing naked, and looked good without make-up. She had an all-over tan. Her book was full of flattering semi-naked pictures. She was very popular with the Japanese market. She was perfect; her boyfriend was 55 and definitely not willing to appear naked with her in photographs, even if Laura had wanted him to, which she didn't.

Stella was still in the office when the male models

8

began to arrive. She knew the first one, Guy, from recent assignments in Miami and Europe. He was a hunky, golden-haired, six-foot Aussie who worked out, rode horses and looked healthy and fit. They seemed to get on well and were not averse to getting into a clinch for art's sake. Laura was never turned on by male models: their good looks were too plastic for her taste – too finished and perfect. But she could certainly appreciate the work that had gone into their making – the discipline of hard exercise and expensive orthodontistry. The others arrived and showed her portfolios full of smouldering looks and oiled bodies, boxer shorts and fitness clothes.

All three men were apprehensive about the full-frontal shot. One had a hairy stomach. Did he have a hairy bottom, too? She thanked them all and said she would be in touch with their agents. She immediately phoned Guy's and Stella's agencies and booked them.

Guy and Stella smoked incessantly. Wrapped only in loose dressing gowns, so that no unsightly marks would spoil their bodies, they chatted in the dressing room as the make-up person gave Stella the 'natural' look and the hairdresser put her long tresses into large heated rollers.

Paul, the photographer, opened an icy bottle of Vinho Verde and sat with Laura in the studio, while she sketched the picture ideas that had been decided on. The studio was heated to a comfortable eighty degrees – comfortable, that is, if you were naked. The silken tones of Frank Sinatra filled the room. He had died recently and suddenly everyone wanted to hear his voice.

'So, first shot: man and woman, standing, facing camera.'

Stella gave her dressing gown to Laura and stood, unabashed and gloriously bare. Her blonde hair hung

9

in waves to her breasts, and delicately wound in tendrils around her pale flat nipples. Her slit was visible through the darker shade of pale of her sparse pubic hair.

'OK, Guy. Your turn.'

Laura took the towelling gown from the young Australian, and walked back to the camera. She turned and looked at the couple standing on the roll of white paper which curled under them to give a neutral background to the first shot. Guy had a good face: rugged but not too handsome. It was too young to look lived-in, but he had a humorous mouth. His body was good – not as overdeveloped as those of many male models. His circumcised cock hung heavily, straight down over his plump balls. Thick golden hair framed this vision of health and fitness. He looked like a Greek god or a modern-day Tarzan. However, he didn't have an all-over tan.

'Um, yes, very nice, good, good.' Paul turned to Laura. 'What do you think?'

'Guy – back to the dressing room, please.'

The make-up artist and hairdresser had gone off to another assignment, as there hadn't seemed to be much point in their staying for the shoot. Stella could patch up her own make-up if necessary and Laura could brush her hair.

'Here's the fake tan. Can you manage?' said Laura, handing him the bottle.

Guy stood in front of the full-length mirror and rubbed the liquid into his thighs and stomach, painting in the pale patch left by his shorts. Laura tried not to watch too closely as his heavy cock leapt up and down and waved at her.

'Do you mind doing my backside?' he said, giving her his boy-next-door smile and turning his buttocks to her. She took the bottle of liquid with trembling hands and began smoothing the fake tan into the pale skin. She looked round his body into the mirror and saw the

10

heavy pink penis flicker and lift. It began to grow. She rubbed rhythmically, squeezing more liquid on to his muscular white buttocks.

'Hey, I can't go in front of the camera in this state,' said Guy. He grabbed her hands and pulled them round to his cock. She was behind him still, her hands over his lengthening sex, his hands over hers. She watched herself in the mirror. Her small hands could not hide his bigness – it grew and throbbed inside her fingers. She pressed up against him, feeling his nakedness through her thin cotton dress. Wetness and warmth filled her knickers. He came very quickly and without much noise, into her palms. His sperm spurted on to the mirror like liquid from a faulty garden hose.

'That'll do it. Good on ya, thanks Laura.' Guy grinned and washed his still-erect cock at the wash basin.

'You're drinking a lot of wine today, Laura, are you all right?' asked Paul.

'Just a bit warm.'

The sixth shot was the simulated intercourse picture. Laura directed the action. Guy was lying down, Stella on top of him, sitting on his cock – or pretending to do so. It was difficult to see what was happening, but it looked fun. Her long wavy hair hung over her lowered face and on to his chest. They were beautiful. Their perfect bodies met and rejoiced in each other. Their hands intertwined. Guy whispered and smiled at Stella. Her small, round breasts shook as she laughed. Her head and neck arched backward and her glorious hair fell like a waterfall on to her slender back. Her nipples were hard nubs.

Laura's knickers were very wet.

That evening, Laura showered and poured herself a whisky. She sat in front of the television and watched the news. Her mind wandered back to the photo session and she smiled to herself.

Next day, Paul brought in the transparencies of the shoot. They looked great. Laura and the editor were pleased with the results. Her editor remarked on the extent of Guy's all-over tan: 'Mm. It seems to have included his private parts, too. Still, I don't suppose the readers will complain.'

Chapter Two

The Expert

June had arrived and London was looking its best. The parks were greening; roses grew on trellises in leafy suburbs. Elderflowers blossomed in Laura's little garden and she determined to find time to make elderflower champagne, just like her grandmother had. She remembered huge white flower heads steeping in large bowls of sugared water. Laura loved early summer. She spent the first Saturday afternoon of the month pottering on her balcony, having spent a small fortune on geraniums that morning at a nursery.

It was only June but already text was needed for the September special issue on sex. Laura needed a medic to write some of the serious stuff. She would do the fillers and captions and introduction. She looked up in the files all the people who had written for them before on the subject. There was Kali Pagean – but she was too frivolous. They needed a professional sex expert. The magazine's features editor gave her the number of a man she had met at a party recently. She said he was nice and ordinary, and would lend their feature authenticity.

Dr Rosen's secretary answered the phone.

'Yes, please hold, I'll put you through.'

'Hello! You don't know me. My name's Laura Mackay and I work for *Health and You* magazine. Joanna Andrews gave me your name. She says you could write us a piece about sex therapy. Is that right? I wonder if I could come and meet you and have a chat about what you do, exactly.'

A softly modulated Oxbridge voice purred, 'Of course,' and she noted the time of their appointment in her Filofax.

The dreary London hospital looked dismal in the June drizzle, but fresh green leaves dripped prettily from the plane trees in the street on to sodden Londoners. The lift took her to the third floor and she followed arrows to the Family Therapy Clinic. She knocked on the door and went in. The secretary smiled and waved her through to a small inner room. She knocked again and the warm, friendly voice she recognised from the telephone call said, 'Yes, come in.'

'Dr Rosen, hello, I'm Laura Mackay.'

'Yes, hello! Do sit down.'

They sat either side of his desk and she felt like a patient with a problem. She giggled nervously.

He leant forward towards her, and looked over tortoiseshell half-glasses into her eyes. His brown-flecked grey eyes gazed at her steadily. His face was lopsided and mobile. His very thick, curly hair was cut short. His large ears wiggled when he smiled, which he did now – with devastating results.

Laura gulped.

Something had hit her in the pit of the stomach. She tried to speak, but only a strangled 'Er, Er' came out. She felt a blush spreading across her face and neck.

'Are you all right?'

'Oh, yes, fine, fine. Sorry, I, er, I'm fine.' She was

14

certain her quick wit and intelligent conversation impressed him.

The secretary appeared with coffee and Laura promptly spilt it all over her short grey DKNY dress. This was a new experience for Laura – she was usually so cool and in control. She hated flirts and refused to be a competitor in the so-called war of the sexes. She never usually had problems with men. If she liked a man she let him know, or if a man liked her and she wasn't interested, she let it be known in a civil manner. She would never deliberately hurt anyone's feelings. But here she was having the strangest of sensations. She felt sick, then elated, and then sick again. She had no idea how to behave. Her mind went blank. Bells rang in her ears. It was the telephone.

Dr Rosen spoke quietly and firmly into the telephone, replaced it on the receiver, and smiled his devastating lopsided grin at the flustered young woman who was mopping at her very short skirt with a Jeycloth.

'You have a problem?'

'Not until now.'

They sat side by side in the dim lounge bar of the pub nearest to the hospital. She had insisted he come out of the hospital to talk. She felt less in awe of him out of his element.

'As you know, Dr Rosen, we need someone to write two thousand words on sex for a special September issue, and we wondered if you would do it. There's only £200 in it, I'm afraid.'

'£200? I'll do it.'

Dr Jerry Rosen was younger than he looked, about twenty-eight, and had only recently qualified. He was staying in an absent friend's flat in Parliament Hill and he was separated from his wife of three years. He had no children. Laura managed somehow to elicit all this while they chatted about the forthcoming issue. At least her investigative powers hadn't failed her completely.

He was six-footish, thinnish and rangy, with nervous, dark, hairy hands like tarantulas. God, she wanted those hands to pounce on her! She gazed, hypnotised, at the smooth, long head that ended in that incredibly sexy lopsided jaw. When he smiled, as he did with disarming regularity, white lines fanned from the corners of his laughing eyes, and furrowed the smooth tanned face. He had discarded his white coat for a pale-brown tweed jacket worn over a dark-blue shirt and khaki trousers, while his large feet were encased in leather brogues.

'I'm not a sex expert, you know. I do have a certain interest in the subject, and I could certainly write two thousand words for your magazine, but I wouldn't like to get the job on false pretences. I'm just an ordinary medic.'

'Oh, you are not ordinary – I mean, I'm sure you'll do it beautifully,' said the besotted Laura, spilling lager over herself.

Ten days later he telephoned the magazine and talked to Laura. He said he wanted to check on one or two things and asked if she could meet him for dinner. She was as nervous as a teenager. Her extensive wardrobe was turned inside out for the right thing to wear. Clothes were strewn all over the floor of her bedroom. She tried a white T-shirt and blue jeans. She tried the navy-and-white flower-print French Resistance dress. She tried the grey pinstripe trouser suit. He had seen her DKNY mini dress once already, so she couldn't wear that, and anyway, she hadn't been able to remove the coffee stains. Her strappy little black dress was at the dry-cleaner's. Her hair wouldn't lie flat, and her hands shook so much she kept smudging her nail varnish.

The red Lycra dress! Of course! It was short, just

16

covering her thighs, with a high neck and long, tight sleeves. Her throat above the close-fitting neck was white and smooth. She wore no jewellery, but her bright-red painted lips were like rubies on her small pale face. Her dark cropped hair shone like a cat's, and her slanted golden eyes were carefully painted to accentuate her feline looks. Her fingernails were exactly the same tone as the dress. She wore nearly-black stockings and black suede shoes.

At eight, exactly, the doorbell rang. Laura opened the door. She tripped on the unaccustomed high heels, and recovered herself.

He was wearing beige cotton chinos and an indigo shirt. No tie. His eyes were whisky brown. She could tell by the look in his eyes that the red dress was a success.

'Do you mind if we have a Greek meal?' he asked. 'I've recently returned from the Peloponnese and I feel like a reminder.'

'Of course not. I haven't had a Greek meal for ages.'

After a glass of Ouzo, two bottles of resinous Greek wine and a marvellously wholesome meal of taramasalata, houmous, squid and roast lamb, they had a fearsomely strong coffee and a shot of Metaxa brandy, sat back in their seats and looked at each other with satisfaction. Laura hadn't spilled a thing.

'Shall I tell you what your dress says to me – as a psychiatrist?'

'All right.'

'It says, "This woman wants to be thought a very sexy lady."'

'Does it?'

'Mmm. Shall I tell you what it says to me as a man?'

'All right.'

'It says, "This is a very sexy lady."'

Jerry Rosen leant forward and looked over his tortoiseshell glasses into her blushing face.

'Would you like to come home with me and find out if your hypothesis is correct?' she whispered.

'Oh, yes, please.'

Chapter Three

Doctor

A little later she thought that maybe she shouldn't have been so eager, but she couldn't help herself. He wasn't obviously good-looking but he radiated sensuality and humour. She found him irresistibly sexy. He was a cross between George Clooney and Daniel Day Lewis, with a lopsided, mobile face and a generous mouth. His large ears wiggled when he spoke, and he smiled with his eyes.

Her hands were in his thick dark hair. His head nuzzled between her spread thighs. She had never felt anything like it – the silkiness of his curls caressing her sensitive skin. He held her buttocks with his tarantula-like hands, squeezing and pinching the inflamed flesh as she sat on the edge of her bed and he knelt between her legs. Her legs wrapped round his head and she felt his teeth nibbling her sex lips and his long tongue insinuating itself into the folds of her labia. He pulled her on to his face, his nose pressing against her pelvic bone, his lips sucking and kissing her clitoris.

He was tender and urgent in his movements – now rough and fierce, nearly squeezing the breath from her small body, now gentle and subtle with featherlike touches that caused her to shiver. Did Jewish men have more pheromones than other men? Whatever it was that emanated from this man it worked on Laura's senses, heightening them to intensity and making her hungry for more.

Her red dress was round her waist, exposing stocking tops, a black suspender belt and inches of white flesh. Her black lace panties were on the bedside lampshade, lending a decadent dimness to the room. She was remembering him behind his desk, in his white coat, the stethoscope hanging from his pocket, smiling at her over his tortoiseshell glasses. Now he was between her legs, sucking noisily at her love juices. His head was held between her red-nailed fingers, and he licked like an over-friendly Labrador as she climaxed. 'Oh, oh, oh, doctor! That feels much better.'

He laughed.

He was still wearing most of his clothes. She pulled at his shirt buttons and revealed his strong long torso. Dark hairs surrounded his nipples. She released the tan leather belt and undid the cotton gabardine trousers. He tore them off and stood over her. His cock was peeping over the top of fine jersey-cotton jockey shorts that fitted him like a soft glove. The bulge was authoritative and lengthy.

'Come here,' she whispered, her eyes glued to the twitching shorts. Her hands touched the hidden penis. He tried to remove his shorts but she said, 'No, let me do that.' She felt the extent of his penis through the soft material. The erection was solid, like an iron rod. The wet tip was trapped at the waistband. She insinuated the fingertips of both hands into the elasticised band and held the bulbous head. It was a miniature copy of his other head: smooth, long and damply glistening. And as she explored downward along the shaft, she realised with an excited shudder that his cock was even more like his head – subtly curved into an erotic crescent, a stiff, fleshy banana. She ripped off the shorts and his interestingly shaped member curved up and away from her. Her fascinated gaze embarrassed him and he covered himself with the sheet.

'But it's wonderful,' she said. 'Let me see you.'

He knelt before her and her pink tongue flickered over the shiny slit. She licked the juice that seeped from the little hole on the exposed mushroom head and stroked firmly. His penis was not too big for her mouth, but because of its slight curvature it was difficult to accommodate. She suckled and licked, holding his large smooth balls and squeezing them. His long, curved column was hard as rock. She felt it pulsating in her mouth. She stopped the intimate caress and held the quivering cock firmly at the base until he had regained control over his impending orgasm. They stood close; her head came to his shoulders. He lifted her dress over her head and kissed her hard nipples.

'Like bullets,' he said.

She shivered as he lifted her up into his arms and carried her, still wearing her suspender belt and stockings, to the bed.

She bent her knees so they were up by her chin and offered her sex to his long fingers. Her mouth full of salty flavours from his sex, she kissed his wide, generous lips, and stroked his hair. His fingers examined her expertly, parting the slippery sex lips and rubbing his palm over her entire vulva, before inserting a long finger into her and performing a deep penetration. She felt like a naughty child playing doctors. She raised her plump mound to his sweetly pumping fingers and felt the pressure of his wide palm on her clitoris. She came, moaning into his ear.

He raised her straightened legs over his shoulders and knelt before her, holding her by the thighs and buttocks, his smooth doctor's fingers pressing into her flesh, marking it. His curved cock bounced and pressed against her sex, and divided the wet, slippery lips. She drew in her breath as the long kinked penis slid into her, touching every part of her sex, with extra pressure from the outside curve. It was as if there were two men inside her, doing things to her that she had never experienced before. She watched the pink column dart in and out of her, the sticky tip leaving globules of love juice on the curly dark hair of her swollen mound. Her breathing became short and laboured, and her mouth opened wide. Her head thrown back, pelvis pushed forward to meet his powerful thrusts, she panted and moaned.

His penis grew harder. She knew he was ready to explode into her. She abandoned herself to the ultimate fuck. Like an animal on heat, she pumped and writhed, bucked and twisted, rose and fell, her legs wrapped round his smooth, lovely head. His face lost its humour, the lips drawn back over clenched teeth. His thrusts suddenly accelerated and, as she felt the waves of an endless orgasm overwhelm her, he cried out.

Later, she held the soft, flaccid flesh and moulded gently. She had always loved the feel of a soft penis. She also loved to feel it become fat in her sly fingers, but first she wanted to lick and suckle the malleable fruit before it became engorged. Her mouth softly sucked. Her teeth grazed the warm flesh. Her flicking tongue darted like a viper. She ordered him not to get an erection. She wanted him soft. But the fruit grew in her mouth and filled it, pressing on the roof of her mouth and against her teeth. She released it.

He lifted her on top of him, so she was lying with her back pressed against the length of his front, her legs together. His penis curved up into the cleft of her buttocks and the weight of her body pressed it wonderfully. She writhed and gyrated slowly like a snake, and her arse caressed his cock. Her legs opened into scissors and she lifted her buttocks to release his cock. It swept up across her vagina, and juices mingled on her pubic hair. With both hands she felt the fatness of his cock and the hardness, the iron hardness, of the underneath curve.

'I love your curved cock,' said Laura. She held it high and dropped it on to her genitals, a firm, soft hammer on her swollen flesh. She repeated the movement again and again, beating herself with his penis. It was delightful torture.

His long fingers were free to stroke and fondle her wetness. Her pelvis lifted to meet his touch. Her buttocks writhed on his stomach and she lay open to him, to his insinuating, curved cock and his doctor's fingers, which opened her wide and examined her thoroughly. She sucked her juices from his fingers, which she suckled as if they were little penises, and felt the bigness of her nipples.

They explored the unknown territories of each other's body, felt the satin flesh, tasted the honey of lust, and were deafened by moans of love. They were the only two people in the world. They ate each other, drank each other, became each other.

'Was that nice?' he asked.

'No, it was terrible! Do it again.'

Chapter Four
Total Nudity

*L*aura had always been proud of her thick bush of dark pubic hair. But lately she had wanted a change. At first she simply trimmed her pubic hair short, and discovered that sensations were magnified. The feel of her underwear against her pubic mound was deliciously erotic. The silk of her knickers caressed her secretly.

Jerry admired her short-trimmed bush and asked if she had ever shaved her pubic hair completely.

'No, I haven't. Would you like to do it for me?'

'Yes, please,' he said, grinning widely.

After a leisurely Sunday lunch of chicken and tarragon with a good bottle of Chardonnay they went to bed and he set to work with scissors, razor and cream, a bowl of hot soapy water and a large bath towel.

Laura trusted him absolutely not to hurt her. If she hadn't felt like that about him, she couldn't have let him come near her with the razor. He placed a large towel on the bed. He sponged her entire pubic area, then smeared the shaving cream over her dark mass of hair. She lay flat, with legs slightly apart and raised. He parted them wider to get into the folds and soaped everywhere. She was excited at the nearness of his face

24

to her sex and the novelty of the operation. Vague erotic memories of first sexual experience flooded her mind – fingers and naive fumbling. His eyes were alight with desire. His soft, lovely mouth almost snarled with sensuality. The cold blade caressed her mount of Venus and ploughed furrows through the dark harvest of her hair. He lifted her buttocks to shave between her sex and her anus.

The lips were the most difficult and needed a sure, steady hand, though both of his shook at the delicacy of the operation. To finish, they took a hot bath, which caused her to sting and squeal. He dried her in a large towel, carefully dried the bare mound of newly exposed flesh and smeared Vaseline to soothe the smarting.

'How do I look?' asked Laura.

He held her tightly against his damp, hard body and kissed her almost brutally. He lifted her bodily and pressed his pelvis against her exposed slit. His penis was ready to explore this wonderfully bare sex.

She suddenly felt very vulnerable, as if she were a young girl being touched by a big man, and she could do nothing about it, he was so much stronger than she was. She knew he shouldn't be doing these things to her, but she liked it too much to try and stop him.

His fingers were all over her and inside her and her bare sex was hidden in his big hands. He rubbed hard on her naked mound and she strained against his hands. He carried her, her legs around his waist, to the bed. Her hands were above her head, surrendering to him. He moved his hard cock up and down over her slit, pouring baby oil on to himself so that his cock was silky, wetly smooth like nothing else could be. It was exquisite! All sensations were multiplied, as if she were drugged with an aphrodisiac. The slightest, delicate, featherlike touch was a shock to her heightened senses.

She came suddenly, like an explosion in slow motion. She watched as if it was happening to someone else. She turned her head away as if she was a young girl ashamed of what was happening to her, unable to cope with the mixed sensations and emotions.

The sight of her bare slit with the strong hands and swollen cock juicily squeezing across it was exciting her again, even as her first orgasm was fading. Now he pushed two pillows under her buttocks so her pelvis thrust upward and he knelt facing her. His head went down to her naked, immature-looking fanny and he delicately licked it like a cat drinking milk. The lovely sight of his head buried between her legs and his tongue coming in and out of her bare pussy was too much. She pushed his head away and begged him to put his cock inside her.

He pulled her legs over his shoulders and held her thighs fiercely as he went into her. His eyes were squeezed tight shut and his mouth twisted in pleasure. He always looked most unhappy when he felt the most pleasure. That position was fatal to him – she knew. It was the ultimate in sexiness. And for her too, the position was just right: the pressures inside her, his cock hitting just the right place, his balls banging against her bare fanny, her anus stimulated by his gripping fingers. She came again as he came. For both of them it was a long, noisy orgasm.

He arrived late one night, wearing his white doctor's coat. She insisted he wear fine rubber gloves and examine her genitals. She wanted him to push his latex-enclosed fingers up the side of her loose-legged French knickers, and into her damp folds of flesh. Pretending she was his patient, she lay immobile, eyes chastely closed while he played with her sex and pushed a finger into her puckered anus.

She lifted his white coat and pressed firmly on the curved bulge beneath his fine cotton trousers. He obligingly undid the zip and loosened his clothing, so she had access to his warm thickening member. She drew him closer and lifted her head to lick the tip of his sex. Her neck curved, her soft lips opened, and her small sharp teeth glittered.

Her moist vulva was swelling and pulsating, wanting his cool touch. His hands were surrounding her sex, moulding the soft flesh, kneading the labia between his palms. The pressure of his very smooth cool hands caused her clitoris to grow and tingle. Her excitement was increased by the idea of the hands being those of a doctor. She was a beautiful patient under her doctor's power. He could do what he liked with her.

His latex-encased fingers flicked her nipples and he leant over her and licked and sucked at the dark peaks, drew them into his lopsided mouth and made them large and erect. She pulled at her knickers with her free hand, drawing the silk into her cleft, pulling it tight so she was split in two down the middle. His fingers flicked at her clitoris and she came in a rush.

The young doctor's penis was in an interesting state of pulsating stiffness, the curve more obvious as the penis grew and fattened. He helped tighten the silk of her knickers into her cleft, drawing it back and forth over the dark folds of swollen flesh, while her flowing white juices smeared and wet the material. Her mouth enclosed his penis and sucked on the warm flesh, drawing the skin up and over the top and down again to the base. She fondled his balls and stroked the root of his cock behind them. Pressing it between her fingers, she sucked his delicious cock in time with her stroking.

His moans began; he thrust his loins towards her face, and pressed her small dark head into his thighs. She sucked and fondled and concentrated utterly on his satisfaction, and he kept the knickers sawing into her vulva, his knuckles banging nicely on her clitoris. They came like this, his cock deep in her throat, his latex gloves wrapped in her knickers and covered in her juice.

They undressed completely and got into the bed and held each other in grateful arms. This aftermath of lovemaking was wonderful. She felt safe in his quietness and gentleness. Laura realised that she was in love with this man. Her heart pounded with fear and joy.

Inevitably, they started spending more time together. When he was not on duty at the hospital on Saturdays they sometimes went to Camden Passage and looked at the antiques. Their taste was very similar. He bought her a nineteenth-century pink lustre bowl. She bought him a first edition Wilfred Owen. They read poetry to each other in bed. She felt safe and loved. He was everything she had ever wanted in a man. She never asked him about his wife, noting his unease when she had been mentioned. He did not offer any information about her and Laura wanted to pretend she had never existed. She hoped she would just disappear from his life.

All she knew was that his wife was still living in the flat they owned and Jerry had been able to borrow his friend Max's flat while he was working in Australia.

'You have never invited me to your place, do you realise?' she said one night.

'I'll put that right soon, sweetie, but it is very grand. It isn't me. He's a strange bloke, is Max.'

'I can put up with grand and strange. Try me. Anyway, what do you mean by strange?'

'Well, he has some pretty strong videos and there's a collection of spanking magazines. And I get lots of phone calls from women who seem to think I'm him.'

'Really? He sounds interesting.'

Two days later, he rang. 'Laura? Jerry. Wondered if you wanted to come over this evening?'

Straight to the point. No messing about with niceties like 'How are you?' Laura smiled at the telephone.

'I'd love to. See you soon.'

Laura looked at herself in the long mirror in her bedroom. She was thirty years old, slender and small, with glossy short dark hair. She looked ruefully at her skin and decided she needed a good facial, but on the whole she was not too unhappy at what she saw.

She took off her old grey marl Lonsdale tracksuit and chose black silk knickers with loose legs, a brown-and-black silk lace bra, black stockings and a brown silk suspender belt. She put her tracksuit on over the top and slipped on a pair of canvas sneakers. There was no point in dressing up – Jerry was only interested in her undressed, though she knew from experience that even he would appreciate her choice of erotic underwear.

She drove to Parliament Hill in ten minutes. She parked in the secure underground car park and spoke into the door phone. A click and she was inside the block of flats. She moved quickly up the stairs and on to the second floor across polished wood floors. Potted plants sat at junctions on the stairs and in the lobby. It was a luxuriously appointed block overlooking the Heath. Jerry's door was ajar and she walked in.

Jerry greeted her warmly. He was naked, his semi-erect cock curved on his slender muscular thigh.

'Bath's ready,' he said. 'Get 'em off.'

She laughed and removed her tracksuit and sneakers. He admired her underwear.

'Mm, you look as delicious as usual, Laura, sweetie.' He tweaked her nipples gently through the softness of silk and pressed his swelling penis up against her belly, crouching to reach her.

She felt an immediate stir of desire. He steered her into the bathroom. The bath was large enough for both of them and the water was deep and hot. He poured some lemon oil into the water and stepped in. She

29

placed her underclothes on a rail and stepped in with him. She sat up against him between his legs and he soaped her breasts and kissed her shoulders and arms. She leant back and felt his cock hard against her buttocks. He soaped her belly and thighs and slipped fingers into her.

'It's like dipping my fingers in hot candle wax,' he chuckled.

'My turn,' she said, and he pushed her away and she sat opposite him at the other end of the bath. She took one of his feet and started to massage it with soapy fingers. His feet were rather beautiful. Strong, broad, not misshapen at all: his toes were straight and his heels and ankles well made. She soaped the other foot and he groaned in pleasure and nearly went to sleep. His powerful calves were kneaded and rubbed and she felt the knots disappear. His muscles relaxed and softened. She drew her fingers up his legs and towards his scrotum, where she lazily stroked and fondled the loose sacs. His cock was flaccid, floating like a bobbing worm, white in the bluish water. She ignored it. Jerry liked to wait. He leant towards her and kissed her cheek. They got out of the bath and he cleaned his teeth at one of the basins. She oiled her legs and arms lightly from one of the expensive oils that sat on a shelf, and then she put on her suspender belt, stockings, knickers and bra again.

He sat on one of the three black leather sofas and drank Coke from a can.

'I'm hungry, Jerry. You never feed me,' she grumbled, pacing up and down in front of him, half-naked, her buttocks swaying. She noticed the many silver-framed photographs of a beautiful black girl. In one picture the girl was kissing another woman.

'Who are they?' she asked.

'Max's wife and a friend.'

'Very friendly friend,' said Laura. 'Where's my dinner?'

'I'm only hungry for your delicious pussy, sweetie.'

She sighed, and gave up nagging him. Luckily, she'd had a proper lunch for once.

'Get over here, Laura, and stop moaning. You know I can't abide a complaining female. I'll have to chastise you for that.'

She noticed that the pile of magazines on the pink granite coffee table were all to do with flagellation and spanking. She threw herself down on the sofa next to him and held off his hands.

'Let's look at these,' she said. She picked up the top magazine from the pile and flicked through the pages.

'Wow! Look at that cock!' A young black man was spanking a slender blonde girl – it looked very like Stella, the model Laura had used for the sex issue. His huge blue-black erection was shining with oil. He held it with one hand and spanked the girl with the other. She was bent over a leather stool. Laura felt very wet.

'That's enough visual stimulation for you, my girl, look at your nipples! I shall definitely spank you. Come here.'

'Not fair!' She leapt up and pretended to run from him. He rose and chased her around the large, carpeted room, caught her from behind and threw her over the end of the nearest sofa. Her bottom was upended and he brought a large hand down firmly on one pink buttock.

'Ouch!'

'You're a naughty, naughty girl! You shall have six of the best.' He spanked her thoroughly and she felt herself getting wetter and warmer. His hand insinuated itself between her open buttocks and slapped her swollen pubis. She moaned in pleasure.

'Your bottom is very red and round and I am going

31

to spank you some more, because you shouldn't be enjoying it. You are naughty, naughty, naughty.'

She knew he was holding himself, rubbing his cock as he spanked her. He did not finish her off yet. He dragged her to his low, six-foot wide bed and threw her on to it, bottom up.

'Kneel!' he ordered her, and she knelt, her breasts hanging, her bottom high. He removed her knickers with one swift tug and he undid her bra so that it fell off over her arms. Now she wore only the suspender belt and stockings. The silk cut into her hips and the fasteners on the suspenders dug into her thighs. She wriggled her bottom at him.

'No, no, no! That's very naughty.' He sighed and she felt his warm sperm softly hit her buttocks and run down her thighs.

'Come to bed and cuddle,' she suggested.

He slept for a while and she rested by his side. He stirred as her fondling fingers wrapped around his flaccid cock and drew the blood into it with her insisting strokes. He turned over and kissed her roughly.

'Want some more?'

'Mm, please, Jerry.' She sat on his belly and admired the taut masculinity of him. His limbs were clean, hard. His chest was not too hairy. His thighs were rock hard. He lay there passively while she stroked his balls and rubbed herself on his cock. She took it in both hands and rubbed herself up and down, feeling the soft silky rod become hard. It grew in her hands – the magic that always made her wet – and she pressed herself on to him. He thrust upward and she rode him to her own climax. He came too, his orgasm triggered by hers.

'Do you know what, Laura?' He was seeing her to the door.

'What?'

'You are the only woman I have ever met who has not wanted something from me.'

'See you, Jerry.' She stood on tiptoe to kiss his smooth lips and stroked his chin.

Laura had become eroticised by the rough caresses of her doctor lover. She began to fantasise about spanking. She wanted him to hurt her more. She trusted him not to really harm her; she simply wanted to feel the twin pleasures of pain and desire. They had repeated the spanking episode several times. She enjoyed looking at the photographs in Max's magazines. One particular image excited her tremendously. A man was whipping a woman's upturned arse, and she was bent over and licking a second woman's sex. The man was fully dressed except that his erection stuck out from his trousers and he held it. Both women were naked. The expression on the face of the woman who was being licked and sucked was ecstatic. Laura felt that she would enjoy being either of the women – the whipped one who was sucking the other woman, especially.

'How do you fancy that scenario?' she asked Jerry.

'I don't suppose I would say no, given the opportunity,' he said, grinning wickedly.

Next time they went to Camden Passage she found him another present. It was an antique leather riding crop, very beautifully made, with a plaited leather loop at one end and a silver handle.

'But I don't ride,' he said as he unwrapped it that evening after dinner in his flat.

'Yes you do.' She put her tongue in his mouth and wriggled it lasciviously. He held her tight and his cock thickened under his corduroy trousers.

'You can try it on me if you like.' She offered her buttocks.

'You naughty girl – you aren't wearing any knickers! I should horsewhip you.'

She ran from him and he chased her, pretending he was on a horse, galloping around the huge expanse of the borrowed flat. He caught her and laid into her buttocks, lifting her skirt and holding her down. She yelled as the leather cut her.

'Are you all right?'

'Yes, yes, do it again!'

Later, when Jerry was in the bathroom and Laura was languishing on a sofa in a towelling dressing gown, the phone rang.

'Hi! This is Elizabeth. Is Max there?' said an American voice.

'Max is away for some time, I'm afraid. Can I take a message?'

'No, it's OK, only I think I left something there last time I was over. I'm only here for a few days from LA. I was wondering if I could come and find it.'

'Well, I suppose it would be all right. Are you in London now?'

'Yeah, I'm at Hampstead tube station.'

'Oh, well, you'd better come over, then. I'm sure it'll be all right.'

'Thanks a lot. See you in a few minutes. I'll get a cab over.'

Laura put the phone down.

Jerry came naked out of the bathroom and hugged her briefly. 'Shall I feed you now?' he said.

'Well, actually, we are about to have a visitor. A friend of Max's is coming to look for something she left here. She'll be here any minute.'

'I'd better put something on, then.' He disappeared into the bathroom and the door bell sounded.

Laura put a hand through her dishevelled hair and opened the door. A stunning tall black woman in ankle boots with four-inch heels stood outside. Her slim figure was defined by a red leather suit: a short skirt that came to mid-thigh, and a fitted leather jacket. Her legs reached her armpits – or looked like they did.

'Hello, you must be Elizabeth. Come in. I'm Laura.'

She was overwhelmed at the sight of the very sexy black woman, who strode into the room and looked around.

'Would you like a drink? Whisky, wine?'

'Yeah, thanks, Scotch on the rocks.'

Laura poured drinks and handed the woman hers.

'Thanks.' She sat down on one of the sofas, her leather skirt rasping on the leather upholstery. Elizabeth had a small, round head defined by the extremely short hair and large gold loop earrings. Her wide mouth smiled and showed glistening teeth. Her breasts were round and swelled from under the red leather jacket, which had somehow come undone to reveal a deep cleavage.

Laura felt very underdressed in the white towelling dressing gown.

'I hope I haven't interrupted anything?' The LA drawl was seductive and she looked hard at Laura's legs, which had slipped out of the dressing gown as she sat on the opposite sofa.

'No, not really.'

'Not really? Does that mean yes? Well, don't let me hinder you. Perhaps I can even lend a hand?'

'Er . . .' Laura was flustered and folded one leg over the other.

'You are so pretty, honey.' Suddenly Elizabeth was on the floor in front of Laura and had lifted the towelling gown away from her thighs. Laura didn't know what to do. She was paralysed by the suddenness of the sexual advance. Elizabeth's long brown fingers caressed her white thighs and drew them apart. Her lips found Laura's and Laura swooned.

The American woman slid her hands over Laura's nipples as they hardened and she squeezed the small, round breasts.

'You are more beautiful than Max's wife. Do you eat pussy?'

'What?'

35

'Do you eat pussy?'

'I don't . . . I haven't . . .'

'Ah, well, honey, there's always a first time.' Elizabeth's tongue had somehow found its way down Laura's belly and had slid into her slit. Laura was overwhelmed at the intensity of her sensations. She opened her eyes to see a rampant Jerry standing behind the black girl. His cock was in his hand. Elizabeth was bent low over the prone form of Laura, whose legs were wide and welcoming. Laura nodded at him and he lifted the leather skirt up over Elizabeth's thighs and buttocks, revealing what Laura had guessed – that she wore no panties. Elizabeth glanced once over her shoulder, smiled, and went back to her tender ministrations.

He caressed the brown skin. She wiggled her arse at him.

'Don't you think she needs a spanking, Jerry, for what she is doing to me?'

He needed no other urging. His cock beat on her buttocks. Laura came as the female tongue searched and found her erect clitoris. She moved to one side and started to undress the black girl. The leather jacket fell from her bare breasts. Her skirt was unzipped and lowered over her long legs. She left the high-heeled red booties. They were perfection. Elizabeth lay back on the black sofa, her legs splayed, her belly and breasts exposed to their gaze. Laura, whose towelling dressing gown had long been discarded, gazed hungrily at the naked woman and wanted to explore her open body. She was hardly aware of Jerry, who was standing, slowly rubbing his swollen cock.

Laura knelt over the lounging girl and kissed her lips and her long smooth throat. She stroked the full, round breasts and sucked on the swollen nipples. Her areolae were huge and brown, quite unlike Laura's. She stroked her belly and her thighs and found the almost hairless sex lips with her tongue. Behind her she felt the insistent pounding of Jerry's cock.

'Spank me, Jerry,' she said. 'Hard.'

He happily complied, and as the umber-skinned stranger bucked and moaned under Laura's tongue, Jerry slapped Laura's tingling buttocks and slipped his fingers into her wetness. Elizabeth urged her to suck harder. Her arms were flung back in abandon. She came loudly. Laura took one look at the ecstatic face. Jerry's cock slammed into her and he thrust hard as she sucked and licked and caressed the unfamiliar swollen dark-red labia. She drank Elizabeth's flowing juices and orgasmed as Jerry slapped her genitals and thrust his banana-shaped cock high into her.

'Wow! And I only came for my video.'

'Your video?' Laura laughed. 'We haven't even seen it yet. Or I haven't.'

'I have.' Jerry was blushing.

They had all bathed and were lounging on the sofa together, wearing only dressing gowns. Elizabeth had found a white linen kimono of Max's in his bedroom.

'Do you want to watch?' asked Elizabeth.

'Yes, I do,' said Laura. So this was what is was like to have sex with a stranger, she thought. She felt no jealousy of this beautiful woman, who was obviously used to bisexual scenes with Max, or lesbian scenes with sado-masochistic overtones. She had introduced her to a part of her own sexual nature which had been dormant. She didn't feel that she was in competition with her for Jerry. Jerry had obviously been perfectly happy watching the two of them enjoy each other.

Elizabeth found the video, pushed it into the slot, turned on the television and clicked the video switch. She turned down the dimmer switch and lit one table lamp.

They sat together, in semi-dark, on one sofa, Elizabeth in the middle, and watched the video.

The scene was very familiar – it was the sitting room of Max's flat. A semi-naked white girl was lying on the low pink granite table, her face completely covered by a black rubber mask. She wore only the flimsiest silky silver-grey slip, so fine that one could discern every curve and moulding of the body underneath. Her small breasts were flattened, her knees bent, and she wore high-heeled silver sandals. Her ash-blonde hair hung to the floor. Her wrists were tied together above her head with a strip of velvet ribbon. Her lips were scarlet. Her body curved up and her hips gyrated slowly. A pillow cushioned her hip bones from the unforgiving surface of the coffee table.

'Who's that? Someone we know?' asked Laura, aware of Elizabeth's long fingers caressing her thigh.

'Yeah, that's Max's wife,' said Elizabeth, and Laura saw that she had slipped her other hand into the opening of Jerry's dressing gown, at his groin.

Another figure came into view. A brown hand touched the flattened belly of the blonde. The video was well filmed, not at all amateur, and the close-up of the white girl was replaced with a long view of the room. Now one could see that the other person was Elizabeth, of course. The American girl wore a long transparent gown of white chiffon – probably Donna Karan, thought Laura. She carried a long white feather. She lifted the grey silk slip up over the blonde's hips to her waist and stroked her thighs and between her legs with the feather. The blonde bucked at the touch, and groaned. Her pubic area had been completely shaved and her slit was a like an open rosebud. In the film Elizabeth took a stick of lip rouge and began to paint the girl's labia the same colour scarlet as her other lips. When she was satisfied with her work, she kissed the newly red lips. Now the camera was close up to the black girl's face and the voyeurs saw the labia swell and ripen. Elizabeth teased the other with the long feather, tickling her belly and then plunging the stiff filaments into her slit.

While they watched, Laura and Jerry swooned under the long fingers of the African-American. She lightly caressed them both, casually fondled, and smiled.

Then another figure entered the video scene.

It was Max. He was rampant, naked and held a whip. Before the 'surprised' Elizabeth could stop her Sapphic games he had laid into her with the long whip. He tore the flimsy chiffon from her and Laura winced – what if it really had been Donna Karan? Elizabeth's long legs ended at jutting buttocks. The brown skin reddened under the ministrations of Max and his whip. He held himself at the root of his fatly swollen cock. Elizabeth was again sucking the rouged sex lips of the bucking blonde, whose legs were behind the black girl's shaved head. The camera moved into close-up to show the open petals, the long red tongue, the swollen labia and erect clitoris. Max's wife, still masked and tied, came loudly. The camera moved to show Elizabeth battered by another weapon – Max's rock solid cock. She took it calmly and slid down over the prone white girl, so he could get proper leverage. He fucked her from behind, leaning into her and touching his wife's body under Elizabeth's.

Laura, meanwhile, was very wet and slippery. She raised her hips to meet the delicate touch and Elizabeth took the hint and stroked firmly, rubbing her palm across the whole sex. Her other hand was wrapped around Jerry's cock, which stuck out rudely from the dressing gown. As the 'stars' on the video groaned and came loudly, so did Jerry and Laura. Laura fell back in a swoon and Elizabeth kissed them both lightly on the lips. She rose and went to the bathroom. Jerry and Laura slid together on the leather sofa and instinctively joined their bodies, still throbbing and excited by the film and the sexual adventure with the stranger.

When Laura kissed Jerry, she could smell Elizabeth's scent on him. She sucked his softened cock to erection again and smelt the black girl's perfume on his balls. He lay back in total luxury while she sucked him and licked his balls. She felt a hand on her thighs. Was it Jerry's? She did not know. Someone rubbed oil over her buttocks and pubis. Then a hard slippery wet phallus rubbed her thighs and buttocks. It could not be Jerry – Jerry's cock was in her mouth. She lifted her upturned bottom to the leathery touch of the phallus and it slid into her vagina. It was thrust in and out lightly at first, nearly to the top and then almost out of her. She rose to each assault, sucking in time to the piston thrusts. Jerry was moaning and holding her head, and she licked him and wrapped her tongue around his balls. Her assailant held her buttocks open and pushed hard into her. She felt long fingernails digging into her flesh. Then a feather touch on her inner thigh. She shoved her buttocks upward to reach the phallus, which obligingly slid into her again to the hilt. It was held there while Laura writhed and churned on it, until she had reached the point of no return. She sucked slowly but firmly on Jerry's hard cock, holding it at the base, and rubbing his balls. He bucked under her head, holding her to his groin. She came as his sperm went down her throat.

She sank on to him and closed her eyes.

When they awoke Elizabeth had gone – and had taken the video film with her.

'Can I come to your place again?' Laura asked Jerry when he next phoned to ask her out. 'I'll bring some food and cook it there if you like.'

'No need to do that. I'll get some smoked salmon and cheese. We don't want to waste time cooking, do we?'

'OK, see you soon.'

Laura chose a short navy pleated skirt and over-the-knee black woollen socks. She wore a V-necked navy cashmere jumper over a white shirt. She looked like a sexy schoolgirl. She also put her hair up into the shortest of plaits. She had kept her pussy hairless since Jerry had first shaved it for her, and loved the feel of her thighs rubbing together under the skirt. She wore no panties.

She took a bottle of white wine with her and her favourite grey marl cotton tracksuit – for afterwards. His door was open. She went into the semi-dark room and he grabbed her from behind and turned her round to kiss her.

She noticed he already had an erection under the linen kimono which Elizabeth had worn.

He slid a hand under her short skirt and stroked her naked flesh. She sighed and opened her legs.

'First things first, my girl. A drink for you and me, yes?'

'Yes, wine, thanks. What about food? Eat now or later?'

'Later, when I've chastised you for being a naughty girl.'

'How am I naughty?'

'You aren't wearing knickers. How many times have I told you about that?' He grinned and grabbed her waist. She pressed her belly to his crotch and felt the hardness of him. Then she broke free of his grabbing hands and slipped behind one of the sofas. He went into the kitchen to pour their drinks. When he came out she had hidden from him, between the vertical blinds and curtains, which were closed.

'Laura? Where are you? Come here at once or I'll spank you.'

She giggled. She was wet with anticipation.

'Laura, where are you?'

She kept still, and could hear his heavy breathing. He

moved the curtain and found her. He pulled her out roughly.

'What a wicked girl. Bend over my knee,' he said, and pulled her across his naked lap on the sofa. Her skirt was over her waist and her over-the-knee socks revealed white thighs.

'Ooh, look at your naughty bottom! It just begs to be spanked,' said Jerry. He smacked his lips loudly and put on a different voice. 'I shall give you six of the best, Miss Naughtiness, and see if you behave yourself after that.'

He spanked her firmly, his big hand rubbing between her legs after every wallop, to ease the pain and give her pleasure. Her bare fanny tingled as his spanking got harder and he managed to get his fingers deeper into her. She felt his cock stiff under her bare belly. She wriggled and felt it harden more. She got a hand under her and held his erection. She rubbed it on her belly and he squirmed under her. He stood suddenly, lifting her and wrapping her legs around his waist. He sat on the edge of the sofa and she sat on him, still wearing her pleated skirt and shirt and long sexy socks. He held her by the buttocks and slid into her. He lifted her so that her legs wrapped around his neck. She was lifted up, her legs wide, his cock fully buried in her soft flesh.

Her neck extended, her head fell backward and he fucked her hard.

A month after they had met, Jerry phoned and asked her to go away with him for the weekend to a small country hotel on the Isle of Wight.

'Yes, please, that would be lovely,' she agreed.

The first night on the Isle of Wight was spent in a four-poster bed, the air hot with the scent of honeysuckle, whose tendrils curled through the latticed window. She lay in happy exhaustion, the white cotton sheets spread around her like a veil.

'Laura, I have something to tell you,' said Jerry.

'What?'

'My wife is returning. We have two more weeks together and then I must leave you.'

'But, I thought she'd left you.'

'She wants to come back to me. Give it another go.'

Laura pulled the sheet over her suddenly cold flesh. 'I see,' she said.

She cried herself to sleep on the far side of the huge bed, while he slept peacefully, unaware of the storm that raged in her breast. She had thought he loved her. She had given herself completely to this man. What a fool she was! What a stupid fool!

He asked to see her again when he drove her home on Sunday evening. She said no, she would rather not. He looked hurt, puzzled.

'So this is goodbye?' he said, holding her hand as if she were a stranger.

'Yes, goodbye!'

The idyll was over.

Chapter Five

Sick Leave

*L*aura was devastated. She left the phone off the hook; she failed to paint her toenails; she only washed her hair every other day; she missed her appointment at the hairdresser's; and she drank too much whisky, on her own, when she returned to her smart little flat each evening.

'You're falling apart, Laura,' Sally – the *Health and You* editor – said two weeks after Jerry had delivered his disastrous message. 'Look at this text. It's full of rhubarb. What's the matter with you?'

Laura burst into tears, which she hated doing because her eyes immediately became puffy and her nose went bright red and looked like it was smeared all over her face.

'Oh, come on, darling, it can't be that bad, can it?'

Apparently it was, to Laura. She really had fallen badly for the young doctor, and she was lost without his desire for her.

'He's gone back to his wife,' she sobbed on the magazine editor's shoulder, while the kind-hearted woman tried not to mind that her new navy-blue silk-and-linen Nicole Farhi suit was being stained with tears.

'Men are bastards, darling, you should know that by now. Why don't you give yourself a treat? Go away for a few days. You can do the rewrite for next Friday. Fax it to me. Go on, Laura, it'll do you good.'

Laura spent the weekend crying in her flat. She didn't have the energy to drive to Cornwall. Instead, she stayed cloistered in the flat, with her telephone disconnected, and watched old black-and-white movies on the television; ate bacon and eggs and fried bread; drank too much whisky and cried some more.

On the Monday, Sally brought a glass of wine to the dark corner where Laura had chosen to sit in the brasserie, and placed it in front of her. Laura picked it up and drank it in one go.

'Laura, we need to talk.'

'Yes, Sally.'

'What's wrong, hon'? You look dreadful. And your work stinks. You know it does.'

Laura let out a loud sigh. 'You're right, I know you are. But what can I do, Sally? I feel so dreadful. I want to cry all the time.'

'Have you seen a doctor?'

Laura burst into tears. 'That's the whole problem, I have seen a doctor, and I'm in love with him.'

'Look hon', how about you take a few months off – say two, three months? You could still do some work for us, on commission as a freelance. I would buy anything you write, you know that. If it was suitable for us. But you could get yourself together again. Take a break. Go on sick leave.' She patted Laura on her shoulder. 'I'll make sure you get paid sharpish for the sex issue. I'll do a rewrite on anything that needs it. Don't worry.'

Laura put her head on her hands on the table and sobbed gratefully.

* * *

Before she could take leave of London, Laura had one more feature to write – an article on London auction houses for *Young Living*, a magazine that had bought several of Laura's features in the past. She had chosen to work with an unknown young photographer who had brought his portfolio in to show her recently. She enjoyed giving new photographers the chance of work. He was a chirpy, dark-blond German lad of about twenty-three, seriously enthusiastic about working in England. His work was unusual, and Laura thought it had a freshness that might bring a spark to the rather dull feature. He shot interiors and still lifes from strange angles. He was also good at people pictures and used a fish-eye lens that made everyone look weird. It was the sort of thing that *Young Living* was known for: innovative, quirky photography.

She and Heinz travelled by cab to Bond Street and went into the auction house as arranged, just before an important sale of silver and plate and precious metal ware.

Heinz set up his tripod and lights and shot a few still-life pictures of the items that were to be auctioned. He put away the heavy equipment and used a hand-held 35mm SLR Nikon to shoot the people pictures, moving among the staff and buyers with alacrity, shifting his viewpoint, changing lenses, doing it all quietly and with no fuss. Laura interviewed an auctioneer and Heinz photographed him in his handmade shirt and dark grey suit. He shot about six films and Laura had enough material on tape. They stayed for the actual sale and she watched, fascinated, as Arabs in white robes, their wives totally shrouded and masked, bid for the treasures, paid high prices and beat the would-be purchasers from Japan and Europe. There was a pair of solid silver candelabras that went for an absolute fortune, and Laura saw a tall redheaded woman stand and smile smugly before leaving. She tried to follow the woman to get an interview with her but she was stopped by a burly grey-haired man in a cream suit who looked like a villain from a Bogart movie.

'Sorry, madam,' he said with a West Country burr to his voice, 'Miss Stallone doesn't give interviews.'

'Never mind,' said Laura to Heinz, 'I'm sure we have enough material for the feature.'

Next day, she evaluated the transparencies with Heinz and James, the bisexual editor of *Young Living*. James was pleased with the shots and thought the text was all right. 'It lacks sparkle, Laura, but then, so do you, dear. What's the matter? The pictures will make it – we'll cut the text and just use it as captions. Double-page spread of small pics, like a cartoon strip.' The editor had spoken.

'By the way,' he said, as she fled gratefully from the office, 'I hope you're going to invite me to Cornwall this summer, Laura. May I bring a friend?'

Chapter Six

The Village

*L*aura drove to her Aunt Celia's in Exeter and stayed with her on Friday night.

'Laura, you don't look well, dear.' Her aunt looked hard at the bags under Laura's eyes and Laura turned away from her penetrating gaze.

'Working too hard, Aunt Celia, that's all. I need a break.'

The journey from Exeter to Cornwall was awful. Her Beetle did not like the traffic queues and kept cutting out. Her timing needed adjusting. The AA took her from St Austell to Porthzelah as part of her Relay option with the association. It was wonderful. She relaxed in the Range Rover while her little car rode behind her on the trailer.

'You're lucky, living in Porthzelah,' said the AA man.

'Yes, I know. I've just inherited a house there.'

'Is it true what I hear about the place?'

'What's that?'

'My brother went there on holiday last year. He said there was a rubber club in the village.'

'What?' she laughed. 'A rubber club in Porthzelah? I don't think so.'

'Oh. He's a bit of a drama queen, my brother. He said there were all sorts going on there.'

'Really? Not that I've heard.'

'Ah, well, perhaps I'll go to Ibiza again this year, in that case.' The AA man grinned at her.

She dialled Ethan's number on her mobile phone and told him she had broken down

'I'm with the AA. I'll be another hour or so, Ethan.'

'If I was with an AA man I'd be a lot longer that that, darling.'

She laughed.

'You should have let me know you were coming, Laura. I'm going out this evening. I could have cancelled.'

'Don't worry, Ethan, I'm not very good company at the moment. I just want some peace and quiet. And I do have work to do.'

She picked up bread, a newspaper, fruit, whisky, and bacon and eggs at the local shop. As the AA vehicle with her car on the trailer rounded the last bend and she saw the little terrace of houses on the hill, with the sea sparkling behind and a tumult of gulls circling above in the cloudless sky, she felt she had come home after a long absence.

The AA man got her to sign a form and he left. She unpacked her small bag and turned on the immersion heater so she could have a bath.

Over the lichen-roofed houses of the village herring gulls gossiped and screeched and chatted; Laura was as amazed as ever at the variety of their vocabulary. She looked out of the attic window at the dark-green sea and white horses beyond the harbour wall. It always gave her a thrill, this view. She could hardly believe she owned the house now.

Her grandmother had lived in this little Georgian house practically all her life. Laura had spent much of her childhood here with her beloved grandparents, when she wasn't in Devon with her adoptive parents, Aunt Celia and Uncle John.

Laura had promised herself she would have a quiet time and do some work – her own work, not journalism. After the funeral Laura had looked at the house with a stranger's eyes and seen the mess, the rubbish that filled the place. She had wanted to have a spring-clean and make the place hers. But now that she was here, she only wanted to relax and perhaps do a bit of drawing or painting. She had always meant to keep up with her painting. Here she would do just that, she promised herself. Cleaning the house could wait.

She walked down the hill into the village. In the art shop she chose a couple of small canvases on stretchers, six hog's-hair brushes and all the tubes of acrylic paint she needed. She loved the names of the colours – Prussian Blue, Zinc White, Titanium, Cadmium Yellow. She had decided to use the attic room to paint in. She could throw open the sash window and let in the sea air and take inspiration from the changing sea and sky.

On her way up the hill she met her neighbour, Mrs Poldhu. The old lady was sitting on a wooden bench halfway up the steep hill, resting with her heavy bag of shopping.

'Hello, Mrs Poldhu! How are you?

'Oh, hello, my dear, how are you? You are a stranger. You didn't hear about my husband?'

'No, Mrs Poldhu. What about your husband?'

'He passed away in January. Cancer, dear of him. It were a lovely funeral down at the parish church. I should have let you know, cheel.'

'Oh! I am sorry. How old was he?' Laura had not heard about the death of Mr Poldhu, who had been coxswain of the lifeboat in years gone by. Last summer she had only caught sight of him once or twice as he pottered in the garden. She noticed that Mrs Poldhu was now wearing dark glasses and had a white stick.

'He was only sixty-nine, dear, and I do sadly miss him.'

'Oh dear!' Laura patted her old wrinkled hand. Mrs Poldhu was older than her husband had been, surely. 'And what about your eyes?' she asked.

'I'm practically blind now, you know. It's only cataracts, but they can't do anything for me for some reason. I have to wait.'

'You poor thing,' said Laura. She knew that Mrs Poldhu had loved to read. She had seen her in the library many times, choosing books for her husband and herself.

'Are you able to read, still?'

'Not really, dear, only when someone gets a large-print book for me, but they haven't much that's good here. Anyway, I won't keep you. You must have better things to do than talk to me.'

'No, I haven't. Let me carry your things up for you. I'm going home.'

'Well, that would be lovely.'

Laura took the string bags full of tinned carrots and baked beans and tucked her canvases under her arm. She walked slowly to keep pace with Mrs Poldhu and returned her bags at her gate.

'Are you sure you don't want me to take it in for you?' she asked.

'No, dear, you go on, I'm all right now, thank you. Don't be a stranger, now,' she added. 'Do you know you are very like your grandmother. Your voice reminds me of her. I do miss her too, dear of her! First my best friend, then my husband.'

Laura took her purchases indoors and made herself a coffee. She felt suddenly guilty at her own youth and freedom from sickness and grief. Poor Mrs Poldhu! How awful for the old dear, losing her husband. She had had no children, Laura knew, and so who was there

51

to look after her? She and her grandmother had been good neighbours and friends for forty or more years.

She took the paints upstairs, placed them on a table with the canvases and found an old jar to hold her brand-new brushes. She gazed out of the window. It was too chilly to open. The glass was covered in a fine film of salt from the winter winds. It was difficult to see out. The roofs and harbour were blurred as if seen through tears.

She went downstairs and looked through her grandmother's book shelves. Laura had not yet moved the objects that her grandmother had loved. The pair of black-and-white Staffordshire dogs still smiled from the mantelshelf. The upright piano, sadly in need of tuning, was propped on the badly sloping floor. She tripped on the torn Turkish carpet that her grandfather had brought home from some foreign voyage once, and that Grandmother had been so proud of. Her eyes scanned the old books. Her grandmother and grandfather had had an eclectic taste: everything from Winston Churchill's *The Gathering Storm* to *Born Free* and Neville Shute's *On the Beach*. There was even a battered, presumably well-read copy of *The Joy of Sex* by Alex Comfort. Laura's mind boggled at the idea of her grandparents making love.

She looked at the novels. She chose a book and went down her path, opened her gate and went next door to Mrs Poldhu's house. Her neighbour's gate was hanging by one hinge. It looked sad and neglected: the brave red paint was peeling. The sky had turned a green-grey and the gulls were complaining loudly. It was cold.

She knocked on the door, and when there was no answer she opened the outer door and knocked again on the storm door, which was half-glazed, with blue and red panels. No answer, but she opened that door a little way and saw Mrs Poldhu, in the tiny back kitchen – more of a scullery, really – sitting at the yellow

52

Formica-topped table, her head in her hands. The radio was on. Old-time dance music came floating through the dim passageway like an echo of days gone by.

'Mrs Poldhu, it's only me, Laura,' she called out, and the old woman turned towards her voice.

'Oh! Hello, dear, come on in. Can I make you a cup of tea? I'm just having one. People generally come in the back door, you know.' It was almost an admonition.

Laura sat in the cramped, chilly room, seeing the dust and grime on the work surfaces that Mrs Poldhu could no longer see or be bothered about. She told Laura to find herself a cup and saucer – no mugs in this household – and Laura did so, choosing a blue-and-white fine china cup and saucer with a willow pattern. It was a bit dusty and she surreptitiously wiped it on her shirt.

'No milk, thank you,' she said.

'No milk! There you are, then. How about a biscuit?' And out came the biscuit tin, which was pitifully empty. 'Oh, I forgot to buy some biscuits, silly me.'

'Oh, that's all right, really, I'm not hungry, thank you anyway.' Laura sipped her too-strong tea without complaint and wondered how to broach the subject of the book without embarrassing her neighbour.

'Er, have you read this? Daphne du Maurier's *Rebecca*? It was my grandmother's, and I wondered if you would like me to read it to you.' She went on before Mrs Poldhu could stop her. 'I would really like to reread it myself and I love reading aloud. You really would be doing me a favour if you let me read it to you.'

'Would I, dear?' The old woman smiled wanly. 'All right then, if you like.'

'Where shall we sit? Here or in the front room?' asked Laura. It was cold and uncomfortable in the kitchen, with no fire and only a linoleum floor. In the old days there would have been a Cornish range here or a solid fuel Rayburn stove keeping the room warm while it cooked. Mrs Poldhu and many of her contemporaries had updated their houses, done away with dirty, time-consuming stoves and put in night-storage heaters and electric ovens.

'In the front room, Laura, my bird. There's an electric fire if you need it.'

So they went into the south-facing room that overlooked the harbour, and Laura admired the black-and-white photographs of Mr Poldhu in his lifeboatman's kit. Mrs Poldhu told her to turn on the fire. Laura put on one bar of the little portable fire and rubbed her hands together. There were paintings on the wall: real paintings.

'What a lovely picture of the yachts!' Laura said.

'Painted by an artist that lived here, a friend of my father, he were. Gave it to him for something he did once. Can't remember what it was.'

It was a good oil painting of the Newlyn School. The colours were as bright as the day it had been painted.

Laura knew that many of the townsfolk had decent works of art hanging in their humble cottages. The locals had come to appreciate the art that had been produced in their town over the last century, and took it for granted. They had grown up with good paintings around them in artists' studios and in the galleries. Painters and locals talked in the pubs, grew to tolerate each other's peculiarities, and even became friends.

Laura did enjoy reading aloud. It concentrated her mind on the words. She sat and read for an hour and a half and had another cup of tea to keep her throat lubricated.

Mrs Poldhu nodded off in her green uncut moquet armchair, smiling, the photo of her husband, a broad-faced, handsome man with bushy eyebrows, in her wrinkled, blotched hands. Laura put a slip of paper in the book as a bookmark, placed it on the table and quietly left.

Next day she did the same thing, arriving mid-morning with a packet of chocolate biscuits. Her canvases remained virgin, her paintbrushes clean. The tubes of acrylic paint were unsqueezed.

Evenings she spent with her old friend, Ethan. They had an easy relationship that carried on each time they saw each other as if they had never been apart. Ethan had 'no side to him', as Laura's grandmother would have said. What you saw was what you got, with Ethan. He did not know how to be devious or sly: his nature was open and sunny. He had 'come out' years ago and had many friends of all inclinations in the village. He was a large, huggable man, like an over-friendly, plump cocker spaniel, and Laura was very fond of him.

The sun shone on the little village and Laura gradually came out of her shell. Cineraria grew wild in the corners of Laura's garden – bright-blue and purple and deep vermilion, like plastic flowers. Daisies littered the long grass. She sank into a deckchair in a sheltered, secluded corner and spread her London-white limbs to the healing sun. She had put plenty of sun-block on but needed to feel the heat seeping into her. Her dark head was covered in an old straw hat of her grandmother's.

The sun helped stop the hurt she was suffering. Its power filled her with heaviness, filled her limbs with languid grace. She felt the ghost of Jerry's hands part her thighs. An oily stickiness seeped from her sex. She pulled the swimsuit down over her hips, pressed fingers under the elasticated gusset and felt her own wetness. Her mouth opened and she licked her lips. She rubbed her fingers over the shaved pubis, admiring her own pouting flesh, then pulled the elastic to one side so her sex was fully exposed and rubbed with the palm of her hand. It felt very wicked to be exposed to the sun in the garden. What if someone should come through the gate and see her abusing herself? She became excited at the thought of being seen. She'd always fantasised about being watched while masturbating in public. She idly stroked herself and let her imagination fly to London and Jerry, his thick hair rasping the delicate flesh of her inner thighs. She came, leaving her fingers inside, feeling the clasp of her flesh as the spasms went on and on. She sobbed.

Later she went to Ethan's cottage and had tea with him. He was going out that evening to a fellow teacher's dinner party.

She watched the sun set over the sea as she walked along the cliff path, drinking in the pinkness of the thick clumps of thrift.

She became aware of turbulence on the calm surface of the sea. A black fin rose and a curved dark creature arched out of the water and dropped again. A dolphin! Her heart missed a beat. Another dolphin appeared and another. Six dolphins leapt and played in the little bay. She sat on a lichen-covered rock and watched them. They must be fishing, she thought. They dived and danced and circled in one spot. After thirty minutes – it could have been a lifetime – they headed off towards the point and disappeared. She felt healed of some awful sickness.

She went back to her grandmother's house and sat in the attic room and looked out at the garden. Her garden. Bamboos whispered in the wind, and there was still a chill in the air. But summer was here in spirit. The herring gulls had hatched in June and ugly baby gulls were bleating on the rooftops; they hunched their grey mottled backs, and looked pitiful, waiting for food to be dropped into their gullets.

The small fishing village was bathed with sunshine. Herring gulls floated in the air above the huddle of granite cottages, whose slate roofs were turned gold by lichen.

She sighed. This was a good idea, coming to Cornwall for the summer. She could sort out the house, enjoy her own company, and read lots of books and paint and draw, as she had done years ago at art school. She had spent many happy summers in this house as a child, though she had been scathing of the town's lack of amenities when she was in her teens. Now, however, she appreciated its very particular charm. Maybe she would delve into the secret that shrouded her parents' death. Her grandparents had never mentioned the accident. She only knew that her pretty mother and proud father had left one evening to go to a dance in Newquay and had not returned. Her grandparents in Porthzelah had offered continuity and security. She had loved them unconditionally, even more than she had loved her adoptive parents.

She spent days in the sheltered and secluded part of the garden, sunbathing naked, safe in the knowledge that no one could see her. The garden was protected by tall pines, through which, from the upstairs rooms of the house, she could see the harbour and all the boats bobbing safely in the crook of its granite arms. On one side was the end terraced house of her neighbour, Mrs Poldhu. A new house was being built, she noticed with annoyance, on the hillside above. How hideous it was – the grey breezeblocks like a brutalist air-raid shelter. But the builders were working on the other side of it and couldn't see her. She turned off the telephone and simply relaxed, feeling all the London greyness and workday cares slip away from her. As soon as she felt her skin begin to tighten, she went into the shade and put on her bikini and a T-shirt.

She drank a whisky and ice in the bath. She treated her body to an after-sun lotion that would enhance her tan. In the mirror, her face was relaxed and pink. She chose her new summer dress. Its deep-blue cotton made her sun-kissed flesh look brown. Ethan had insisted she go out on the town that evening with him.

As she admired herself in the long mirror, she thought of how she had dreamt of bringing Jerry here. She shut her mind to thoughts of his long face, his mobile chin, his brown eyes peering at her over his tortoiseshell glasses. Damn him!

Ethan knocked and walked in, embracing Laura in his plump arms.

'How are you, gorgeous?' the young man exclaimed. 'Oh, it's disgusting how pretty you are! You look tired, though. Give us a drink.'

'Where shall we go?' said Laura, after a second whisky.

'Do you want dinner?'

'Of course! What restaurants are good this year?'

The standard of eating-places in the small town of Porthzelah hadn't always been good. Places opened for a season or two, restaurateurs made their fortunes and left, or failed to make enough money and left. Premises changed hands each season, or the chefs left in a huff, or fell out of love with the waiter, or got a local girl pregnant and fled. It was a part of life in a small Cornish town.

'The Galleon has good food these days, and we can sit outside on the balcony upstairs. It's out of the wind,' said Ethan, his mouth watering at the very thought of grilled lobster or mussels and chips.

'Lead on,' said Laura.

They walked out the front door, down the path and passed Mrs Poldhu's house. The old woman was taking her washing off the line, and Laura waved at her.

'So. Tell me, what have you decided to do?' said Laura. Already she had forgotten the world of deadlines and photo shoots, editorial meetings and models.

'I told you about Eugene, didn't I?' said Ethan.

'The gay Irish vegetarian?'

'You make him sound like a bad joke,' admonished Ethan.

'Sorry, darling, I didn't mean to hurt you,' said Laura, smiling.

They walked along the cobbled lane, arm in arm, admiring the great swathes of white valerian that hung from the walls and the dark-blue cineraria that had seeded itself.

'Anyway, he and I are opening a health food shop together.'

'Really? Great! Where? Here?' said Laura.

'Yes, of course. Just off Back Hill.'

'What, where that useless grocer's is?'

'Was. It's closed, haven't you seen?' said Ethan. 'We're opening in four weeks' time. A bit late, I know, for this season, but the builder let us down and . . . Oh, it's too boring to go into.'

'And where's Eugene?'

'Oh, he's gone to his parents' wedding anniversary do, in Kilburn.'

'And didn't take you?' Laura asked, archly.

'They don't like gays. Or rather, they prefer to pretend their son isn't one.'

They had reached the wharf and had to push their way past crowds of red-faced holiday-makers. The water was high in the little harbour and the brightly coloured fishing boats bobbed cheerfully. Laura felt wonderful. She did not mind the crowds of northerners and midlanders and Londoners who gawked and gaped at pizza menus, hanging baskets and fishing-trip signs and ate their fish and chips from polystyrene cartons. The herring gulls gossiped and hung overhead, waiting for a chance to swoop and steal a sausage or a chip from an unsuspecting child or its pot-bellied father.

'Ee up, Davey, watch out!' cried a young woman in too-tight jeans and brief bikini top as a beautiful large white-and-grey bird descended with a flurry of wings and squawks, like an avenging angel, and deftly removed the pasty from her husband's hands.

Ethan and Laura smiled and passed by.

They pushed open the door of the popular pub. It had expanded its premises in recent years and they made their way past smoking, ancient locals and fleshy young visitors to the stairs up to the balcony restaurant.

'Do you love him?' asked Laura, over the sticky toffee pudding.

'Of course,' said Ethan, licking his lips. 'How about you Laura? You're looking a bit peaky. Are you in love?'

'No, of course not.'

She couldn't tell Ethan about Jerry, yet. The hurt was too raw, still, and she felt she had made a fool of herself.

'So you're a free agent!'

'I suppose I am, yes,' said Laura, smiling and crossing her legs. 'Completely free. No man – just me to think about and please.'

'Sounds wonderful! You'd better make the most of it.'

After they had eaten, they went downstairs and sat outside in the fresh air, at one of the circular metal tables in the flowery courtyard. The wind had got up and Laura wrapped a woollen stole around her bare shoulders.

'That's nice. Where did you get it?' asked Ethan, fingering the pale-grey cashmere.

'Oh, on a trip with *Young Living* – Kerala, in southern India.'

'Never heard of it! You do have a glamorous life, Laura. It's gorgeous!' said Ethan, using his favourite word.

'Who are they?' asked Laura, leaning towards her friend and moving her eyes to the right of where they sat. A group of men were standing, leaning and laughing, their voices raised. They looked like fishermen, dressed as they were in jeans and sweaters, and with the deep tan of the sea. One in particular had caught her discerning eye. He was stockily built, not tall, with narrow, foxy eyes that were bright blue. His mouth was hidden under a short beard of brown wiry hair. His nose was proudly Phoenician: large and hooked. His hair was a lighter brown than his beard, curly and long. She was not attracted to men with facial hair, as a rule, but his laughing eyes, and his obvious interest in her, made her rethink her prejudice. He had been staring admiringly in her direction for the last five minutes, ever since they had come out of the door of the pub.

'It's Bill Montpelier and his divers. They dive for lobsters, usually, but they're working on a wreck, I've heard, somewhere off the Scillies. You don't want to mix with him, Laura, he's trouble.'

'Who, that gorgeous bearded chap?'

'No, that's Aaron. It's his uncle who's the nasty piece of work.'

'In what way?'

'Oh, the usual male chauvinism with a bit of sadism thrown in, I believe.'

'Is this village gossip or do you really know something about him?'

'Just gossip, Laura, I suppose. Ex-girlfriends appearing with black eyes, that sort of thing. His niece is a sexy minx, too. Too ripe, too young. He treats her with a little more than avuncular affection, if you know what I mean.'

'Incest? Well, well! But, Ethan, you mustn't spread these rumours.'

'Well, I think it is rather more than rumour. But the main thing is the whole family is trouble, if you ask me. It was Bill Montpelier's brother who was involved in the stolen goods affair I mentioned. He's inside.'

'Inside?'

'Prison.'

'Oh! The curly haired one is rather lovely, though.' said Laura.

'I don't like men with facial hair, it tickles when you

kiss,' whispered Ethan, and Laura giggled. Just then, Bill Montpelier turned and faced her. She had seen him somewhere before, but she couldn't think where.

Later, in the cool sheets of her new double bed, alone, Laura sighed blissfully. She had a feeling that this summer could be wonderful, if only she could forget about Jerry. No responsibilities except to produce a few features before the end of the three months. Heaven! And that golden-fleeced young man. She supposed he must be about twenty-four or five, just a few years younger than her. Then she remembered where she had seen Bill Montpelier, the uncle. It was in the London auction room, with Miss Stallone. He had been her minder, or bodyguard. The mystery deepened!

As she had promised, next day, she went to visit her neighbour, taking a packet of biscuits with her, and a packet of the teabags she knew Mrs Poldhu liked.

'You shouldn't have done that, my flower. How much do I owe you?' The woman looked around for her purse.

'No, it's a present,' she said, lightly.

'I can't be accepting presents from you, my cheel.'

'Really, it's nothing. I'll help you drink it.' Laura refused the money.

'Oh, all right then, thankee.'

'Shall I bring another book in for us to read?' Laura said enthusiastically.

'If you must, my cheel, though why you should want to waste your time with an old woman like me . . .'

And so the pattern continued, and Laura looked forward to her reading sessions with her grandmother's friend. It brought her grandmother back to her, somehow. The soft tones, the lovely Cornish expressions: 'my cheel' – my child; 'dear of him'. She told Laura of the town's happenings: the sea rescues, storms that had been particularly furious that year, damage to her roof. Laura saw that she'd had her gate repaired.

'Who did that for you?' she asked. She needed several maintenance jobs on her house and wanted a reliable workman.

'Young Thomas over the way in the terrace below. You know him? That Anna's son.'

'Oh yes, Tom! Does he do carpentry then?'

'Oh, he can put his hand to anything can Thomas. Fixed my frozen pipes on the outside toilet he did.'

'When did it freeze?'

'Just after Easter. We had snow for two days and it froze my pipes. Burst they did. Water pouring everywhere in the back yard. Thomas fixed it.'

Laura intended to visit her old friend, Anna, Thomas's mother, as soon as she was settled.

That night she went to the pub alone. It was the sort of town where a woman on her own didn't get hassle entering licensed premises. The town was used to independent women – artists had been coming here for a century at least, and the locals were accustomed to their ways, tolerating their eccentricities, accepting their drinks, even taking their paintings instead of rent, or payment for work, sometimes.

Laura had arranged to meet Anna and her husband. They were nowhere to be seen, so she went to the bar, pushing through the cheerful crowd, and ordered a whisky.

'Hello, my flower, didn't I see you here last night with that Ethan?' It was the diver.

'Yes, hello!' Laura blushed. The young man was pressed close to her in the crush, and she smelt his musky sweat. His arm felt huge next to hers, subtly pressed against her. His laughing eyes looked down into hers, then dropped briefly to her cleavage. He tore them away and smiled, opening his very expressive lips to show her his white teeth.

'I'll get that,' he said, passing over money to the barman.

'All right, thanks,' said Laura. No point in being coy, she thought. Remember what Ethan said – make the most of it!

She followed him to a quieter corner, by the window. She stood so her hair was backlit.

'I'm Aaron. What's your name?' he asked.

'Laura. Cheers! Good health!' She clicked her glass on his and they drank, looking at each other over their glasses. There was an obvious and immediate sexual attraction, and she felt inclined to go with it, let it happen.

'Are you a diver? Ethan thought you were.'

'Yes. Are you a dyke? Bill thought you were.'

She laughed, showing her throat. 'No, I'm not gay.'

'Good!' Aaron smiled and his eyes spoke volumes.

'Here you are!' Anna pounced on Laura, like a hawk on its prey, and Charles, her husband, was close behind, grinning inanely and waving a cigar.

'Hello, Anna, Charles.' Kisses and hugs were exchanged and Aaron smiled benignly, amused at this middle-class ritual.

They looked expectantly at the diver, and Laura introduced him, embarrassed that she had forgotten his last name.

'It's Aaron Montpelier. Nice to meet you. I have to go.' He turned to Laura, apologetically, and said, 'But perhaps I can see you on Monday, here at ten?'

She nodded, taken aback by the sudden invitation to an assignation, but pleased.

'Good night,' said Aaron. He nodded to them all and disappeared through the throngs of holiday revellers that filled the harbour road.

'He seems a rather jolly young man,' said Anna, longingly.

'Jolly' meant sexy, if Laura read her friend's lustful expression.

'Mmm, he probably is,' she said, smiling. 'How's Thomas doing?'

'He's happy enough. You know boys. They never say what's going on in their minds. You'll see him at the weekends. He's got a building and labouring job this summer. We've got my mother with us, too. She's a dear, of course, but the house feels small with the four of us there. My men are so big!' she bragged, happily. 'Come and have lunch on Sunday. Just the family.'

'Great! Thanks! I'd love to.'

So on Sunday she went to Anna and Charles's place, a small Georgian house just a few hundred yards from Laura's with lovely proportions and a splendid view of the harbour town.

Thomas was unrecognisable as the gauche, awkward adolescent she had seen three years before. He had grown taller, broader in the shoulders and chest, and his blue eyes were like cornflowers. She was astonished at the metamorphosis. He'd had the misfortune to be a plump child and had suffered from severe shyness. Now he was more sure of himself. He smiled and shook Laura by the hand. She laughed. 'Is it really Tom? Well, well! You're so handsome!' He laughed but turned red and left the room. 'Now look what I've done,' she groaned. 'Oh, Anna, I didn't mean to make him run away.'

They laughed and drank the icy wine and nibbled the olives and pistachio nuts that a beaming Charles handed round.

Chapter Seven

The Fetish

Maybe it began when she was much younger, and couldn't sleep, holding her hot-water bottle between her legs and rubbing herself against it, pretending that it was a horse she was riding naked across a beach. She would place the hot, quivering rubber across her belly and pull the sheets over her head, breathing in the warm smell and enjoying the weight of it on her stomach. She would hold the stopper and the handle down between her legs and rub gently until she fell asleep. She had worn knickers in bed and had loved to feel the tight cotton against her budding sex. Even now when she was alone she used a pair of her own panties to rub against and excite herself. And a rubber hot-water bottle was still a favourite aid to masturbation.

No matter how it had begun, rubber itself had become a fetish for Laura. She would find her gaze drawn irresistibly to men, even really unattractive ones, in Wellington boots. And in this fishing village young fishermen in waders were supreme objects of desire. Her eyes hungrily watched the bulge of the loins, swelling against denim jeans, the edge of the rubber waders cutting into the thighs just below the balls. She imagined the young men naked except for their waders, their balls and loosely hanging penises jogging up and down against the silky rubber. She saw their buttocks rising firm and muscular above the waders, and ached to handle them. She wanted to press herself against the boots so that the cool hard rubber rubbed at her sex.

She was walking along the harbour, very early on Monday morning, before the hungover holiday-makers were about, doing her food shopping, her mind on swimsuits and sun oil, when she saw Aaron, wearing waders. He walked straight towards her. She gulped.

'Hello, my flower.'

'Hello!'

'Where are you going?' he asked.

'I was going to have a coffee.'

'Come and have one with me?'

'Oh! Where?'

'My cottage in Love Lane.'

'Who could resist?' she laughed.

He pushed open the unlocked stable door of the small granite cottage and she found herself pressed close to him, crushed by his strong arms.

'Do you want me?' he whispered in her ear.

'Yes!'

'Let me wear them,' she asked Aaron, later, while they were lying together in his small room, with a view of the boats in the harbour.

'How do you mean, my flower?'

'Your waders – let me wear them in bed, now.'

'Do you mean it?' he laughed.

'Yes, yes, I want the feel of them on my thighs.'

'But they're not very clean, my lover.'

'I don't mind.'

He raised himself from the bed and fetched the thigh-high rubber waders, brushing at them with his large, roughened hands. He laid the waders across the bed and she slid into them, the tops of them reaching high up to the tops of her thighs and the edges touching her sex. She lay back, laughing with delight, the whiteness of her belly made whiter by the black rubber that lay against it.

'They're so heavy – I won't be able to move.'

'Don't you worry none about moving, my bird – you just lie there looking like a Belladona lily what comes from the Scillies. It has no leaves. Just a naked, tall pinkish stalk with a bright-pink blossom on top.' His penis showed appreciation of the unexpected vision of beauty and he moved quickly on top of her. The feel of the rubber against the lips of her sex was wonderful. The more he moved his hard body against her, the more the edges of the waders rubbed and excited her. With his help she lifted her legs and wrapped them over his muscular back.

'Oh, that feels good,' he said.

'I love it, I love it,' she panted. With her hands she pulled at the rubber waders and kept them tight against her thighs and arse. They were both sweating now and the waders had begun to give off a soft, hypnotic smell. She sniffed and licked his fingers, which smelt of her sex and the rubber mingled together, and she was in ecstasy. Her orgasm was long and lovely. He rubbed his penis all over her thighs and the wader tops, obviously enjoying the feel of the rubber on his sex, and when he came the semen ran down her legs and into the tops of the waders.

'Do you still want to meet me tonight?' he asked, smiling.

'I think so, yes.'

She spent the rest of the morning doing domestic things – washing all the musty curtains and rag rugs and hanging them out to dry on the washing line. The smell of the air was so good here, she thought. It was a simple delight to hang out washing and watch the cloth waltz in the brisk wind. The herring gulls swung and gossiped to each other or stood on roof-tops near their nests and screeched at each other. Their young jumped up and down in frustration and flapped vestigial wings. She did not miss London streets, grimy window sills, traffic noise, pigeons. She heard children laugh as they ran down the hill towards the beach. She tended the garden, which was luckily not very labour intensive. Her grandfather had loved his garden and had learnt to grow plants that did not need much care and that tolerated the salt-laden gales. There were hardy camellias, rhododendrons and fuchsias, palms and bamboo. Cineraria had seeded itself all over the garden and she was amused at the thought that in London, each of the bright coloured plants would have been sold in a pot at an extortionate price. On her way back from Aaron's cottage she had bought some scarlet geraniums in pots and when the florist delivered them she arranged them on the terrace. Her day was relaxed and domestic. She threw out old cushions and magazines, turned out cupboards and cleaned shelves. She felt wonderful. Instant sexual gratification had lots going for it, she thought.

That evening she dressed in a short, flattering summer frock of cotton. Her tan was enhanced with baby oil spread all over her brown legs and arms. Her limbs glistened and shone.

'Hello, Laura.' Aaron was smiling and handed her a lager. 'You look good enough to eat. Shall you come back to my place again?' he whispered in her ear.

Her dress had slid up her thighs as she sat on the high stool by the bar. She grinned.

'I might,' she teased. 'What have you to offer me in the way of entertainment?'

'Whatever you like, my flower.' His brown beard was soft on her face as he kissed her cheek.

His cottage was cool and dark, though untidy, with clothes and papers thrown around and food left out on the worktops of the kitchen. They did not bother with preliminaries. He led her upstairs to his bedroom, where the lights from the harbour shone on the low, sloping ceiling. He pushed her against the wall and kissed her. He undressed her slowly, lifting her short dress up over her thighs.

'Tie me down, and do rude things to me, Aaron, with your waders on.'

He put on his thigh-high waders and rubbed up against her, so the rubber pressed her belly and thighs. He pushed his fingers inside her knickers and rubbed her flesh.

'Tie me down,' she begged.

'No, I daren't. I might get carried away.'

He took his leather belt from his jeans and undid his flies so his erection stuck out rudely above the waders. He slid the belt between her legs and her knees buckled.

'I must lie down,' she said.

He picked her up and lay her across his bed. He placed the leather belt under her buttocks and between her legs. Her knickers and the belt sawed into her vulva. She felt herself open to the pressure of leather and silk. His fingers slid between her buttocks. He pressed his cock against her belly. Her hands went to slide the belt and wrap his cock in it. The waders rubbed her legs and thighs. The leather sawed her tingling flesh. He breathed hard and his beard hurt her face. He kissed her breasts and bit the nipples. Her wetness was staining the belt. He pressed his cock under the leather and into her. She held his balls and buttocks and smelled the strong scent of rubber. Her cries were drowned in his as they climaxed.

Laura and Aaron did nothing sociable together. They only had sex. They met in the pub, usually, or at his cottage during the day when he was not diving, and had sex. This suited Laura. She only lusted after him, and wanted the rubber boots. However, she noticed that there was another female presence at his cottage. She saw tights hanging in the little bathroom, and white cotton knickers. She had decided not to mention them, thinking it was none of her business who else he had sex with, but then it occurred to her that he might be married.

'Aaron, do tell me to mind my own business, if you want to, but I was wondering who the flimsy underwear belongs to, in the bathroom.'

He laughed. 'Ha! That's Becky. My little sister! She lives here too.'

Becky and Laura's paths had not yet crossed.

Laura was content with her 'rest and recreation' from the war of love. She stayed in bed until eight-thirty most mornings, going for a jog along the beach before having a shower, washing her hair and then having a simple breakfast, usually on the terrace. Then she would go and see her neighbour and ask if she needed any shopping. After a trip to the shops, before the tourists were out and about, she went to read to Mrs Poldhu.

Then her time was hers for the rest of the day.

She toyed with a few ideas on her laptop. She looked out of the attic window and started the outline of a painting of the view from the house. She had lunch alone, again on the terrace, if it was warm enough. She heard the call of the boatman: 'Trips around the lighthouse, leaving in ten minutes. Get your tickets on the boat.'

Sounds carried from the harbour up the hill. She watched as gannets stabbed the waves to dive for fish. Cormorants bobbed, their bodies almost submerged, their snake necks high. Little sailing boats with brightly coloured sails were swept along by the wind, and kites flew in the blue sky.

71

One morning, as usual, she went for a walk along the beach. The tide was high; waves licked her bare feet and she felt the clean fresh air filling her lungs. A few surfers slid on the high rolling corrugated waves and she admired their grace and skill. She loved the look of them – the tight-fitting neoprene moulding their slender, youthful bodies. She thought maybe she should learn to surf. Was it too late? Was she supple enough, young enough? She loved the idea of the rubber-like suit on her body. About two weeks after she and Aaron had started to sleep together, he surprised her with a present.

'Wherever did you get them?' Laura exclaimed in amazement as she undid the wrapping paper and exposed a pair of fine black latex rubber sheets.

'I sent for them – mail order.'

'Let's pretend I'm a Turkish whore and you are my client,' said Laura.

'Why a Turkish whore?'

'Because I read in a magazine somewhere that they have rubber sheets and use lots of baby oil.'

They arranged large cushions over the floor and covered them with one of the rubber sheets. The log fire gave a soft pink glow to the darkened room and their naked flesh. At first they shivered on the cool rubber but soon warmed each other and wrapped the other sheet on top of themselves. When they were quite warm she sat up and reached for the baby oil and began to massage him with it. First she made him lie on his stomach, his legs close together. She started at his feet, firmly holding each foot and massaging with the oil. Then she moved up his legs, one at a time, gently but firmly kneading each calf muscle, and moved gradually to his thighs, slipping her fingers insinuatingly between his tight-closed legs for a moment before kneading his small firm buttocks. His legs relaxed and she pushed her hands between them to stroke his scrotum with the oil. Then, sitting naked astride his thighs, she slowly massaged his back, moved up his spine to his neck and along his shoulders and arms to his fingers.

'You are finished on that side, sir. Turn over, please.'

Laura's 'client' turned over, his penis already swollen. She poured more oil on her hands and on to his stomach, casually dribbling it on to his balls and penis. Rivulets of oil ran down between his thighs. She massaged his chest, shoulders and arms and left his belly wet and his penis swelling against it. Her small, strong hands soothed all the knots in the muscles of his lower legs and then moved inevitably to his thighs and the bulge of his scrotum. He was completely covered in oil now and sliding a little on the rubber sheet. She rubbed oil over her own body and then stroked his swollen penis with the whole of her body, up and down, so that first her mouth, then her small, pointed breasts, then her rounded belly and well-oiled thighs rubbed silkily over his sex. She concentrated her whole attention on his sex, making him feel that there was nothing else in the world but his very desirable wet prick. She took the other rubber sheet and covered him with it and he shivered with the shock of its coolness. She found his penis through the rubber and held it tight in her hands, then pushed and fondled the rubber-encased rigid penis against her own sex, sitting astride him, her legs wide apart. The dark lips of her sex curled back to take the rubber baton.

Moaning, he tore the sheet from his body and hurled it over her so that they were both inside a black tent of rubber, oiled on both sides. The smell was dark and forbidden and she breathed it in deeply. He wrapped the top sheet round her while she was still above him and enveloped her thighs. Then he pushed his fingers, half folded in the rubber, between her legs and stroked her, torturing her with his tantalisingly delicate touch on her open sex.

73

'Push the rubber inside me – please, please!' she begged, and came immediately he did so, without meaning to – the excitement was too much. He pushed his hard, slippery cock inside her and held the rubber sheet tight against her buttocks, almost tearing the sheet as his fingernails dug into her flesh. The rubber was all round them, caressing their hot skin. Their mutual sweat mingled sweetly with the dark smell of sex and rubber.

He pulled her over on to her belly and sat over her buttocks. He covered her head, back and arms with the rubber sheet so she was completely hidden from him except for her firm, upward-thrusting bottom. The under sheet pressed against the mound of her sex and he slapped her slippery oiled buttocks until they stung. Every time he slapped, her sensitive sex mound pressed into the rubber beneath and all she could feel was the sensation of rubber. The smell was thick in her nostrils. Her teeth and lips pulled at the rubber sheet that slid beneath her body. She could see nothing and this heightened her other senses. He lifted her bodily so his hands were surrounding her sex and entered her from behind, shoving her pink buttocks into his belly. Her juices ran thick and warm. He kept pumping her disembodied arse, holding her pressed against his belly. The rhythm of her moans quickened, and they came together.

Their animal smells mingled with the rubber and warmth.

Chapter Eight

Thomas

Aaron was going with Bill Montpelier on his boat to the wreck-diving site in the Scillies.

'Tell me about the wreck,' asked Laura, as he left her bed.

'Oh, it's a four-masted barque, the *Elizabetta*. Foundered off Bryher in the eighteenth century. Should be interesting. I'll be back in about three weeks' time,' he told Laura, and she waved him goodbye regretfully.

'I'll miss you,' she said, honestly.

She could smell the rubber on her hands for many days afterwards. Then she roused herself and made efforts to be sociable again.

Anna had told her to drop in any time; she loved a gossip and a glass of wine and craved company. Laura would go and see her soon. Meanwhile, she went for long walks along the cliffs, sometimes taking a sketchbook and pencils. She took great delight in the craggy coast, the wild wind and rough seas. Fishing boats dropped into deep watery valleys, disappeared momentarily, then rose, pushing the wall of water aside with their prows. She was exhilarated by the light, the space of sky and sea.

She decided to join an art class. There were several artists in the town who gave individual painting lessons, but there was only one studio that catered for a group of daily students. She bravely signed on and went to her first session, at four o'clock one Monday afternoon. She climbed the rickety stairs and went into the old studio. She had seen postcards of the historic premises. It was one of the things that had attracted her to the lessons. It was a high wooden room with horizontal boarding, painted white, and there were six long windows facing north. There were a dozen students, mostly holiday-makers, she assumed. She sat at a donkey – a stool with an easel attached – and took out her paper and charcoal. She pinned the large sheet of paper to the board on the easel, like the other students were doing. The artist was a man of about sixty. He had long white hair tied in a ponytail.

'Good afternoon, people,' he said, in a melodious voice, 'I am your tutor. My name is Stanley Gibbs. I hope you have all paid? If not, see me now, please.'

There was a flurry of scraped chairs and stools and an easel crashed to the ground.

'Oh dear, oh dear, never mind,' he said as he went to help an elderly woman with the overturned easel. Laura stood to help him. 'Thank you, my dear,' he said to her. His smile was kind. Laughter lines radiated from his brown eyes. She suddenly thought of Jerry.

She really enjoyed the two-hour life-drawing session. The model was a largish lady in her forties and her flesh was firm and rosy; her face was sweet, round and mild. Laura had signed on for eight weeks' lessons. She would go on Monday, Wednesday and Friday afternoons. It was good discipline, she knew, and would teach her about line and form, depth and movement. She left her drawings in the corner of the room at the end of the session and put away her things in her old rucksack.

'Do you fancy a beer?' said her tutor. 'We usually go

to the Galleon after these lessons. Anyone can come along.'

'Why not? Thanks, I do fancy a drink.'

Four other students went with them.

She saw a few people she recognised in the pub, and Stan knew everyone. Every man and woman who entered the bar greeted him.

'Have you lived here always?' Laura asked him, sipping her lager.

'No, not always. I come from London, originally, but fell in love with the place in the late sixties, like lots of my friends who used to come on holiday here. I simply didn't go back to London one autumn, but stayed and tried my luck painting.'

'And do you make a living?' another student asked.

'Not from my own painting, no, but I do sell the odd work now and again. I'm having a retrospective exhibition in the Seagull Gallery in the square soon. Come if you want to see what I do.'

There were enthusiastic murmurings and the holiday students wanted to know the details to see if they would still be in town. Laura made a note of the exhibition dates.

'There's a private view next Saturday, if you're interested,' he said to her.

'I am interested, yes,' she said.

'I'll get you an invitation.'

She didn't miss a drawing session. She dressed in jeans and T-shirt, or a sweatshirt when it was cool. She had a stack of drawings of different nudes – male and female, young and old. There was a young girl she loved to draw. Her body was slender, flowing, her face angelic. She could have been only about sixteen, and was just formed, perfect. Her grey eyes were haughty in the knowledge that she was beautifully made. Her long blonde hair fell from a high round forehead to her waist. Laura noticed that the atmosphere in the studio was charged when this particular model posed. The students became voyeurs, enjoying the feast of absolute youthfulness, the smooth, unblemished flesh, the poise of the young girl. Talk was kept to a minimum at most sessions, but when Rowena was modelling, there was silence, just the occasional sigh. All felt a reverence for female perfection.

Laura smiled at the thought of the young men and the older ones lusting after the untouchable model. She was like a perfect doll in a window: the easels, the pencils and paper were like sheets of glass between them and the naked girl. She was to be gazed at longingly, not touched. Rowena always went home after the modelling sessions. She did not come to the pub. 'She's too young,' said Stan once, when one of the men asked her if she wanted to go for a drink. 'Hands off Rowena,' he said, mildly.

'How old is she?' asked the young man.

'Seventeen,' said Stan. 'She's my daughter.'

'Oh!' said the young man, and smiled timidly.

Stan hadn't dressed up for his private view. He was, as usual, in baggy corduroy trousers, with a checked work shirt and suede shoes. No allowance was made for the fact that it was summer and rather warm.

Laura took Ethan and Eugene with her to the exhibition. She wore a short cream linen dress with thick-soled sandals in transparent colourless plastic. Most of the other guests still dressed in the fashion of their youth: long seventies skirts in flowing purple and black, and crushed velvet jackets.

Ethan and Eugene wore bright-coloured dungarees and floral shirts – updated seventies. Eugene was small and slender as a ballet dancer.

'Wow!' exclaimed Ethan, sipping his warm white wine.

'What is it?' said Eugene, standing on his toes to see over taller people's shoulders. 'I can't see a thing.'

'The paintings are all of one model, by the look of it. And she's gorgeous.' Ethan rolled his eyes in mock ecstasy and Eugene punched him playfully.

'I'm going to take a closer look,' Laura said, and pushed through the crowds of chattering people, who did not seem to be looking at the paintings at all, but consuming as much free wine as they could get their hands on. She noticed one of the painters who always attended Stan's classes: Odile, a Frenchwoman. Odile was tall and slim. She wore an extraordinary outfit: a one-piece, long-sleeved and long-legged cat-suit made of a fine black latex. It fitted her tightly and showed off her rather pointed breasts and narrow waist. Many people wore eccentric clothes here, but this was really something. It shouted her sexuality. It made her look naked even though she was completely covered. It was very like a wetsuit but was better designed, more subtle, sinuous. Laura could not take her eyes off Odile.

Laura noticed that on the drinks table there was a box with the notice CONTRIBUTIONS GRATEFULLY ACCEPTED, but she had only seen two people put cash in it. Many more had helped themselves to wine without paying a thing.

As the crowd thinned Ethan and Laura drew closer to the wall of paintings. Stan's model was his beautiful daughter, Rowena. The paintings were in oil, mostly, some in water colour, and there were a few drawings in pastels. All were of Rowena, but not the modest teen-ager that Laura had drawn in the studio. This Rowena was running, naked, hair wild, legs wide, or lying in an abandoned wide-legged pose. Laura was moved by the exuberance of the work. It was full of passion and love. There were portraits of her face: close-up drawings of her eyes and nose only, or her mouth, the moisture and arch of her upper lip so real that Laura almost wanted to wipe it dry. But then she noticed the date on the painting in front of her. It was an oil painting of a young girl on a swing, her long legs thrown high in violent movement, her head thrown back. It was dated 1951. It was now 1998. The model in this painting could not have been Rowena. Yet it looked very like her. She examined the rest of the dates on the work. They had been painted years ago. Of course, she should have known: it was a retrospective exhibition.

The crowds were thinning. The wine had all been drunk. A few red dots studded the wall where paintings had been sold. Stan stood talking to an old man with a stick, a grizzled old local who was laughing loudly and uninhibitedly. Stan chuckled. Laura approached them.

'Hello, this is Laura, one of my more intelligent students,' he said to the old man. 'This is Tom.'

'How are ye, my cheel?' The old man wiped his dribbling mouth. 'Don't I know you?'

'I don't think so. I'm sure I would have remembered you,' she said, turning on the charm.

'Yes, I know your pretty face. You must be the maid of May Trehearne as was. Look just like 'er, you do.'

'You knew my mother?'

'I knew your grandmother, too. Lovely woman she were. I were at 'er funeral, Christmas gone.'

'Oh yes! Of course you were. Thank you for going. I'm afraid I wasn't very sociable that day.'

'That's all right, my maid. When you've been to as many funerals as me, you'll learn how to be sociable.'

Next day Laura went to Anna and Charles's house. Anna's mother was alone in the house.

'Do come in, Laura. Sit down! Anna's out, I'm afraid. She won't be long.' The elderly woman made Laura comfortable in the sitting room and brought her a cup of tea. Laura liked Anna's mother very much, and had recently done several sketches of her in the garden.

'Oh, there's Thomas arriving home.' The old lady rose and went into the kitchen.

He gave Laura a wide smile through the open back window.

'Hello, Thomas!'

'Hello,' he said. He was covered in red mud, which made him look vaguely African – like a Masai warrior, thought Laura. He went upstairs to the bathroom and Laura heard his grandmother moving about in the kitchen. Laura felt almost sick with anticipation.

Thomas reappeared, a towel around his bare shoulders. He wore blue jeans and his feet were bare. His fair curly hair was still damp from his shower. Laura could hardly keep her eyes from his naked chest and strong arms. They sat in silence watching the television news, interrupted only by the old lady's solicitous questions to her grandson.

'Shall you have tea, Thomas? Do you want a piece of my fruitcake? I made it today.'

'Sit down, Gran, sit down and behave yourself, why don't you!' He spoke in a gentle tone of admonishment and she smiled and gazed at him lovingly. Laura liked his open affection towards his grandmother.

'Thomas, are you available for work at all? I mean, I've got one or two jobs that need doing at the house, nothing huge, just checking the dormer frame and sashes.'

'Well, I am working full-time at the moment, but I could do something weekends, if you like.'

She agreed to pay him cash and he said he would come that weekend. Soon Anna arrived home and Laura joined her in the kitchen for a glass of wine and a chat.

Anna had been shopping and wanted Laura's opinion of her new clothes. They took their glasses of wine and went upstairs to Anna's bedroom.

'What do you think, Laura? Does this make me look fat, or not?'

'You look good in that, silly. Not fat, just right, voluptuously sexy.'

'Oh, dear, does that mean tarty?'

'No! Stop it, Anna. It's flattering, that's all.'

'Oh, good, thanks, Laura. Mind you, Charles likes tarty!' She grinned and took another swig of wine, admiring herself in the mirror.

Saturday came, and Thomas arrived at eight thirty in the morning to see what Laura needed. She showed him the broken sash in the attic dormer, and the rotting door frame at the back. He got on with the work and she made him coffee and watched surreptitiously as he raised his muscular arms and his shoulders bulged under the faded blue vest. She had to go away from him so he wouldn't see the desire in her eyes.

Next time she saw Anna she tentatively asked if Thomas had a girlfriend. Yes, apparently there had been a year-long relationship with a young girl student, but they had broken it off when he came back to Cornwall.

'So, is he a virgin?'

'Well, how should I know? I'm only his mother. Anyway, why should it concern you?'

'Ah, it's all this sea air, Anna. It's making me frisky.'

'Hmm! Did I tell you we're taking my mother to Charles's mother in Devon? They got on so well last time they met, they have decided to have a holiday together. I think they're going to talk at each other rather than talk to each other, but I don't suppose either of them will notice.'

'Sounds a good idea. When are you going?'

'Saturday. We're taking some time off too, just staying at good restaurants with rooms for a week or two.'

'What about Thomas?'

'Well, perhaps you could look after him, eh? Make sure he has the occasional decent meal? Otherwise, he might live off pasties and get revoltingly fat.'

'I'll look after him, darling. Don't you worry.' Laura

smiled broadly and went pink at the thoughts that ran through her head.

A few days after his mother and father had taken his grandmother off for her stay in Devon, Thomas arrived at Laura's door with a bottle of wine and a bunch of sweetpeas. He wore clean blue jeans and a denim shirt. His short curly hair was still wet from his shower. He had not been able to scrub the dirt from his finger nails, and his hands were calloused and ingrained with red earth. He tried to hide them behind him.

'Don't be shy, Thomas. You know I like your work-man's hands, don't you! I'll draw you, if you like, one day.'

He blushed.

'Come on, come and sit down in the kitchen and talk to me, while I finish the cooking.' She led him into her kitchen and gave him a glass of beer.

'I'm very thirsty,' he said and she watched the muscles in his thick, strong neck as he threw back his head and drank the cold golden liquid.

She chopped leaves and arranged a salad in a large pottery bowl. She had found lettuces still surviving in the vegetable plot in her garden, and fresh herbs, and had incorporated them in the meal. She had cooked a chicken with tarragon sauce.

He ate with enjoyment and drank several glasses of wine with her. She watched him relax and bloom under her encouragement. She wore a brief summer dress in a soft fluid pale-cream fabric. It flared over her bottom and ended halfway down her tanned thighs. Thin straps dug into her suntanned shoulders. Her cleavage was just visible. Gold flat sandals showed off her narrow, brown feet. She leant over him to pour coffee and her breast touched his shoulder. She felt him stiffen.

'Do you mind if I do a quick sketch of you, now?'

'Er, well, no, all right.'

'Take off your shirt, will you? I want to see your back and shoulders.' She quickly gathered together a large sketchpad and pencils. She sat on the floor and told him to sit opposite her on the sofa. He did as she told him, pulling off his shirt over his head. He flopped down on the sofa, unsure of himself again.

'That's it. Just relax. It won't hurt.' She touched him lightly on the shoulders. 'Lie back and put your arms behind your head, like that. Yes, that's good.'

The smell of his warm, clean body assaulted her senses. She breathed it in. 'Yes! That's fine. Stay like that for a few minutes if you can.'

She drew quickly, the lines flowing. She looked hard at his strong, tanned shoulders, noting every curve and bulge. She worked fast, almost forgetting him as she saw only the beauty of his lines, like a young horse. She drew the hips and belly and was aware of the quivering bulge at his crotch. She sketched the rise of his thighs, the strength of his youth. It was almost Germanic, her drawing, like a thirties illustration of idealised Aryan beauty. His round head grew from the thick stem of his neck. His shoulders held the neck perfectly in balance. His bulging arms and naked chest glistened with a faint misty perspiration. His underarm hair was golden. She imagined she could smell the scent of his lust for her.

'What time is it, Thomas? '
  'Midnight.'
  'Do you want to go home?'
  'No, I want to stay here, with you.'
She took him by the hand and led him upstairs, leaving the dishes piled in the sink, her drawings on the sitting room floor. She went immediately to the bathroom and when she entered the bedroom dressed in a blue kimono, he was lying face down and naked across the bed.

She knelt over him on the bed and touched one arm above his elbow.

'You're beautiful,Thomas.'

'Am I?'

'I should draw you like this, now.'

'I would rather you did something else.'

'Shall I massage you?'

'Mm, yes please,' he whispered.

She took a bottle of baby oil and dripped it over his shoulders. She spread the soft cool oil over his body, enjoying each ripple of muscle. He shivered as she touched his waist. Firmly she stroked and massaged the young man's perfect flesh. He was so smooth and new. She stroked his rough hands with the oil, working into the scars of his workman's hands and fingers. Her hands firmly moved down the length of his spine, the weight of her small body pressing on each vertebra. He groaned with enjoyment. She pressed down on his waist where his tan finished and his white hips began. His buttocks were white as marble.

She poured more oil on to his back and moved her firm-fingered hands down over his taut buttocks, circling them and digging her fingers into the flesh very slightly. She sketched lines on them with her sharp nails. She was very wet. She had grown her pubic hair again. An attempt to forget Jerry. She slipped her fingers between his thighs and they slid open slightly to allow her access. Her oiled fingers dug firmly into his sensitive inner thigh. He writhed on the bed, groaning in erotic pleasure.

'Turn over,' she commanded, quietly, and she knelt back on her heels so he could turn over on to his back. His face was flushed and his eyes dilated. She had a glimpse of his penis as it leapt up at her, before he grabbed her and pulled her roughly on top of him. She felt his short but very hard penis thrusting against her body through the silky stuff of her kimono. His lips

sought hers and his tongue pushed between her lips.
She pushed him away gently.

'Wait, wait. Patience!' She poured the oil on to his
hairless chest and smoothed her slender hands across
his body, taking sensual pleasure in the strength of his
shoulders, the flatness of his stomach, the hardness of
his thighs. His fat cock stood straight and proud, throbbing slightly. She knelt up and placed his hands on her
waist. He undid the bow that held the kimono together
and slipped his rough fingers under the edges. She
shivered in delicious anticipation. He roughly pushed
the garment from her shoulders and let it drop, revealing the slim brown body.

'You are the most beautiful woman I've ever seen.'

She smiled at the flattery, arching her back so that her
belly and breasts were pushed towards his eager hands.
He touched her with a gentleness that belied the
strength behind his caresses. Her nipples were hard
little volcanoes, as erect as his thrusting penis. His
battered, rough hands felt marvellous on her, scratching
the fine skin made taut by too much sun. His hands
covered her breasts and squeezed them firmly, allowing
the nipples freedom between his fingers before he
pinched them lightly. She almost purred in appreciation.

'Am I doing things right?' he whispered in her ear,
kissing her cheek and her hair.

'You know you are.'

He let one hand wander down over her round belly
to stroke her dark mass of sex hair. Laura leant towards
him and felt his hand slide between her legs. Her body
pressed his and her breasts squashed against his hard
young chest. She opened her legs so she was still
kneeling over him but only supported by his body. He
groaned and held her tightly, his penis pressed hard
against her sex. One arm held her hard against him, the
other was behind her and his hand came up between
her damp thighs and stroked the engorged flesh. She

moved her buttocks in circles to feel his fingers all over her sex lips and her plump mound of flesh covered in curly hair. He grabbed her writhing buttocks and slammed his hips upward, his penis finding her slit immediately and making her cry out in shock. His cock was very stiff and aggressive, touching her wetness with a force and intensity that was very exciting. She had to hold back her orgasm. She wanted to savour the first one longer than this, but Thomas was having trouble making his lovemaking last, too. His face and chest had the strong flush of sexual arousal: his pupils had grown huge. He had the glazed look of a wild animal.

She resolutely lifted herself off and away from his urgent cock and lay down by his side, all the time stroking his hair and face soothingly. His chest rose and fell heavily and he groaned and put an arm across his face.

'What's the matter?'

'I find it difficult to control my orgasms.'

'I can help you, don't worry,' she said. He opened his Germanic blue eyes and looked at her. She was smiling, reassuringly.

'Let me make you come first,' he said.

She raised her arms in surrender and lay still, her eyes closed, her mouth slightly open. His soft mouth was on hers, his insistent tongue searching her mouth. He was over her, his legs wide apart, his cock in one hand.

'Touch me, Thomas, touch me.'

He released his cock and it sprang upward to his belly. He pushed both hands between her legs and buried them in her wetness. His fingers found her outer labia and rubbed them, then parted her inner lips and pushed roughly into the juicy purse. She put her hands on his shoulders to feel the strong young body, the clean muscular form – he was like a storm trooper bearing down on her. She almost swooned at his eager, naïve touch. He reached behind her to hold her rounded buttocks in one hand while he stroked the palm of the other pitted hand across her sex, and held her up from the bed by her buttocks and her sex. He held her close to his loins so that she could feel his cock throbbing and hard at the entrance to her vagina. She began to orgasm and he carried on pressing against her, his palm rasping against her pubic hair and his hard cock just at the entrance of her sex. His fingers rubbed slowly and firmly as the waves of orgasm rolled through her body in spasms. She fell back exhausted and satisfied.

Wow, that was quite something, she thought. This lad was no virgin. 'Thank you, Thomas!'

'Thank you,' he said smiling widely.

'Well now, what would you like me to do to you, Thomas?'

He answered by lifting her on top of him.

'Do anything to me. Whatever you do will be marvellous.'

She began to kiss his face, his nose, his mouth, his chin. Her head moved to his shoulders and trunk. She nibbled his nipples. He groaned and moved away from her mouth.

'What's the matter, Thomas?'

'Don't touch my nipples. I'll come straight away.'

'Really?' She moved away from his over-sensitive nipples and kissed his broad shoulders and licked the length of his arms. She then concentrated on his hard, strong, battered hands, licking between the fingers and to the tips, sucking on each fingernail and finally on his fat thumbs, digging her teeth slightly into the rough skin. Laura was in an aroused state again with the novelty and beauty of the lovely youth beneath her. Her lips ran down the line between his breasts and tugged at his nipples.

'No! You wicked woman!'

She laughed.

She licked and bit gently at his taut stomach and belly and just scraped her teeth against his short, stiff penis just for a moment before leaving it to lick his thighs. Her mouth wrapped around his balls while her nails pressed softly into the base of his penis and scratched gently up the length of the shaft, pulling the loose skin over the tip and holding it there for a second before pushing it back down and scratching gently down to the root.

Thomas groaned softly, his head shaking from side to side in an ecstasy of excitement. Laura placed herself on top of him, her buttocks next to his face, her sex pressed up against his chest, and she took his penis into her mouth, holding it firmly at the base and stroking his balls. His lips sucked at her sex, his strong arms holding her and moving her across his wet lips and teeth. They swayed together in an oily orgy, his tongue inside her, thrusting and darting, sucking at her labia, holding her buttocks apart with strong hands, exposing her wet, swollen sex and anus to his ardent mouth.

Laura squeezed lightly around the base of his thick cock to stop him from coming. She sucked his penis to the hilt and suckled it, her teeth digging in a little. She felt the change in his breathing, the quickening of his blood. She loosened her hold but sucked strongly on the thick shaft. He came silently inside her mouth with little spurts that hit the back of her throat before she swallowed the hot sperm, coming almost immediately after him.

They freed themselves from each other's embrace and curled up like exhausted children, his head resting on her belly.

In the morning they woke very early to a blue sky. Laura was concerned with her age in the harsh morning light but he was blind to her tiny imperfections. He made exquisite love to her that morning. She came with his hard little prick inside her. Her sex seemed to close in and surround it, holding it firmly like her mouth had done. It felt strangely aggressive – an exciting blunt weapon – and his rough fingers rasped her smooth skin. He flushed rosily red all over his face, neck and chest when he was about to come. They tasted each other's sex juices on their fingers.

'I love your breasts,' he said, sucking the nipples hard. 'And your arse,' he said, squeezing the plump flesh.

'I want you inside me. Stick your cock into me. Fuck me!'

He plunged into her. She clawed at his white buttocks and raised her knees, wrapping her legs and feet round his back, hugging him to her. They rhythmically rubbed together until they became one writhing sex organ. Her orgasms came in tiny flutters and deep spasms. Her face changed every time he made her come. First it was lascivious, her lips dry, her eyes mad and unseeing. Then she was softened, gentle, her mouth open, relaxed, her lips swollen, her eyes closed, her face pale, her damp hair flattened on her forehead, exhausted.

It was then, when she was quiet and seemingly finished by his efforts, that she felt the most thrill. She was wide open to him. He was her young storm trooper, violating her, raping her, filling her with his rough youthfulness, his overwhelming passion and lust.

As she lay quiet and open and passive, he lunged at her, attacking her with his stiff cock, filling her, overpowering her with his strong arms, his thighs pressing her to the bed, his rough hands bruising her tender flesh. She came loudly this time, groaning as she felt the spurt of his seed inside her.

Chapter Nine

Dinner with Thomas

*L*aura had been for a long walk along the cliffs. The telephone rang almost as soon as she opened the door of her house.

'Hi!' It was James. He had been a newspaper journalist before he changed direction and started *Young Living* magazine. When they had first met years ago at a party he had wanted to sleep with Laura but she grew to value his friendship too much to spoil the relationship. He was always in love with someone, male or female, usually much younger than himself.

'I phoned Thursday evening, but you weren't there. Where were you?' he asked.

'Out at an opening. I am allowed out, you know.'

'Who with? Anyone I should know about? Look out for those artists, Laura. Their morals aren't as high as yours or mine.'

'Huh!' Laura nearly choked with laughter.

James was a terrible gossip and loved to hear anything scandalous. 'Laura, I've met this beautiful boy, Guido. May I bring him for a weekend? I want to know what you think.'

'Well, I am a bit busy at the moment, James. You don't need my approval anyway, do you?'

'I just want to show him off, darling.'

'I'll ring you when I've looked in my diary and fix a date for you to come. I have to go. See you!' She put down the phone firmly, smiling to herself.

'So, where are you taking me?' she asked Thomas as he opened the car door for her. She was pleased at this show of gallantry, hoping that he hadn't done it out of deference to her age.

'To eat in the Aquarium Restaurant at Porthleven.'

He drove his mother's Rover. Laura sat back and relaxed. Thomas was in charge tonight. Laura eyed him as if he was a work of art. He had fine lines. He was not tall but nicely built, compact and muscular. He wore a white cotton shirt open at the neck to show his smooth throat. She wore her red dress – the one she had worn the first night she slept with Jerry.

The waiter showed them to their corner table, which had a large pink linen tablecloth and huge pink linen napkins. The lighting was seductive and low.

She drank whisky and then more wine than Thomas did.

'Do you think I feel smooth and soft?' She took his hand and slipped it beneath her dress to feel her silky thighs. He blushed and pushed his hand higher to discover that she was naked. They sat close together in the semi-dark of the restaurant, his hand at the top of her thighs, slowly caressing the furry mound with two fingers, then moving to her inner thighs to stroke the fine skin between her stocking tops and her sex. She leant towards him and delicately traced his lips with her tongue. Before he could take her lips with his she turned her face to caress his ear with her tongue, and very gently nipped the lobe with her sharp teeth.

'Wow!' he yelped like a puppy dog, and the waiter came running.

'Yes, sir?'

Thomas's hand had resumed its place on the table, and Laura smoothed down her dress so that her legs were covered.

'Another bottle of the same,' said Thomas, smiling at the waiter.

'That was very good. Are you sure you can afford it? she asked, when the waiter had gone. 'I'll share the bill with you.'

'No, certainly not, thank you, I have enough. I've just been paid.'

'Well, then,' she said, when the wine had been opened and poured. 'Where were we?'

He unclasped his hands and reached under the table to take the hem of her skirt and slide it upward to expose her thigh. She was very wet and knew she must be staining her dress with the love juices that flowed in lovely anticipation. She moved closer to him and let her hand drop into his lap. She played her fingers lightly over his inevitable bulge and used one to trace the length of his straining cock, pressing it deeper and deeper into the cloth of his trousers, her fingernails scratching the material.

'My God, don't go on! I can't bear it!' he begged.

'Don't worry, Thomas, I won't overexcite you. Relax and enjoy it.'

'No, it's too public. We can't . . .'

She smoothed her hand across his crutch over and over and felt the straining of his sex to escape the trousers. He closed his eyes and sat back in his chair, having given up his fight only too easily. She undid the belt without looking, and saw in her mind the leather and metal unhook from each other, the wonderful moment of freedom about to happen. She unzipped him and his swollen cock leapt to rear its head under the table of the restaurant.

She took his resting hand and placed it over her slit.

He instinctively felt for her wetness and pressed into it. Her hand enclosed his penis firmly and with determination began to rub the shaft and draw the hood over the glistening tip, squeezing and caressing. He moaned gently.

'For goodness' sake, you can't mean to . . .?'

She laughed softly into his ear, 'But I am going to come, Thomas. You are going to make me come, here, in this restaurant.'

His wet fingers burrowed and fondled, stroked and grabbed the soft warm wetness of her flesh. His other arm was around her, pulling her close, and she moved her thumb and third finger smoothly up and down his hard erection to keep time with his own caresses. As she felt the tide of passion rise in her she held his sex tight at the base and didn't move her fingers except to squeeze tightly. Her orgasm rose and took her over as his fingers slid in and out of her slippery lips and she buried her head in his neck to stop the moans.

Thomas asked the waiter to fetch Laura's coat and she hid herself in it, concealing her love-stained dress.

'Did you enjoy your meal, sir?'

'Oh, yes, thank you. We'll come again, I hope.'

They laughed together as they got into his car and drove back to Porthzelah.

'May I stay with you?' he whispered, as they reached the cottage.

'But of course.' She kissed him lightly and got out of the car. Laura took him to her room – the room which had been her grandmother's. She'd had it redecorated.

'Make yourself at home,' she said, and went into the bathroom.

Thomas looked around. The wallpaper was a wide pale-pink-and-white stripe. The room was like a warm, pretty Edwardian boudoir, with a collection of small boxes on the dark mahogany chest. Cream Holland blinds edged with lace hung at the white sash windows.

Long mirrors reflected the white bed. White Egyptian cotton pillowcases were crisp and inviting. The dark wood floor was scattered with rag rugs of pink and green. Pink glass shell wall-lamps were each side of the large, high bed and threw flattering beams on to it.

Laura reappeared, wearing a loose pink satin wrap over her damply glistening, slim body. Thomas was lying on her bed in all his clothes.

'You know, there's nothing quite like freshly laundered blue jeans and a white cotton shirt, with a leather belt, of course, holding everything together.' She leant over him and stared into his dark-lashed blue eyes.

'I'm glad.' he said, smiling in self-congratulation.

'Would you like me to dress up for you?'

'How do you mean?' he whispered as he kissed her and held her small body close to him.

'What do you like? Do you like stockings and suspenders?'

'Mmm, yes, I love them. But I don't care what you wear – you always look lovely.'

She drew away from him as he lay on the wide bed with his arms behind his head and legs crossed. He had kicked off his sneakers. She disappeared into her dressing room and Thomas lay there almost asleep, waiting in the soft pink glow of the pretty room.

Her light fingers moved across his chest to the open neck of his shirt. He didn't open his eyes yet. She undid the buttons deliciously slowly. She saw his desire rise as his penis fought to escape his tight jeans. Her hands moved to his legs and caressed each thigh, almost accidentally touching the bulge of his sex, and moved quickly over his waist to undo his metal-buckled leather belt. He opened his eyes.

Her rosy breasts were pushed into a black silky bra that was like a set of straps holding each breast apart and upward. Her fully exposed nipples were extraordinary, dark, erect and quivering on her tiny, perfect breasts, and pointing directly at his mouth. Her body was encased in a tight-fitting black satin waspie – a corselet – tightly laced at the back, and boned and shaped to make her waist very tiny. It started just below the breasts and stopped at her hipbones. Fine red silk ribbons were threaded through and tied in tiny bows front and back, and elasticised suspenders covered in black satin were taut against her thighs and fastened on to fine black stockings. She looked like an exquisite, gift-wrapped doll, her sex parts exposed and offered, the rosiness of them matching the red nails of her fingers and toes.

His mouth opened and one small, rosy breast moved to fill it. The nipple was firm and pushed deep into his mouth like a tiny penis. She could tell he was almost in a swoon of delight and expectation. She deftly removed the belt and undid his zip carefully, allowing his swollen penis to slide out of its prison and lie comfortably on his belly inside his boxer shorts. She pulled his jeans down over his feet and removed his socks. She then slid her smooth, satin-encased body over his hips and thighs, causing his penis to rise up and peep over the top of his pants. Her breasts now stroked his silky smooth sex and pushed down his pants. His hands grasped her slippery waist and pulled her higher over him. He took her nipples into his mouth, first one, then the other, the silky straps moving across his face. Her warm, sweet breath was in his eyes and swept over his cheeks, hypnotising him into a sort of dream.

His sex had never been so hard and huge. She admired it with her small fingers, lightly stroking and murmuring. He had hardly any pubic hair, just a soft halo of fine hair at the base of his penis. She moved over him and let her lips and tongue caress his hard young penis.

'Lovely, lovely cock,' she whispered. 'So sweet and fresh.'

She licked and suckled gently, her hands moving lightly to encase his balls, which retracted at the shock of her touch.

'You have balls like a boxer dog.' She laughed and licked her lips. 'I like them.' He was very excited now and made her stop sucking his cock. He removed his shirt and pants so that he was completely naked, and knelt over her, kissing her open mouth furiously and then her dark, animal nipples, catching them between eager teeth.

'Shh, Shh!' She gently slowed his too-eager enthusiasm and he smiled and said,

'Yes, it's too good to be over with quickly, but I'm so excited.'

His firm fingers traced the shape of her small, slender body trapped in the silky case of the corselet, felt the sharp peak of her hip bone and moved down to the creamy softness of her thigh. The exposed flesh between the black stockings and the corselet was an inviting spread of paleness drawing him to the centre where lay her dark triangle of bushy hair, waiting for his touch. His fingers circled the soft bush of hair and slid immediately to the centre fold of her sex, which was moist and hot – a waiting, alive crevice, which folded over his fingers and hid them inside her. She moaned appreciatively.

His penis lay pointed towards her sex, hard and quivering and swollen. Her hands guided it slowly over her thighs and let the tip touch her mound, and then she moved it up on to the silky surface of her corselet. His hands were all over her. He knelt above her, a smooth, clean youth, inexperienced in the ways of love-making, only aware of the mechanics of the business. But her extra twelve years' experience in the art of pleasing another's body was a wonderful tutorial for this eager student.

She guided his fingers back to her sex and he pushed

his firm body impatiently on hers, pressing her suspenders hard against her legs. She enjoyed the feeling of being held down and hurt almost too much, with the pressure of tight-laced satin enclosing her panting body. His penis was leaking small globules of white juice on to her shiny black corselet.

She let him inside her and gently held his smooth, tight buttocks, only allowing small movements inside her, holding her excitement back to suit his.

She could see he was in a swoon of erotic excitement. His belly was against the shiny black satin and her animal nipples were rubbing his chest. His penis was pushing hard and deep inside her tiny body, as if it would tear her apart, but she didn't cry out in pain: she moaned sweetly, enjoying the thrusting of his young sex.

'It's good, it's good,' she whispered. She held his buttocks tightly, digging her red nails into his flesh.

'Now!' she said. 'Now! Come now!' And he let go into her, with a deep thrust and spurt, and he cried out. Her orgasm came as she felt his wetness flood her.

Chapter Ten

Odile

*T*he next days passed in an erotic haze. Laura felt ten years younger, revitalised by the young man's strenuous demands. Her body glowed with health. But although she felt grateful for Thomas's love and didn't want to hurt his young ego, her love for him was almost purely sensual.

Her morning sessions reading to Mrs Poldhu and the art lessons every other day gave a pattern to her indolent life, punctuating the sexual excesses with disciplined work and a sense of purpose. She felt that she was beginning to become part of the community.

She particularly enjoyed the life class when Rowena was the model. The young girl's body was a joy to behold. Her long lithe limbs were like a ballet dancer's – she was like a reed swaying. Her small budding breasts sat high on her rib cage and her long blonde hair was a curtain from under which she gazed at lesser mortals with dark-lashed navy-blue eyes.

One afternoon Rowena was modelling a series of quick, difficult poses, where she moved every five minutes and the students had to produce an immediate sketch of her shape. Stan, apparently, had other business, and Odile, the Frenchwoman who had worn rubber to his exhibition, took over the class. She was not as relaxed as Stan was, with his slow, careful examination of the students' work. She raced around, smoking, exclaiming and swearing in French at their errors. She said something to Rowena that Laura didn't hear. Rowena scowled at the Frenchwoman and stood, her hands on her hips and said, 'That's it! I'm leaving.' She disappeared behind the screen that was there for her to change in private, came out in a very short flared skirt and T-shirt and left the studio without another word of explanation.

'Ah! Merde, alors!' said Odile, and lit another cigarette.

Later, when Laura was walking along the harbour in the dark, thinking about Jerry, and what she should do about Thomas, she saw Rowena with two middle-aged men, who looked like holiday-makers. They both had moustaches and were beefy and unevenly tanned. The girl was between them and looked drunk. The men were half carrying her, laughing and talking loudly in Birmingham accents.

Laura walked over the road to confront them. 'Rowena, are you all right? Do you want help?'

'No, why should I want help?' The girl was slurring her words slightly, but looked sensible enough.

'Are you sure?'

'Yes, quite sure.'

Laura followed them, keeping well back so they wouldn't see her. The girl was holding both their hands and running and stopping, dragging them almost. She was certainly inebriated. Laura felt like a spy. The night was starlit and the lights on the harbour lit the streets. They went down an alleyway and Laura crept up to a high granite wall and peeped around the corner. One of the men was undoing his flies. The girl was up against a wall. She was giggling. She lifted her flared white skirt, like a dove wing in the starlight. Laura held her

100

breath as she saw that Rowena wore nothing under the skirt. Her white thighs flashed and she opened them wide.

First one man fucked her against the wall. She made no noise, did not fight or cry out. She wants it, thought Laura, disgusted at herself for watching. The man grunted and thrust quickly and was finished. The other had been watching too, and was already holding his erection, pink and glistening, in his hands. He moved over her, covering her with his huge shape, like a cloak enveloping her. He took longer, and the other man watched, leaning against the same wall, smoking a cigarette. The second man was drunk and couldn't finish what he had started. Laura saw that the first one had an erection again, and was rubbing himself while he watched. His drunk friend eventually gave up his frustrating efforts and slipped down on to the cobbles, sitting there stupidly. His mate took over and fucked Rowena again, holding her roughly. She didn't flinch. Her hips writhed towards his, and her neck arched away from his leering face. She pushed her slender white belly into him and Laura saw her hands go down to it. After they had finished the men moved away from her up the alley and into another, disappearing into the night. Laura slipped behind the wall so Rowena wouldn't see her, but she went the other way.

Laura was aware that the girl was only seventeen. The men had not been doing anything illegal, but if the girl was prostituting herself, Laura thought her father should know about it. But how could she let him know?

Next day was not an art class day for Laura but she sought out Rowena at the beach. There was a crowd of teenagers who sat together on the beach most days during the school holiday. Laura wandered down to the shore and looked back up the beach at the hundreds of holiday-makers with their encampments of colourful

101

windbreaks, picnics and beach umbrellas advertising Coca Cola. The local youths and their girls were in a huge group together. Like mating gulls, thought Laura. The boys preened their feathers – showed off their surfing muscles and tans. The girls pretended not to notice, giggling together and preening also – their little tits and bums bobbing in minuscule bikinis, their quick eyes hidden behind dark glasses. It was a ritual of youth: the viewing of each other's charms, the mating calls, the roughhousing, the playing, the pushing each over in the sand and tickling. Rowena was there in the centre and there was no hope of talking to her in private. Then Laura saw skinny Odile sitting with the young people. She was talking to Rowena and a pretty, plump, dark-haired girl of about the same age or maybe a bit younger. Laura walked past them, throwing a quick glance at Rowena but not catching her eye.

She went to the art school in the afternoon in the hope of seeing Stan, who gave lessons every day, but there was a notice saying that class had been cancelled for that day.

'Ethan, do you know anything about a French-woman? Odile her name is. She teaches art with Stan.'

Laura was in the pub with Ethan and Eugene having a beer.

'That anorexic bird?' piped up Eugene.

'Yes, that's the one.'

'She's new here, I think, only arrived this year, any-way. She's a nasty piece of work, I think.'

'Ethan, you think everyone is a nasty piece of work,' said Eugene.

'No, really, I don't know anything about her,' said Ethan. 'But I don't like her thin lips. She looks sneaky to me.'

'The rest of her is thin, she can't help having thin lips,' said Eugene.

'I think she might have some evil hold over Rowena,' said Laura.

'Go on, why?' said a fascinated Eugene.

'It's just a feeling I have.'

'That's how gossip begins, be careful,' said Ethan. 'Malicious gossip does not become you, dear.'

'No, you're right. I'm sorry,' said a contrite Laura, but she resolved to find out more and to watch Odile and Rowena.

Her opportunity came rather sooner than she expected. Next day she attended her usual art class. Stan was still not there but Odile was taking his class. Laura arrived very early for the class, wanting to work at her most recent drawing.

She heard a voice as she went up the stairs.

'Yes, I'll come to your place tonight with Rory. Thanks, Odile.'

'*D'accord*, Rowena. I'll see you later.'

'If you let me meet Rory in private I'll let you cane me,' Rowena giggled. 'You can watch us do it, if you like.'

'Thank you, I would like that.'

Laura heard the unmistakable sound of lips on flesh. She coughed and made as much noise as she could entering the room, and the woman and the girl separated. Rowena said, 'Oh, I forgot to tell you, I can't model today. I have to do something else.'

'But it is too late to tell us now, how are we to continue the class without a model? Really, Rowena!' Odile was furious, but the girl tossed her ponytail and ran down the stairs, her short white skirt lifting and showing her perfect, tanned bottom.

'Well, what was that all about?' asked Laura. The Frenchwoman was tight-lipped and refused to answer.

'There is no model today,' she said.

'Oh! That's a shame,' said Laura. 'Is Rowena OK?'

'*Salope!*' swore the Frenchwoman and turned her back on Laura.

'Shall I do it?' asked Laura.

'What do you mean?'

'Shall I model for the class? Just this once, of course.'

'Would you? OK, that would be good.'

As the students began to arrive, Laura began to be nervous. She had offered her services as a life model on the spur of the moment and now she was getting cold feet. What had she been thinking of? I must be mad, she thought. However, she had let herself in for the job and now she had to do it.

The class of twelve people sat around her in a straggling circle, their paper pinned to their easels. Laura slipped out of Rowena's kimono and sat on the low wooden podium. She kept her back straight and her stomach in, remembering how she had noticed models she had hired do the same thing. She remembered Guy and the fake tan. She was tanned all over and her pubic hair was black and glossy. She wasn't ashamed of her body: on the contrary, these past weeks with Thomas making love to her had given her a confidence she hadn't had before. His adoration of her breasts and belly had made her proud of herself and she felt that she was as good-looking as the young model who had abandoned the podium.

Odile eyed her curiously. The thin woman wore a vicious look, as if she was jealous of her. She told her to sit any way she wanted and the class started. The poses would last fifteen minutes each. Fifteen minutes was about all that Laura could take. She had not realised how tiring it was on the back muscles to sit still for that length of time. Her muscles ached and she concentrated on keeping still. Her knees were bent. Her head and shoulders were thrown back and her hands supported her from behind. It was a difficult pose to keep for any time. When the time was up she determined to go into an easier position. She sat with her head on her hands on a low table, her legs bent under her, half-kneeling. It was much easier.

After the next break Odile asked her to bend over the table with her bottom up high and her head down. She did as she was asked, but felt the indignity of the pose, with her buttocks up high and her pubis exposed beneath, pressing on the table. She felt as if she was about to be caned by the Frenchwoman, who was behind her, arranging her limbs. In the large mirror on the wall she could see herself. Her pelvis pressed closer to the wooden table and her pussy became wet. She could almost feel the students' eyes pierce her flesh, slide in between her buttocks. She imagined the young girl, Rowena, with her pale buttocks high like this, in a room full of men taking turns to whip the white flesh. She closed her eyes and saw the red weals stripe her bottom. She heard the squeals and saw the lascivious glances of the men. When she opened her eyes she was shocked to see the students, who were all men today, staring at her. She was aware that her pussy was very wet and that she had probably been making noises of sexual satisfaction. She moved from her lewd position and sat on the offending part. She coughed and asked what position she should take next. The students were looking hot and sweaty and one young man had covered his crotch with his hands. Odile was licking her lips and smiling at Laura.

'You have done enough, I think, for today. *Merci, Mademoiselle.*'

Laura did not offer to model again. There was a male model at the next session. He was a good-looking slender-hipped youth, with long blond hair that was sunbleached from surfing. Laura recognised him as one of the regular local group on the beach. She had seen him waxing his surfboard with Dr Sog's Sex Wax, as it was unbelievably called.

'Rory, stand up, please, for the next pose,' Odile commanded him. He moved from his prone position and did as he was told. He had a long, thick penis, and small tight balls nestled in golden pubic hair. His thighs were long-boned and his whole body was athletic and graceful. His pretty face was almost girlish under the unruly locks.

Laura sighed. How lovely was youth and how easily freshness and beauty was squandered. She had been guilty of the same crime – not aware of how quickly time changes skin, flesh, muscle. She admired the young man's muscle tone, the way his pectorals flexed. He had a hairless chest and his nipples were dark pips on his tanned flesh. Where he had worn a wet suit his tan stopped and pale skin began. She remembered the male model she'd had to cover with fake tan for *Health and You*, and the impudent way he'd encouraged her to masturbate him. She felt wet. Thomas was shorter and chunkier than this long-limbed youth, but his body was hard and strong and she liked to imagine him holding her down fiercely. Thomas was, in fact, a very gentle young man and didn't like to use force, though she often silently begged him to. Why wouldn't the men she slept with tie her down? Perhaps they were afraid of their own strength and the brutality that might come to the surface if they were given the chance to have complete physical control over her. She thought of Jerry. She would trust him not to hurt her more than she wanted to be hurt. She pulled herself from her reverie and carried on drawing the boy.

'OK, Rory, you can stop now,' said Odile.

After the session Laura went to the pub with a group of the students and Rory went too. Laura bought a round of drinks. She gave him his lager and asked if he was at school or college.

'I'm still at sixth-form college, but I hope to go to

university after that, if I do well enough. I want to be an architect.'

'Oh, do you? Great!' She was aware of the salty tang of his sweat as he sat near her. Just then Rowena came into the pub and went up to Rory and kissed him on the lips. Laura was surprised to see her here. She knew that the girl's father would not approve.

'Is your father away somewhere?' she asked Rowena.

'Yeah, he's off on a trip to London. I've got my aunt staying, unfortunately.'

'Ah, I see.' Laura felt like a disapproving aunt, herself. Rowena went to the ladies' cloakroom and Laura followed her. 'Rowena, I want to talk to you.'

'What about?'

'I think you ought to be careful about who you . . . go with.' Laura felt embarrassed.

'What business is it of yours?'

'I don't mean Rory, of course not. I mean, I saw you with those two Brummies – the middle-aged men, the other night.'

'So?'

'So, they were fucking you.'

'You cow, you were watching?'

'You didn't hide yourself too well.'

'Yeah, well, are you jealous or something?'

'You must be joking! But why go with them? You're very young and pretty. Don't waste yourself – don't give your body to just anyone. It's dangerous.'

'No it isn't. I take precautions.'

'It didn't look like it.'

'Look, why don't you mind your own business?' Rowena shut the door behind her and went back to the bar. Laura left, depressed beyond words that this beautiful young girl should be throwing herself away.

Odile, Rory and Rowena left the pub together, at about nine o'clock, when the place was filling up with tourists. Laura had not arranged to see anyone that night and she followed the trio, curious as to what Odile was up to with them.

She hung back as the Frenchwoman opened the gate to her little cottage in the old part of town and the two young people followed her, clinging close to each other. Laura waited until they had opened the front door and gone inside before she went into the dark little yard, which was hidden from the alleyway, and stood by the window. She could see clearly into the small room through a crack in the curtains. The dim light of a small lamp threw huge shadows of the naked Rowena and Rory on to the whitewashed wall and ceiling. Laura watched as the perfect bodies kissed and caressed. She did not see Odile, but guessed that she watched also.

Rowena was kneeling, her mouth around the long white cock of Rory, who held her head to him. She moved slowly, drawing the cock deep into her large mouth and then letting it almost out of her lips before sucking it in again. Laura stood in the shadows, a guilty voyeur. She watched the two lovers entwine their perfect bodies like snakes coupling. Then she saw Odile, who was also naked, except for a long apron of black rubber, which left her buttocks and legs bare and showed her breasts either side of the bib top. It tied at the back around her waist. Her breasts were rounder than Laura had thought and her waist was narrow. She looked better with no clothes on, more shapely. She wielded a cane, which was made of bamboo or some other fine, whippy material. The Frenchwoman came towards the window and Laura thought she had been spotted. But Odile only closed the chink in the curtain.

Laura was close to the open sash window, but now could see nothing. The cane sang in the air before Odile let it fall. Laura heard its swish and the unmistakable thwack of cane on flesh. She couldn't see whose flesh was struck. She heard grunts and sighs and cries of pleasure and pain. She could only imagine what position the girl was in. Had Odile made her lie with her bottom up as she had posed Laura in the art class? Laura grew hot listening to the sexual games and her excitement was magnified by the frustration of not being able to see what was going on. She felt her thighs throb. Then a breeze lifted the curtain briefly and she saw the white backside of the slender Frenchwoman bending over and stroking someone with the cane. Was it Rory she touched, or the girl? Laura went home through the dark cobbled streets and went to bed on her own.

She wished she had not left the rubber sheets at Aaron's cottage. She needed them now. The sight of the rubber apron that Odile had worn had brought back the longing for the scent of rubber, the silky feel of it on her nakedness. Thomas was away for the night. She tossed and turned, thinking of Jerry and his head between her legs, his large hands spanking her pubis. She thought of being spanked by the woman in rubber. Perhaps the apron would caress her back and thighs. Perhaps she would let Laura put her hands under the rubber to press the flesh beneath. Laura fantasized about the Frenchwoman. Did she do this sort of thing to many of the town's young people? Was she allowing them to take their youthful lovers to her house to fuck in private in return for certain favours? This was how it looked. It was a safe haven for the town's youth, who had nowhere to kiss except back alleys, sand dunes and seafront shelters, and it provided voyeuristic fun for Odile. Laura eventually slept, dreaming of surfers in wetsuits and Jerry in a rubber apron.

Odile must have had similar dreams, thought Laura, for at the next art class there was Rory modelling in his wetsuit. It clung to his narrow frame, outlining his muscular back and the long penis. His long fair curls hung down his back. His lips curled in a smile as he saw Laura's eyes narrow.

'Undo the back of your suit. You will be cooler,' said Odile.

He pulled the ribbon that hung from the heavy zip and unzipped the suit to reveal his perfect back. He slipped it down over his shoulders and arms and left it, like a half peeled snakeskin at his waist. His shoulder blades were like the vestigial pale wings of an angel. His tanned torso gleamed with oil. His thighs and buttocks were encased in rubber, or neoprene. Laura had sat close to the model today and could smell rubber and the youth's body smells. His salty sweat mingled with the heady rubbery perfume and she felt faint. Laura drew fast in charcoal, outlining the shape he made. She saw him, not as a person, but a shape in space, the weight of his hip, the curve of his spine as he bent. He was like a young horse, she thought, all legs and mane.

Odile smiled lasciviously at the youth and touched him on the bare shoulder. '*Merci*, Rory, that's enough for today.'

Weekends, Laura and Thomas escaped from the town, driving through narrow lanes, looking for isolated meadows where they could make love. There was nothing better than sunbathing naked next to an ardent young lover, she thought, with the sound of insects humming and seed heads bursting. Butterflies and bees were the only witnesses to their hot-skinned couplings; hovering skylarks made music above.

Weekdays, he came straight from work to her house, still covered in dirt and dust. She adored him like this. He was like a miner, covered in thick dirt, the whites of his eyes bleached in contrast. He kissed her, trying not to touch her clothes, just their lips meeting. But she tempted him, pressing herself against his filthy overalls, licking dirt from his face. She lifted her cotton dress, revealing her bare belly and sex, offering it to him with a sensuous writhing of her hips, like a belly dancer. She danced closer, her pelvis nudging his thigh. His penis strained through his overalls to meet her pushing, thrusting belly, offered to him like a ripe fruit. She pulled her dress over her head and rubbed her naked body against him. She undid his buttons and drew out the eager cock. She knelt down on the kitchen floor, the bare boards hard on her knees, and sucked the pink, flickering penis pointing at her. They had no contact except her mouth surrounding his sex.

He was completely clothed except for the undone flies and found it difficult to stand with Laura kneeling at his feet, sucking hard on his swollen cock. He reeled, and held on to the pine table, regaining his balance. He groaned. She instinctively knew he wanted her to stop, and she released his throbbing cock. Laura got on to the table, sitting with her legs off the floor, her hands braced on the table behind her. His cock was almost, but not quite, at the right height for penetration. It just reached her sex, and he used his hands to grab her round the hips and pull her closer to him.

'I'm so dirty, I'll make a terrible mess of you,' he said.

'Yes, you will. Please do!'

He bent over her, her sex displayed on the edge of the table like an open flower, glistening with dew. His work-blackened hands smeared her clean tanned skin. Her small breasts were tasted and sucked, the prominent nipples nibbled to erection. His work-dirt transferred from his face to her body. His sweat was strong and sweetly pungent, and she breathed it deeply. She spread her legs and put her feet on the tabletop, lying back across it. He stood, still fully clothed, playing with this lovely naked toy. Her sex was spread open, sex lips swollen and dark. Her clitoris was a little pearly peak. His desire was too much and too young to hold back from immediate gratification. He fell on her, his penis finding her wetness and entering her completely,

111

fiercely piercing the too-tempting sex, like a knife piercing a soft ripe fruit. Her head fell back and her throat swelled towards his mouth. Her mouth was open, her breath laboured. Her naked body was smeared with dirt from his overalls and his hands and face. She felt he could be raping her, spoiling her clean fineness. He was in control. He was strong. He was enjoying his strength and potency. His penis had her impaled on the table. His hips undulated, gyrating his penis inside her, churning her swollen sex, which pulsated like a sea urchin, clutching at him and holding him tight.

Yes, she thought, he was a very lucky young man.

Next morning the sun rose red and the sky was a clear pale blue. Another perfect day! The sleek little black cat slithered between her feet and mewed at her. She wondered who it belonged to as she fetched it a saucer of milk and stroked its soft warm coat. She was semi-naked on the terrace. There were trees protecting her on one side and the sea in front. There was only the one other house above on the hillside – the new building, high up, overlooking the sea. It was an eyesore, and the trees didn't quite hide it from the terrace. The builders had finished it recently and she hadn't yet seen the new owners.

She wore a one-piece black swimsuit, rolled down to her waist, so that her lightly tanned breasts were exposed. She swept the terrace free of leaves and settled down on the sun-lounger with her third cup of coffee, a sketchbook and brush, and a small box of water colours.

It was a perfect early summer's day. The sun was not too high in the sky. There was a light breeze blowing from the sea. Laura painted several sketches of the views all around. The house had dazzling white walls and a slate-tiled roof covered in orange lichen. Brilliant pink and red pelagoniums spilled from old, lichen-covered earthenware pots on to the terrace. The sea was turquoise and deep blue with little ruffles of white where the wind hit the surface of the water and furled it into waves. The sun glinted sharply on the water and pierced her eyes. It was getting warmer. She rolled the swimsuit down over her hips and slid out of it completely, leant back on to the deep blue canvas lounger and closed her eyes.

Into her sun-drugged mind came the long-forgotten image of Jenny, a childhood friend. Jenny had a way of stroking a cat that made the hairs on Laura's neck stand on end. Jenny's hands were strong and she had caressed Laura's tabby cat with firmness, slowly and with animal enjoyment of the softness of the creature. Her every movement had been sensual. She had been like a brown-haired gypsy girl, with slanted sleepy brown eyes, more animal than child.

Laura sighed deeply. She reached for the paintbrush and drew a line from her belly button down to her pubic mound. The paintbrush tickled her warm flesh deliciously, arousing her. Her other hand cupped a breast and allowed the nipple to peek between her fingers and be squeezed by them. The paintbrush stroked and insinuated its way into her slit, parting the black curly hair. The sun beat down on her nakedness, warming her open slit. She opened the tender folds of flesh to the sun, pushing her pelvis upward and opening her legs. The paintbrush continued its tracing of her opening, in and out of crevices and channels of tingling flesh. The tickling was a torture to her senses, self-inflicted and wonderful. Her other hand squeezed her hot breasts and pressed her belly, then slapped and stroked the yearning sex, aware of the warm intimation of mimosa and sea scent emanating from the damp folds. She sucked her fingers and tasted the salty fragrance and pushed her fingers inside her plump sex, which was like a flower, open to the sun's rays. The brush traced her own work of art, its perfection displayed to the sun and the blue sky. She thrust her hips up and met the fingers as they slammed into her. Waves broke over her shores. Fiery pelargoniums burst in their glory over her senses. The sun burnt through her eyelids and woke her from her artistic endeavours.

Out of the corner of her eye she saw movement and the glint of sun on glass. She reached for binoculars and saw the disappearing figure of a woman on the terrace of the new villa. A black cat sat on the wall of the terrace, washing itself, and next to it a telescope on a tripod stared directly at her.

'Pour me another beer, will you?' Ethan, who was painting the shelf. They were trying to finish the decorating of the health food shop. Laura had offered to help but Ethan said he would rather do it on his own as long as Laura would pour the drinks and keep them flowing. Ethan was a capable man, in spite of his size, able to fix tiles, saw wood, mend a tap and change a tyre. Laura sighed and watched the man painting, the bare round arm lifting and the paint flowing from the brush.

'What a big sigh!' said Ethan. 'A penny for them?'

'Oh, nothing, I'm just feeling inadequate, a bitch, hopeless. The usual.'

'Why particularly?'

'It's Thomas. He's so young and he's in love with me.'

'Well, don't sound so surprised. Of course he is. I am. I expect your diver is too. You cast a wicked spell of lust wherever you go, you know.'

Laura laughed loudly. 'You fool! Of course I don't, not intentionally, anyway. What a dreadful thing to say! I am not a flirt!'

'No, darling, of course you're not,' said Ethan. He blew a white splattered kiss in his friend's direction and smiled. 'Seriously, though, what are your plans for Thomas?'

'Plans? I haven't any plans. As far as I am concerned

114

this is a holiday romance, a fling. He's a lucky young man to have the benefit of my experience.' She sounded defensive.

'Mmm, and what about Anna and Charles when they come home and find their boy soiled, spoiled, deflowered, and by an older woman?'

'He was no virgin, I can assure you. You make me feel ancient. For goodness' sake, Ethan, get on with your painting and shut up about it.' Laura poured another red wine and dipped her hand into the large packet of crisps she had thoughtfully brought with her. 'Where's whatshisface, anyway? Shouldn't he be helping you?'

'He'll be here later.' Ethan smiled and looked softer.

'Anyway, I can't help it if he loves me. It isn't my fault.' Laura felt guilty. She should have stopped before it became serious. But he was so lovely, such a willing student. She had obviously reached the age when a mature woman lusts after young men, she thought.

Just then the doorbell rang and Ethan stopped painting and wiped his hands, then put the wet brush on the top of the paint tin. He was flushed.

'I'll go,' said Laura and rose from the stool to open the door.

It was Eugene. He was a short man, smaller than Laura, and slender. He wore dusty pink dungarees and looked about seventeen. His dark hair was cut very short.

'Hi, Ethan, honey, how are you getting on?' Eugene went to Ethan and kissed him quickly on the lips.

Laura turned her head away in sudden embarrassment.

'What do you think of our venture? Are we mad or are we mad?' said the vivacious young man.

'It's a great idea, good news for the town, and it's bound to do well. I hope you're going to sell Greek yoghurt and haloumi and huge bunches of coriander,' said Laura.

'Yes, we hope so. If we can get someone to supply us in small enough quantities. We've found a reliable grower of organic veg and a Chinese supermarket supplier of exotic spices and rice noodles and seaweed.'

'Seaweed, even!' Eugene clapped his hands.

'Have some wine?' Laura poured another glass of the red wine for Eugene.

'Thanks! Cheers! The shop looks good, so much brighter.'

'What did you do before?' asked Laura.

'I'm a teacher, like Ethan. Or was until the holiday started. I'm throwing it all up to do this with Ethan, I believe in him, you see.' The small man suddenly looked his age – about thirty-three, thought Laura. He took Ethan's hand and squeezed it proudly. Ethan, a foot taller, at least, looked shy and almost simpered.

My God, being in love is so pitiful, thought Laura. I'm glad I'm not involved. But she suddenly thought of Jerry's long head, the lopsided smile, and she felt bereft.

'I think I'd better go,' she said and picked up her denim jacket and left. The two men were in a deep embrace and didn't notice the door open and close quietly.

Chapter Eleven

Secret Games

*S*tan returned from his London trip full of enthusiasm for the gallery owner he'd been to see. She was prepared to give him an exhibition in eighteen months' time. He came back to his art class with renewed energy.

Laura didn't know whether to mention his daughter's sexual adventures to him. She could hardly admit that she had been spying on Rowena. Instead she kept quiet, but at the same time she was fascinated by the idea that Odile was some sort of rubber fetishistic dominatrix preying on the naiveté of the town's youth. Was she only jealous? Did she perhaps want to join in the fun? She thought it better to let sleeping dogs lie and not interfere. After all, Rowena only looked very young. She was seventeen and old enough to look after herself. Her father was very protective and had been strict with her and maybe that was why she found it necessary to hide her sexuality from him. Laura found these thoughts running through her head as she drew the girl.

Rowena had marks on her buttocks, Laura noticed. Only faint weals, but Laura knew how she had come by them. Rowena was aware of them and had insisted on seated or lying poses. But Laura had spotted the reddened flesh when she stood at the end of the session, before she slipped on the kimono. Laura felt a sudden surge of wetness between her legs. She knew then that she had to involve herself in the rubber and whipping games that Odile was playing.

After the session, when regulars of the class adjourned to the pub, Laura took the opportunity to speak to Odile.

'I've heard that there's a rubber club here in Cornwall, somewhere,' she lied. 'Do you happen to know where it is?'

'*Mais non*, there is no such thing. I would have heard of it. But what a good idea, Laura, perhaps I will start one.' She laughed and showed her sharp little teeth in her thin mouth. She looked almost attractive when she smiled. She should do it more often, thought Laura. The others laughed in mock horror at the thought of a rubber club in this little village.

The ruse worked though. After the other art students had gone home, Odile asked Laura if she would like to go to her place later for a drink, and perhaps a little fun.

'What sort of fun?' asked Laura.

'You will see,' said the Frenchwoman sternly. 'Come at midnight. Wear something loose, and do not wear any undergarments.'

Laura went home and showered and changed from her painting clothes into a long loose antique cotton-and-lace dress. She had found it in her grandmother's attic cupboard. The lace edging and pin-tucked bodice were as good as new, and after several washes and hanging out to dry in the strong sun, the slightly yellowed garment was pristine white. She wore nothing underneath. It was chilly, so she threw her denim jacket over her shoulders. She wore brown leather cowboy boots. Her hair was still damp and she rubbed it with a towel before setting off to Odile's cottage. She felt excited and wicked. She knew that she would be doing something she had never done before. She wanted the feel of the whip on her bottom. She wanted to be whipped by the Frenchwoman in her rubber apron. She was soon at the cottage and she knocked at the door. Rory opened it.

'Hello,' she said, embarrassed.

'Hi!' He did not seem at all surprised at Laura being there. He was dressed in baggy chinos and a sweatshirt with an American baseball team logo on the back. His long blond hair swung on his shoulders. He flicked it back, like a girl.

'Come in, Laura; come in and make yourself comfortable.' Odile was wearing her rubber apron and nothing else. She looked stunning. Her ratty hair was tied back and made her stern features even more solemn. Her body was good: lean and hard, but with fleshy round breasts that strained to escape the confines of the rubber apron. It looked so bizarre.

'You must obey the rules here,' said Odile, 'if you really want to enjoy some rubber games.'

'Oh yes, I do, I will obey.' Laura looked around at the room where she had witnessed the caning – or almost witnessed it. It looked very ordinary, with a brown leather sofa, a pine table and bentwood chairs. Other furnishings were ornate: a large gilt framed mirror filled one wall. On another wall hung a collection of whips and canes. Laura shivered at the sight of the leather straps and the bamboo rods. The polished wood floor had rugs over it. A log fire blazed and a fur rug was on the hearth.

'Good. Remove Rory's chinos and sweatshirt, now.' Laura did as she was told. He was used to being looked at, this lovely youth. But in the art class Laura had not been able to touch him.

'Are you wearing any undergarments?' said the Frenchwoman, lifting Laura's skirt to see for herself. 'Good.'

As Laura drew Rory's pants down over his legs and helped him remove them she saw that he had an erection. He was wearing no underpants. Young men had erections so easily, thought Laura, smugly.

His penis leapt up as she released it. He's a lovely specimen, she thought. Perhaps I could take him to London for Sally.

He stood naked, waiting to be told by Odile what to do.

'Rory, lift Laura's dress above her waist and tie it with this belt above her breasts.' She handed Rory a long leather belt. Laura wished she'd had more whisky this evening. She felt rather sober and nervous. The surfer lifted her long petticoat-style dress up to her waist and caressed her hips casually as he did so. She felt a flutter in her belly. He tied the skirt around and above her breasts so that the cotton was bunched up and she was exposed to their eyes. He looked appraisingly at her body. She felt rather ridiculous, but the Frenchwoman gave her no time to change her mind.

'Tie her over the leather stool,' she ordered the rampant youth. He pushed Laura forward and she almost fell over a stool she hadn't noticed before. It was a low, wooden stool with four legs, padded with leather. She found herself held fast by the wrists, tied with velvet straps to two rings in the floor. Her bottom was uppermost. Her ankles were also tied and held fast. She couldn't move. She felt more naked with her dress tied over her breasts than she would if she'd had no clothes on at all. She could see herself in the long gilt mirror. Her bottom was round and firm and she had no qualms about exposing herself. She watched as Odile kissed the youth on the mouth and handled his private parts. She was oiling him. He allowed her to caress him and stroke his genitals with the oil. Odile wore black rubber gloves to perform this ritual.

Laura watched. Her sex lips were opening. Her legs

were open to their gaze as the woman caressed the boy. Laura was helpless. She wondered how long she was to be kept in suspense before they involved her in the game. She didn't have long to wait. Rory, at a signal from Odile, went to Laura and stroked her with a long bamboo cane, which he had removed from its place on the wall. She held her breath and closed her eyes waiting for the first blow to fall, but no pain came. Instead, Rory pressed the cane between her buttocks and rubbed it gently along her pubis and anus. Odile, suddenly supremely beautiful in her long rubber apron and a rubber mask over her narrow face, took the cane from his hands.

'Remember to hold it the way I showed you, and hit not too hard or you will spoil her pleasure. Hit not too gently either, or she will receive no pleasure.'

She watched in the large mirror as the youth, his genitals held by Odile's rubber-clad hands, took aim and struck Laura's buttocks for the first time. She yelped loudly.

'That hurt!'

'Good! Again.' Odile rubbed the long penis, which reddened and thickened under her thumbs and palm. Laura thought how rude it looked – so red and ripe under the black rubber gloves. She concentrated on her own pleasure as the cane struck several times in fast succession, warming her flesh and sending pleasurable sensations up her thighs and into her womb. Her belly pressed against the leather stool. She wasn't uncomfortable, but she was helpless. She just had to lie there and be caned by the beautiful young man, and watched by the woman in rubber. Laura was amazed at her own excitement. The whippy cane left marks on her flesh. She could see everything that was happening. Odile stopped the caning and inspected the damage.

'Yes, you are doing it well, *petit*. I will reward you.

Watch me stroke her to orgasm. Do not caress yourself, Rory.'

Laura gulped as the French woman knelt over her, pressing her rubber apron and her naked breasts on to her back. She knelt and stroked the sore flesh with rubber-clad hands. Laura thought of Jerry and the latex gloves. Odile breathed heavily and stroked Laura's inflamed vulva.

'You did a good job, Rory. See how she likes it,' she said.

Laura saw the boy lean over to examine her.

'Not too close,' barked the dominatrix.

She rubbed her hand over Laura's buttocks and spanked her firmly while she caressed and pushed fingers up inside her. Laura found herself panting like a dog as the Frenchwoman thrust her fingers deep and caressed her pubis. The spanking continued and Rory watched, his penis straight out in front of him like a flag pole. He didn't touch himself. Instead he stroked the dominatrix from behind, pushing his hands between her legs and masturbating her hard. He didn't press himself against her but his excitement was obvious. The Frenchwoman came loudly and he removed himself from her. Laura was overcome at the powerful sensations that flooded her body: the rubber all over her, the stings from the cane, the dominatrix's rough caresses. She climaxed and felt her womb close over the rubber-gloved fingers in a wave of fluttering spasms.

'Enough for tonight. Bathe her, Rory. Then untie her.'

Poor Rory is not to allowed an orgasm, at least not yet, thought Laura.

He bathed her carefully with warm water and a sponge, and soothed her caned buttocks with a cooling lotion. It felt heavenly and she closed her eyes and almost slept. He was still erect, and she felt the hard, warm penis rub against her flesh and stiffen imperceptibly. She was loathe to leave him like that, but here the rules of the house forbade him to have his satisfaction, it seemed. Laura turned to see that Odile was still in her rubber apron and mask. The room was hot from the fire and the scent of female musk filled the air. The latex smell was overpowering and Laura felt faint. She was still excited, wanting a cock inside her to fill the aching gap. She looked longingly at Rory, and Odile saw the glance.

'You want to fuck him?' she asked, huskily. 'OK, let me see you do it.'

Laura and Rory slipped down on to the fur rug by the fire, and she held his narrow waist and felt the flatness of his muscular stomach. Odile stood over them like a malevolent angel, her long rubber apron down to the floor, her mask hiding her nose and cheeks. Her thin red lips were open and her tongue flicked out. Laura was too much involved in arranging her limbs so that the youth could penetrate her fully to notice. She had lifted her legs up and around his neck. He had her buttocks in both hands and her pelvis was lifted high. He pumped into her without thought for her enjoyment, but she needed no more than his thrusting. Odile smiled under the mask and brought herself to satisfaction with her gloved hands. She glanced over to the window where she knew, behind the heavy curtain, a man watched.

Next day, Laura was surprised to find a bunch of pinks on her doorstep. There was a note: 'From Odile. You are invited to another evening of secret games next week at the same time.' Laura looked forward to it.

Thomas agreed to pose for Laura. The best time was first thing in morning, when the light was glancing and low, so his muscles were defined. She arranged him on the low day bed, one leg bent, the other away from his body, hanging over the edge, his balls and cock neatly arranged on the right thigh. His arms were above his head, stretched behind him.

'Close your eyes,' she said.

He fell into a slumber as she made several large charcoal drawings. He moved into different shapes, each one more beautiful than the last, and she sketched hurriedly, catching the exact mood of the early morning light and the youth's perfect form. She worked frantically, making many drawings, and he slept, unaware of the poem of his body, and the art she was turning it into. She knew they were good drawings: knew it honestly, as a good workman knows.

She washed her hands and put a bottle of wine in the freezer. He was still asleep, but his cock stirred, curving up from his thigh. She watched as it grew and stiffened and turned its head upward to lie on his stomach.

She found his leather belt and tied it around his wrists and attached them to the metal rails of the antique day bed. She lifted her skirt and sat on him, impaling herself. He groaned gently. His eyes opened slowly and she covered them with a silk scarf so he couldn't see her. She moved slowly, raising and lowering herself and holding his cock at the base. He was helpless, totally in her power.

She didn't wait for him but touched herself, watching his cock disappear into her and appear again, swollen and wet with her juices. She pulled aside her labia and watched his cock go into her. When she had finished with him she collapsed on to him, kissing his chest and nipples.

'Right, it's my turn now.'

'No, it's time for you to go to work, my boy.' Laura untied the youth and ran to the shower, locking herself in.

'I'll want my revenge later,' he called after her.

In the shower she touched herself. Her body felt as if

electricity flowed through the skin. Her nerve ends tingled. She imagined his revenge . . .

She was spread-eagled across the large bed, her wrists wrapped round with silk scarves and tied to the iron bedposts. Her long white knife-pleated skirt was pulled up above her waist. Her white cotton blouse was ripped off her shoulders and her breasts were bared. He tore the thin silk pants roughly from her legs, and threw them across the room.

His cock protruded obscenely from his open fly. He was fully dressed in his overalls and T-shirt. Just his strong arms and his penis were naked. He held a wide leather belt between her legs and rubbed it against her pink flesh. She drew breath between clenched teeth, hissing like a snake. Her head moved from side to side on the embroidered cotton pillow. He held his thickened cock against her mouth and holding her nostrils closed to make her open her mouth he forced his cock between her lips. Before he finished he withdrew and stood over her, his dirty hands smearing red clay on to her breasts and belly. He rubbed himself, standing by her and rubbing himself faster and faster. She stared wide-eyed at him, wanting him, but he ignored her eyes. He stared at her triangle of dark hair, parted her sex lips and stared into her. He spurted over her belly and thighs and she writhed alone.

Laura walked alone along a white sand beach. This was a quiet beach, with no vehicular access, so only the serious walkers and beach anglers made the effort to get to it. There were no beach cafés or deckchairs, no ice-cream parlours, just the dunes behind the long white stretch of sand. It was hard work, like marching through a desert. Someone had written in the sand FAT SAM in huge letters, and she saw, high on the dunes, a small, plump child with a red cap.

A woman passed her going in the opposite direction,

with four dogs that ran, barking and leaping, at a ball she had thrown. Laura made her way up to the dunes, where the wind was less fierce than it had been nearer the sea, and she removed her sweatshirt, tying it around her hips. She had brought a sketchpad and pencil and she sat in the shelter of the dune, marran grass whispering at her shoulder, a skylark hovering above.

She drew the sea, the beach, the dunes, the grass, the clouds, and the woman and the four dogs, which were dots now on the far side of the beach. Then she heard voices, laughter, young girls giggling. Rowena, in tattered white shorts and a skimpy vest top, and two other teenage girls sauntered by along the beach into the dune beyond her. They hadn't seen her. There were men's voices, too. Not boys, but middle-aged men. She couldn't hear the conversation over the whispering grass and the pounding of the waves.

Laura carried on drawing and then lay down, feeling drowsy in the midday sun. The sun beat down on her legs and face and arms and she wished she had worn a bikini. She slipped off her T-shirt and lay in her bra and jeans. She became very warm and removed her jeans. Now she was cooler and could sunbathe in comfort. She moved further into the crease of the dune, away from the sea breeze.

Now the voices were clearer. She couldn't see the girls or the men. She didn't even know if they were together, but she could hear male grunting and it sounded like someone was having an orgasm. She didn't know what to do. She hadn't meant to spy. She still saw no one, but heard the giggling and the men's nervous excitement. She suddenly saw one stand up, naked, thigh-high in the grass. She didn't recognise him. What had been going on? Had the girls been fucking with these men? Were the men watching the teenagers sunbathing? Were they gay? Laura did not know. Was it worse for older men to fancy young girls than it was for mature women

126

to seduce youths? How was it she felt disgusted at the idea of the pot-bellied man naked in the dunes, having possibly been sexually serviced by teenaged girls? She dressed and put away her drawing things and walked back to the town determined not to look back in case Rowena saw her and recognised her.

As she walked she remembered a time when she was a young girl and had been swimming in fairly shallow estuary waters, the tide flooding over sun-warmed sand. A man she only knew vaguely, a friend of a friend's parents, had swam too close to her and put his hand into the loose gap of her baggy swimsuit knickers, and clasped her bare pubescent flesh. She had been shocked and mortified and had been unable to tell her aunt what had happened, as if somehow she had been responsible for the too-intimate caress. She had thought, why should a man want to touch me? She had also been secretly proud that he had thought her attractive enough to give her that sort of attention. She had not come across sexuality before, except with her more mature girlfriend who had played doctors with her.

Perhaps Rowena was not so young, and it was none of Laura's business anyhow. She was chastened and sorry that she hadn't simply got up and walked away earlier.

The day came for the rubber games again. Laura dressed as before in a loose garment and with no bra. She ran through the streets to the little cobbled alleyway at the end of a cul-de-sac where Odile's cottage was. Flowers in pots hung in the walls and sat on steps. There were no gardens here, but the townsfolk had compensated by festooning the walls and outside stairs with geraniums and petunias. The wind blew hard and the sash windows rattled. Above the little town the large white gulls flew high on thermals and cackled to each other. There were no stars and the dark night had only the white wings to light the gloom. Laura felt an excitement about this second experience of sado masochism. The first had been a gentle introduction, she was sure, and she wondered what Odile had in store for her this time.

Rory opened the door. He wore his wetsuit, undone to the hips. His torso was oiled. He smiled at her. 'Come in,' he said, holding the door open. She walked through into the now-familiar room.

'Do you want a drink?' he asked.

'Oh, yes please, a whisky if you've got it. Where's Odile?'

'She'll be here soon. Sit down.'

He was more relaxed without the dominatrix, thought Laura. She sat and he scratched his chest with a horny finger.

'Did you surf today?'

'Yeah, I've just come from a barbecue on the beach.'

'You look good in a wetsuit,' she said.

'Thanks!' He grinned and swept his tangled golden locks back from his angular face. She felt wet under her long skirt. She had cheated a little in the form of her underwear. She was wearing split-crotched Edwardian bloomers, in fine white cotton that was embroidered and had fine ribbons threaded through each leg. She felt very naughty. She felt sure that the dominatrix would allow this laxity.

'Do you know Thomas Bligh?' she asked him.

'Yeah, vaguely. He was two years ahead of me at school. We played in the same cricket eleven, though. You know him well, do you?'

She blushed. 'Yes. Are you a good cricketer?'

'I gave it up after school. There's no time for anything but surfing now.'

'Of course,' she said. She imagined him in cricket whites, with his brown throat. The white pads to his thighs.

'It's warm in here,' she said.

128

'She likes it warm. Makes the rubber smell good, and keeps us warm when we're naked.'

'Yes, of course. Rory, do you know Rowena very well? I mean, I know you know her well, but do you know her other . . . friends?'

'If you mean do I know she's the village bicycle, yes. She'll fuck anyone and do anything. She's a scream.' He didn't sound as if he disapproved of her. He was seeing her through other eyes, that's all, thought Laura. 'Her father thinks she's a virgin. Innocent! Huh! What a laugh!'

Just then, as Laura was on her second large scotch, Odile appeared. Her cheeks, usually pale, were flushed from the wind.

'I am late, we must start straight away,' she said. 'You got my flowers and the message, then?'

'Er, yes, I did, thank you.'

Odile removed her long riding coat, which had a rubber lining. Underneath she wore a one-piece cat-suit of rubber, which had holes for her nipples and areolae to peep out. Her hips and legs were encased in the suit but her thighs and pubis were not. Instead, there was a wide rubber strap across her pubis, going under her legs and up to join the waist each side. Her long legs were encased in the black stuff and she wore high-heeled boots. As before, she wore black rubber gloves.

'Show me what you have under your long skirt,' she ordered Laura.

Laura lifted her skirt to show the naughty knickers with the split crotch.

'You are wearing underwear. How dare you disobey me?'

'But . . .'

'Rory, fetch the whip from the wall – the first whip on the right.'

Laura was tied to wall rings she hadn't noticed before. Her face was to the wall and her dress had been hitched up as before. Odile had not removed the offending article, though. Instead, she whipped Laura, making sure that the leather thong struck where the material gaped, so Laura was stung soundly on her thighs and buttocks. The tongue of leather flickered over her genitals with a subtle caress and then the sting of leather on flesh. Laura moaned. She hadn't really wanted to experience this much humiliation, she thought. Her genitals hurt, at first, with the unfamiliar blows, but then she realised that it was only fear that made her flinch. The actual caress of the whip was gentle on her private parts, and she enjoyed the harsh whipping on her fleshy bottom. There was an unexpected contrast between the sensations.

She wondered what the lovely Rory was doing meanwhile. She turned her head so she could see in the mirror. He was on his knees, his head between the dominatrix's legs. She was standing, her legs slightly apart so that she could wield the whip, and he lapped her private parts. His tongue was behind the rubber strap that divided her sex lips. She writhed on his face. His hair was tangled and wild. His rubber wetsuit clung to his muscular legs. He pushed it down further so his cock stuck out the top. Laura could see the glistening pink head leaking. Her climax came suddenly as the whip curled under her once more, oh so subtly. Odile was expert with the whip.

Laura was untied and allowed to clean herself. Odile looked at the clock on the wall and imperiously told Laura to go behind the curtains and watch what happened next.

'You will not make a sound or try to interfere,' she ordered.

There was a smell of pipe tobacco wafting from the velvet. It nearly made Laura sneeze. She wondered what interesting development there would be. She didn't have long to wait. The door opened and Rowena, in short skirt and denim jacket, walked in. She embraced Rory, who was dressed in jeans and T-shirt now. Odile watched avidly as the two young people kissed. She glanced towards where Laura was hidden, behind the long curtain, and narrowed her eyes.

'I want you to make love on the floor, on the rug in front of the fire,' she said to the young couple.

'With pleasure,' said Rowena. She drew her jacket off and threw it on to a chair.

'Have you obeyed the house rule?' said Odile.

'Not wearing any panties, if that's what you mean,' said Rowena and lifted her flared skirt so that they could see she was naked. Laura held her breath. Could she really be playing the voyeur? Only the girl did not know she was watching. Rowena kissed Rory again, passionately, as he slipped his long hands up under her skirt and clutched her buttocks. Rowena's back was to Laura and she saw the white flash of bottom under tanned hands. The girl kept her black vest top on and her skirt, but slipped out of her high cork-soled sandals. She stood on tiptoe to reach Rory's mouth. He leant over her, his jeans straining with his erection. She undid his flies slowly, and pushed her hands under the cloth, pushing the jeans down over his slender hips. He had no underwear on and his cock flopped out of the jeans into her hands. He pushed her on to the fur rug, on her back, and mounted her immediately.

Suddenly Laura saw Odile slash at the youth with a whip. The leather struck him hard and he yelped. 'Christ, why did you do that?' he shouted at her.

'Because you are not obeying house rules. You may fuck each other, but I want to see what you are doing. You cover her and I see nothing.' She struck again and he rose, rubbing his arse, furiously.

'You are sick, Odile,' he said.

'Shh. Go back to your fucking and let me see her this time.'

Rowena was writhing on the rug, her skirt above her waist, her bare belly lifting. Laura's view was perfect. Rory took his now-limp penis in his hands and rubbed.

'Come here and let me do that,' said Odile. She placed her rubber-gloved hands over the flaccid member and expertly caressed him. He was soon hard again. Rowena was fingering herself, waiting for the male presence inside her.

Laura was touching herself, too, unable to stop the excitement that grew inside her like a fire burning hot. She placed her fingers inside the split crotch of her Edwardian knickers and stroked herself.

Rory lowered himself on to Rowena. His knees were either side of her hips, and his cock touched her belly. She stroked it.

'Can you see us now?' whispered Rowena.

'Well enough,' said the dominatrix. She had knelt close to the couple, leaving an area clear so that the hidden Laura could also see clearly. Odile touched Rory's genitals with her gloved hands as the long cock curved into pink folds of sex lips. Rowena's face wrinkled in pleasure as he thrust slowly, held from behind by the slave mistress. His pleasure showed in his agonised face. Laura felt her own wetness. She could see everything: the cock pumping into the girl's body, the girls' belly and thighs and buttocks lifting to meet the thrusts. Odile's hands stroked Rory's tight balls and held him at the base of his cock. Her black rubber gloves touched the girl's genitals also and she rubbed herself against them. Laura came at this point and closed her eyes briefly, swaying as the waves of pleasure ran through her limbs.

When she came to, the others had also had their climaxes, she saw. Rory was still pumping and Rowena lay still. Odile, under her mask, was smiling with satisfaction. She rose and ordered Rory to get up and leave. He did as he was told, putting on his clothes without

132

washing. He left quickly, looking back at Rowena, who still lay, exposed, on the rug, her body lit by the fire's low glimmer. Her long hair was tangled and wound about her breasts. Her thighs were open.

Laura watched as Odile lay down with Rowena and caressed her. She kissed the small breasts and Rowena lay, quiescent. Odile's nipples were large and hard. They fell out of the rubber that cut into her breasts and surrounded them, and into Rowena's mouth. The girl sucked. Odile moaned. She drew her hands down on to Rowena's belly and between her open legs. Rowena shook and writhed as Odile stroked and pushed her rubber-gloved fingers into her pink wetness. The bizarre sight of the dominatrix making love to the semi-naked girl was too much for Laura, who came again on to her own fingers and palm. The smell of rubber filled the small warm room. The two women on the floor became still and languorous. Behind the curtain, Laura leant and sagged, waiting to be released.

Rowena dressed, kissed Odile passionately and left by the front door.

'So, what did you think of that?' asked Odile as she theatrically drew the curtain back and revealed Laura.

'Very entertaining. You'd better not let her father know, though.'

'Huh, he is an innocent, not her. She is willing to do anything, that one. She is hot.'

'Well, I must be going. Er, thanks . . .' Laura opened the front door.

'Next week?' asked Odile.

'Why not?'

She walked back under the dark sky. The wind howled through the steep cobbled streets. She hobbled home, still wet and sticky. Who would think to see the shuttered windows, the closed curtains of the little cottages, that such wild sexuality hid behind the doors?

Chapter Twelve

Depilation

'Shave me, Thomas.'
  'What?'
  'I want you to shave my pubic hair.'
  'Why?'
  'I like the idea of a completely bare sex. Will you do it for me?'
  'But I like your bush.'
  'It'll grow again. Do it for me.'
  'Do you trust me enough?'
  They had finished a good bottle of sparkling white wine, some fresh-picked crab meat, soft granary bread with butter and a bowl of olives stuffed with anchovies.
  'All right, my hand is steady.'
  She lay on her back on a large bath towel. Thomas knelt between her thighs and covered her pudenda with soapy foam.
  'This is fun.' He slipped two fingers inside her.
  'Stop it! Get on with the operation, you naughty boy.'
  Soon her flesh was white and smooth as a snowy hill. He smothered the newly exposed mound in oil.
  'You look like a young girl.' He kissed her belly and

drew his tongue down into her slit. 'But you taste like a woman.'

'And do you prefer young girls?'

'You know I don't.'

His excitement was obvious and she drew him on top of her, drowning in a voluptuousness of intensity. Her flesh was new, alive, tingling with electricity. She closed her eyes and allowed the fantasy to become real. The boy became an old man fingering her bare sex. She couldn't stop him pushing his big root into her – forcing her open, pumping into her frail flesh. She was helpless and dominated by this strong young man.

Later, he whispered in her ear, 'Don't you love me, just a little bit? No, don't answer, I don't care if you don't love me. Just let me love you.'

She was tempted to tell him about Jerry, but she didn't.

Chapter Thirteen

Return of the Diver

Joseph was much kinder and more ardent than most of the older men she had known. But that was no guarantee that love would follow. She didn't pretend to be in love with him. She at least owed him that. She was obviously infatuated by him – but in love? No! She didn't want to hurt him. Was she doing any harm? Probably not, as long as she didn't lie to him. She felt younger, vital, and beautiful.

And so the days progressed, with lazy times spent sunbathing when the sun shone in the morning, one eye on the house on the hill. Thomas worked at his labouring, and Laura typed on her laptop, producing more work than she had thought possible in this balmy atmosphere, where the blue sky seemed to envelope her and cotton-wool air made her feel inebriated, in a dream state. Her drawing and painting were coming along well, too. She spent hours in the local art galleries. It was such a productive, creative atmosphere. In this small town there were more artists, sculptors and potters per square metre than almost anywhere else in England. She even swam: the sea seemed warmer than it had been in previous years. Her muscles were toned, her calves smooth and rounded, her arms and breasts firm. It really was an idyllic place, better than any foreign resort, she thought. The sea breezes kept the air fresh and clean, there were no mosquitoes, and the temperature never became unbearably hot. Who needs Greece or France when they could have Cornwall? she thought smugly.

She gradually tidied the house. Her grandmother had never thrown anything away, it seemed. Old newspapers tied in bundles were stacked high. Her grandfather's clothes still hung in a wardrobe. She took them to the charity shop in a large suitcase. She put the newspapers out by the dustbins, but then saw that they were very old local papers and she thought they might be of some use in her research into local smuggling. She had yet to write an article on smuggling. She took them in again and left them in the sitting room. She noticed the year on one particular bundle. It was the year her parents had died in a car crash. She wondered if there was any mention of the accident, and she began going through them looking at the headlines. There it was, on May 4, 1971:

DOOM ROCK POINT PLUNGE TRAGEDY

Local PC John Mackay and his wife May died when their car plunged off Doom Rock Point. It was their fourth wedding anniversary. The car came off the road on a slow bend. Police cannot explain how the accident occurred on a clear night, with a full moon. The bodies, trapped in the vehicle, were recovered by inshore lifeboat. The car has since broken up in stormy seas. They leave one daughter, Laura, aged three.'

There was a photograph of her parents, taken on their wedding day. It was the same photo that sat on Laura's mantelpiece. She felt a pang of loss, even though she hardly remembered them. They were lost history. Now her grandmother had died, there was no one she could ask about them. Had they been happily married? Had he been drinking? He had been the driver. Had they had a row, or a pact to kill themselves? Her imagination went wild thinking of how they had spent their last moments. Had he lost control; had she grabbed the wheel? Had he had a heart attack? She would never know now. She put the newspapers back in the cupboard.

She had talked to Thomas about their situation and told him she'd decided to tell Anna.

'I feel duplicitous, not telling her, as if there is something to be ashamed of,' she said.

'Fine,' said Thomas.

She realised that, for him, announcing the affair made it seem more important. 'But don't think it means I'm in love with you, Thomas,' she added, gently. 'I'm not, you know.'

'No, of course not,' he said, touching her dark wedge of hair with a horny thumb and forefinger.

Laura wore a navy linen shirt and white linen trousers to the interview with her friend. She felt smart and sophisticated, sure of herself. She felt that she was having to explain herself to a head teacher; guilt flooded her. Oh, God! What a stupid situation to have got herself into!

'Anna, hi!' Laura had a bottle of cold white wine in one hand and a bunch of lilies in the other.

'My goodness, for me?'

Laura blushed and said, 'Yes, open it for God's sake. I have something to tell you.'

'What is it, Laura? You look awful. Well, not awful, I mean, you look ill, dear. Sit down while I put these in water. The opener is there. Will you . . .?'

Laura opened the bottle and poured the yellow liquid into the stemmed cut glasses. She sighed and said it.

'I'm sleeping with Thomas. Did you know?'

'What?' Anna laughed nervously.

'Don't sound so amazed, darling, it's just an affair. He's a big boy now, you know.'

'Oh dear! Laura! But he's only a boy.'

'No he isn't, Anna. He's a man.'

Anna took a swig of the wine and gulped.

'I'm sorry, Anna, I think – I know – he is in love with me. But I'm not seriously involved with him. My intentions are purely dishonourable, I'm afraid.' Laura drank the wine and poured herself another glass, filling Anna's glass too.

'Well, well, well! What can I say? Why did you tell me, anyway?'

'Because, because, I feel guilty . . .'

'I see.'

'But he goes back to college at the end of the summer, and I go back to London, so it will come to a natural end, I hope.'

'But he is in love with you, you say?' Anna examined her friend's tanned smooth flesh, the glossy hair, and the slender form. Laura nodded miserably.

'Does Charles know?' Anna asked.

'Yes, apparently he guessed, or so Thomas said.'

'And what does he think?'

'Oh, drink up, Anna, and stop making me feel such a heel. I do hate myself, you know.'

When Charles came in an hour later, the two women were quite drunk, having opened another bottle of wine, and Charles, miffed that his dinner wasn't cooking, went off in a huff to watch the test cricket highlights on the television in his study.

Laura had invited Charles, Anna, Thomas, Ethan and Eugene for Sunday lunch. The lunch party was the day after Laura had told all to Anna, and Laura felt

139

hungover and grumpy. But she had prepared several salads and a whole cold salmon.

Eugene and Ethan arrived first, their arms full of white flowers.

'Thanks, darlings,' said Laura. The male lovers were so happy together, easy in each other's company, not afraid to touch and kiss.

Eugene looked at the new house on the hill, which had now been painted white and looked less ugly in the bright sunlight.

'You know who lives there, don't you?' he asked Laura.

'No, who is it?'

'It's that woman architect. There's been such a fuss about the house.'

'Architect? I am amazed. It's an eyesore, I think. Did she design it?'

'Oh yes, there was the usual barrage of letters in the local rag, but the planners passed it.

'What's she like?' asked Laura, remembering the glint of sun on the telescope lens.

'Gorgeous! Redhead, big breasts, long legs,' said Ethan, smirking. His lover smacked him lightly on the bottom, and he went, 'Ouch!'

'I'll have to go and knock on her door, just to be neighbourly,' said Laura.

'Take me, please take me along,' laughed Ethan, and Eugene chased him down the garden path.

Anna, Charles and Thomas arrived together, with bunches of flowers and two bottles of sparkling white wine. Anna looked a little jaded, as well she might, after the previous evening's imbibing.

Thomas kissed Laura on both cheeks and then once on her lips. She blushed but smiled and kissed his parents. There was a moment's embarrassment and then the wine flowed and conversation blossomed. They ate the light lunch on the terrace, with the tall fuchsias

140

swaying and rhododendrons casting dark shade over the cedar table laden with salads and fresh salmon.

Eugene was asking Thomas about his plans.

'Well, I go back to college in October, then I have another year to decide what to do.'

He seemed self-assured, quite mature, thought Laura, admiring the youth's bulging arms through his navy-blue T-shirt. Yes, he would survive the love affair, come through it a man, and build on the experience. She had not damaged him.

'Is your diver back yet?' said Ethan, provocatively.

'If you mean Aaron, I don't know.' Laura did not rise to the bait. It had been a sexy summer, all told, she thought, dreamily, satisfied that all was well with Thomas, that he was not too smitten, and that she had handled the Aaron affair satisfactorily.

As if on cue the gate squeaked, and Aaron walked towards them.

'Oh, Aaron, you're back! We were just talking about you.' Laura smiled and stood, and received the fisherman's easy embrace.

'I'm interrupting,' he said, taking in Thomas's sudden jealous flash of anger, which he tried to hide.

'Of course not, it's lovely to see you, join us, please. There's plenty to eat. Oh, my goodness, a live lobster! For me? How wonderful! Have a drink. Thomas, will you get another glass, please?' She touched the boy's arm, caressingly, showing Aaron how things were. Thomas was mollified and allowed himself a smile.

'You do know everyone, don't you, Aaron?'

He shook hands with Charles and Anna and gave Thomas a wry smile as he took his hand. Their hands met in a firm, almost bone-breaking grip, a scarcely disguised exhibition of masculine strength.

Eugene and Ethan laughed spontaneously at this macho display.

141

Aaron laughed too, and released the boy's white fingers.

There was an argument about how to kill the lobster humanely.

'I always slice it through the back of the head with a sharp knife,' said Charles. 'Kills it immediately.'

'I can never hold them down to do that,' said Ethan. 'It takes two people.'

'Well, I'm going to put it into lukewarm water and bring it slowly to the boil,' said Laura, 'It's the RSPCA-recommended method. The warm water makes them sleepy and they are unconscious when it gets hot, so they don't feel the heat and they die without pain.'

'Hope you are right,' said Eugene. 'I think it's all cruel.'

'Well, they shouldn't taste so damned delicious, should they? Then we wouldn't want to eat them.' Charles laughed at his own joke.

'Come on, everyone, eat, eat.' Laura clapped her hands and the tension was broken. She turned from them and put the lobster into a large pan of lukewarm water.

'How were the Scillies?' asked Anna, mesmerised by the handsome diver's bulging arms and his brown neck. 'You were away longer than three weeks, weren't you?'

'As always – flat, warm, sunny. Good for lobster picking, and a few other things, if you know where to look.'

'That sounds intriguing,' remarked Charles, lifting his glass of white wine and admiring the resinous colour.

'Do you mean you really were treasure hunting, Aaron? Do tell us,' urged Laura. She had placed herself between her two male admirers, more to keep them apart than anything else.

'Later, my bird, I'll tell you about it. Can't go letting secrets out, can I?'

Laura saw that Thomas bristled at the 'later' and what

142

it indicated. He had known about her brief fling with the diver but had obviously not expected to have competition now that he was her lover.

This was a moment of decision for Laura. She had as much as announced her interest in Thomas. Now she needed to show him, once and for all, that it was not a serious engagement, that she was her own person, and didn't belong to him.

'Sounds exciting, Aaron, I'll see you at the pub, later, perhaps?'

He smiled his agreement, and Thomas slumped in an adolescent heap of disgruntlement and defeat.

Anna and Charles affected not to notice their son's moroseness, and carried on chatting and laughing. Eugene and Ethan were telling the gathering about their first week as shopkeepers.

'There was this woman came in. Our first customer. A visitor. Asked if we sold instant coffee. Honestly!'

'Well, don't be amazed, darling. We are a food shop, after all.'

'No we're not, we're a health food shop.'

'Don't worry, you'll soon get used to throwing out the proles,' said Charles.

'You could always sell instant coffee, if there's a demand,' suggested Aaron.

Later, when Laura was clearing up the debris of lunch on her own, the telephone went.

'Laura?' It was Tom.

'Tom, did you enjoy lunch?'

'Yes, thank you, apart from that ape, Aaron, arriving. You aren't really seeing him later, are you?'

'Well, yes, Tom, probably.' She made no other comment.

'I see!'

'Tom . . .'

'No, Laura, you can't play with me and then throw me away as if I'm an old toy. Laura, I love you.'

143

'Tom, I have told you time and time again how it is with us, with me. I'm very fond of you, but I don't love you, and there is no future for us, believe me.' She was cross with him and herself and the wine had made her reckless. 'If you don't like it, you must do the other.' What a graceless business it was, breaking off with a lover. She regretted her words immediately, but there was no going back.

'Right then, I'll do the other,' he said, a tremor in his voice, and he put the phone down.

'Oh dear, what a bitch I am,' she said to the dead phone.

The wharf road was full of barely covered flesh, in various stages of roasting. Girls in high-heeled shoes and short dresses stumbled on the cobbles and young men in bulging vests drank beer from cans.

Laura slid into the pub between the overly after-shave-lotioned lads from Nottingham and Derbyshire, and stood on tiptoe to see if Aaron was there.

He waved to her and she fought her way through the throng of happy holiday-makers and locals.

'Hello, my queen,' said an old man with a permanent smile and laughter lines etched into his brown face. 'Ar'right then?'

'Yes, thank you, Bert, how are you? What are you drinking?'

'Proper job, my bird. I'll have pint of best, thankee.'

'You'm a stranger,' he accused, when she brought back their drinks.

'Well, I'm here for three months now, so I won't be such a stranger,' she sighed.

'At your grandmother's house, are you?'

'That's right Bert. It's lovely to be here.'

'Time off work? You're lucky, aren't you? They keeping your job all that time? You must be good at it.' He tipped back the tankard and she saw how thin his neck had become since the last time she'd seen him.

'I'm freelance, Bert. I can work anywhere. Are you working?' she asked. He'd had a job selling tickets for boat trips around the lighthouse.

'No, my bird, my legs is gone. Can't stand up any more.' He pointed to his crutches in the corner. 'Any road, the jobs goes to the young'uns, and that's the way it should be. No real work for a man here these days, any road. No fish since they bloody Spanish came with they great trawlers. And they Russians with the factory ships.'

Laura had heard these spurious reasons for the disappearance of the fish stock many times. There was always someone to blame for bad luck. But it was true, what Bert said about there being no real industry. Fishing had practically died out.

The conversation turned to tin. Cornish tin mining had died a death in recent years because of rock-bottom prices in the world market. Now there was a newspaper report that said because of the worsening economic crisis in Indonesia there was a possibility that tin would be a viable industry in Cornwall, again. The most recent mine closure had resulted in the laying-off of hundreds of local men. Perhaps there was hope again for them, if they could clear the flooded mine. The old man brightened. Then he lapsed into melancholia.

'An' there's 'ardly any farming. Just tourism. That's what the locals have to concentrate on. Bed and breakfast; restaurants and cafes; souvenir shops, and they fast food outlets, encouraging people to eat on the move – encouraging gulls to chance their luck with fish and chips, pizzas, they 'amburgers in polystyrene plates. I 'ate polystyrene plates – float in and out with the tide, they do.'

'Bert, my cock, you moaning on again? What're you drinking?' said Aaron.

'Hello, Aaron,' said Laura smiling up at the foxy face and felt his admiration envelope her. He was wearing clean, faded jeans, which were almost white over the bulge of his crotch, and a bright-blue linen shirt. He smelled good, she thought, as she kissed him on the cheek.

'Whisky?' he asked.

'No thanks, half a lager will be lovely.'

He turned to Bob, the barman, and ordered drinks. The other divers were there, and Bill Montpelier, the skipper, whom she was wary of, only because of his reputation. She had heard from Ethan that he could be violent. She wanted nothing to do with male aggression. He was a burly, fierce-eyed, broad-faced man of about forty-five. She also knew from Ethan that he had been running a team of divers for years in these waters and there were those who suggested he did not hesitate to use strong-arm methods to ensure his exclusive rights to the waters in which he chose to dive.

'Have you met Jason?' Aaron introduced an Australian bottle-blond hulk who looked a bit of a male bimbo. He was leaving the diving team to go back to Australia very soon and this was a goodbye drink. Then Aaron introduced a tall, thin, rangy older man called Andrew, who looked sly.

'Laura Mackay, is it?' said the thin man.

'Yes.'

'Hm!' He turned away from her and ignored her pointedly.

Bill had his huge arm around Jason and was telling a smutty joke. Laura didn't try to listen. She eased her denim-encased bottom on to a barstool and pressed her slender arm against Aaron's muscled, bare, tanned one. He smelt good. Fresh lemony soap.

'I've got you something,' he said. 'I'll show you later.'

'What is it?'

'Something you'll appreciate, my flower.'

146

'I can't wait,' she smiled.

The waders were green, fitted her beautifully, and had straps at the top, like suspenders, to attach to a jacket. They were fly fishermen's waders.

Laura strutted about his room, the rosy glow from the bedside lamp highlighting the roundness of her belly, the pink bareness of her pudenda, the rounded, upturned breasts.

'What do you think?' She laughed at his huge erection, held in his hands. He reached out to her and caressed her buttocks.

'I think you've got the best arse in Cornwall,' he said.

'They feel wonderful, I want to wear them all the time,' she said, lowering herself on to him. The waders dug into her thighs and sex, and the thick edge of the rubber sent shivers of pleasure up her spine. His hands were inside her thighs, under her buttocks, grasping her firmly. He lifted her up and down on his cock, and she threw back her head to show him her white throat. His kisses hurt. The thrusts were strong and deep. The rubber boots became warm with the exertions and she smelt the wicked, yearning odour. Her nostrils flared and she breathed in deeply.

'Right size, are they?' he asked.

'Yes. So are you,' she said. She gripped his strong neck and shoulders, feeling the knotting muscles strain. He slapped her bottom and rubbed the wader tops across her cleft. She moved closer, rubbing herself on him.

'I missed you, my flower,' he said and pushed his solid flesh into her, watched it slide out and the deep-red head slide over her bare lips, before pushing it back deep. She had no inhibitions. She didn't care if he saw her delight, her enjoyment. Her moans were animal and loud. She used him as he used her, and the two found mutual satisfaction in their clever writhing. He came violently and grunted in pleasure.

'Aaron, do you know Odile?' she asked later.

'That eccentric bird with the rubber fetish?'

'Yes. Have you been to her house?'

'No, flower, I wouldn't dare. They say she has whips and such there; a torture chamber or something.'

'If she invited you to join her in some games, what would you say?'

'I don't fancy her, flower, not enough flesh on her. She can keep her rubber truncheons. I like my sex private.'

'Thank you for my beautiful boots, Aaron. I don't know how to thank you properly.'

'You just have, flower.' He fell asleep in the dishevelled sheets, and she rose and washed and dressed, and left, taking the waders with her.

'You slut!' He hit her across the face.

It was Thomas, who had been waiting outside the cottage in Love Lane for an hour or more. He was livid, furious, beside himself and very drunk.

'For goodness sake, Thomas, don't be stupid,' she said, only slightly alarmed at the attack. He stood like a naughty child, not trying to hold her or hit her again. It had been an instinctive lashing out at her because he was so jealous and hurt.

'Oh, Laura, why did you go with him?' he sobbed.

'Come home, Thomas, come on, you've been drinking.'

She led him away down the alley, up steps and through another cobbled lane, finding the 'back doubles', the secret ways through the old town. He let her lead him, like a dog which has tried to make an escape and is taken home on a lead, his tail between his legs.

'We'll talk about it tomorrow,' she said, as he tried to kiss her at her door. She felt guilty, but also sexually aroused because she had just slept with another man and now this boy was trying to make love to her.

'No, Thomas, please go home. Tomorrow we'll talk, if you must.'

'No, I want to be with you, you!'

'Come on, Tom.' She led him to his home, along the dark lane, to his parents' house. In the dark sky gulls tumbled.

She shut the door on his sad face, closed like a book, hiding its emotions and story. She went back to her house and let herself in.

She sighed, smiled at her reflection in the mirror, tried to tell herself she was a free woman, not answerable to any lad who chose to think he owned her. She cleaned her teeth and showered, peered out of the window, just in case Thomas had come back, and curled up under her clean white sheets. She could still discern the scent of the rubber on her flesh.

Chapter Fourteen

Red Sonia

*L*aura woke to the realisation that someone was banging on her door.

'Damn!' She had overslept. She hated being caught in her kimono, unkempt, unwashed.

'Wait a minute, I'm coming,' she yelled.

'Oh, hello.' A tall red-haired young woman stood smiling wryly, her gaze taking in the dishevelled sleepy Laura, who had mascara in dribbles on her cheek.

'Hi! I'm sorry to disturb you so early. I wondered if you would like to come for drinks up at the house,' she said, jerking her immaculate head towards the house on the hill. 'I'm celebrating the fact that it's finished.' She smiled. 'Today. Six o'clock.'

'Oh, er, thanks, thank you.' Laura drew her dressing gown closer over her naked thighs, which had flashed as the wind took the flimsy cotton kimono.

'I'm Sonia Stallone,' said the redhead. Poised, elegant even at nine in the morning, smiling dangerously and arrogantly, she gazed into Laura's sleepy eyes. 'I've seen you on the terrace,' she admitted, 'through my telescope. You are quite a star.' She turned and descended the steps. 'See you later. Bring a friend if you want.'

'Yes, thank you.' Laura's upbringing denied her the opportunity to ask the stranger how she had dared to spy on her while she was naked. Her good manners held her mouth closed and made her feel guilty that she had not been in a decent Christian state at nine in the morning. How disgusting and decadent! She ran a bath immediately.

Sonia Stallone! What a name! A Mafia moll, at least. Red Sonia. Miss Stallone. Of course! She remembered now: she had seen her at the London auction house. 'Miss Stallone does not give interviews.' Had she been buying or selling?

Usually Laura had lazy mornings, reading to Mrs Poldhu, then painting or drawing in the garden before the sun got too high, working in her bikini or with just a sarong tied around her waist. This morning, however, she dropped into her neighbour's house to make her excuses and then she went into the small town, braving the crowds of slow-moving visitors, like cattle ambling along a lane, to try the hairdresser.

'I only need a trim.'

'A style and shampoo? There's a cancellation, twelve o'clock. All right madam?'

Laura picked up the few things that Mrs Poldhu needed – bread, chuck steak for a stew, carrots, spring greens, and sliced white bread – carried them back up the hill and delivered them.

'Thank you, cheel, it's difficult for me these days, in the town. It's so busy and they foreigners don't look where they're going.'

'Don't worry, Mrs Poldhu, I'll do your shopping whenever you want – while I'm here in town.'

'How long would that be, then?' she asked wistfully.

'Oh, a while yet.' Laura did not want to think about going back to London. She felt like a schoolchild with the summer holidays stretching out like an empty white-sand beach before her. She was happy here. Perhaps she should stay? She could get a fax machine, get on the Internet. Her laptop gave her all the freedom she needed to write anywhere. She could spend more time painting.

Did hairdressers all go to the same language school? Were they all taught to say the same things as they tugged and tore, combed, caressed and snipped?

'Are you on holiday? Are you going somewhere special tonight? Who cut your hair last? Oh dear, tsk tsk.'

The girl who shampooed her hair was called Kat – not Kate, she hastened to explain, but Kat. She pressed her large bosoms against Laura's shoulders and they moved up and down as she danced her knowing hands in the dark hair. It was hypnotic: the hair moving on her scalp, the fleshy breasts heaving against her. Kat was not a pretty girl, but healthily plump and friendly like a golden spaniel puppy. She should have been called Pup. Her capable hands massaged Laura's scalp and Laura drifted off into almost a sleep state. God, it was so relaxing here in this little town. The sea air had got to her, filled her with unheard-of longings, a sand-coloured, sea-coloured, sky-filled desire. Her thighs throbbed. She came to as the girl wrapped her wet hair in a thick black towel, and bade her remove herself to another seat.

Why was she anxious, nervous about this drinks party? Who would be there whom she knew? For good-ness' sake, she was a sophisticated woman; her articles appeared in national magazines. She was well paid and highly regarded. How come she felt not desirable, not loved by several men, but small, untalented, ethereal? She had chosen not to ask Thomas or Aaron to go with her. Why? She preferred to go alone, unencumbered. Oh, if only Jerry was here!

Her sharp-cut fringe and slanted wedge of heavy dark

hair shone in the light. She tipped the stylist and the girl who had washed her hair.

'Do you want to make another appointment?'

'Er, no thanks, not at the moment.'

She would be back in her home town, back in reality, London, by the time her fringe grew into her eyes. Her work was fun; she enjoyed it. She loved being a Londoner. She sighed, and admired her tanned, very un-London, legs as she shaved them. She trimmed and painted her toenails a bright red. There was a sudden pang in her chest as she remembered the time she had worn the red dress for Jerry. It was the same colour red, scarlet as new spilled blood.

What was Jerry doing now? His wife? What was she like? Were they ... happy? What is happiness? She should have known not to get involved with a married man – but he had said they were separated, hadn't he? It wasn't fair, to feel so hurt, still. She wasn't getting over him. The sex might be good – was good – with Aaron and Thomas, and Rory, but it was after all only lust she was experiencing, not love. She had really fallen for Jerry in a serious way, had been ready to give everything of herself to him, and she felt lost, bereft, without that warm feeling of love and safety that he had instilled in her in such a short time. She must just try harder to forget him, she determined.

Oh God, a house gift ... a house warming present! She had not thought of it before, and she had no idea of Red Sonia's taste – apart from her Second World War bomb shelter, Brutalist architecture, her antique silver candelabra and her voyeurism.

She wore the red dress, sans stockings and suspender belt, but with silver, flat, strappy sandals showing her red toenails. Her newly cut thick wedge of crow-black hair fell and swept like a dark cloud over the field of her open face.

* * *

153

'I didn't know what you would like.' she apologised, handing Sonia the small, neat parcel. She had chosen it from the newly opened, very good second-hand book-shop in Harbour Street.

The architect wore a navy-blue chiffon floaty shift over a silk slip that reached her immaculately mani-cured slender feet. Her four-inch carmine-red shoes showed her toes and her insteps, which curved like a ballerina's. She looked even taller than before, a veri-table amazon, with one white shoulder bare, her round breasts untethered and the nipples prominent. Laura felt herself blushing and she realised she felt something akin to lust as she watched Sonia's slow smile.

'A first edition Yeats! How generous and what a wonderful present! I shall treasure it always.' She leant forward and kissed Laura on both cheeks, her fragrant breath caressing Laura's burning face. 'I love your dress. Come in and meet people. I expect you'll know some of them.'

She led Laura in through an uncluttered white space under the broad, pale-green leaves of banana plants in a sunken garden. Light entered through a glass roof, diffused by white muslin.

'This is lovely,' said Laura.

'I'll show you the rest of it later.' Sonia steered Laura towards the drinks – champagne with fresh squeezed orange – and introduced her to two men: her business partners.

'This is Jasper Ernest, and this is Jonty Stewart.' At that point more guests arrived and Laura was stuck with the architects. She had not met them before, and they were attentively charming, welcoming an attractive woman into the hothouse of small town life.

'Are you living here?' asked the mustachioed, burly Jasper.

'No, unfortunately. Just here for the summer.'

'What do you do, Laura?' asked the tall, thin young man, Jonty, louche in a pink bow tie and cream suit.

'I write for magazines – freelance – about anything and everything.' She heard herself sounding defensive, as if she was ashamed of what she did. But after all, it was a luxury industry, just like theirs, and nothing to be ashamed of, she told herself.

They were talking architecture, of course, and their own awards, and she soon tired of the subject and wandered off, admiring the shelving, the staircase, the details of the interior. All was in a pale fine wood, which gleamed like nacreous seashell. She had another glass of champagne and orange juice, and wandered outside, through double-glazed doors to a wide expanse of wooden deck, where the black telescope stood on its tripod looking out over the harbour and with a fine view of the terrace where Laura had sunbathed.

The deck wrapped around the whole house, like an open verandah, and Laura admired the design. Suddenly she heard a familiar voice and was astonished to see the diver, Bill Montpelier, in intimate conversation with Sonia, holding both her arms and laughing conspiratorially. He looked almost handsome, thought Laura. His bulk was elegantly draped in an expensive, unstructured, beige linen suit, under which he wore a white silk shirt, undone at the neck to show his tanned neck, a sturdy column of sinew and muscle. His silver hair was cut very short all over and, even though he was balding, he looked virile. Laura had only seen him in his working clothes, the heavy sweaters and jeans and checked shirts the divers wore when they came on shore for a drink. He was obviously not poverty-stricken, she thought. She wondered what the connection was between the skipper of the diving vessel and the woman architect. They certainly seemed to know each other pretty well. She thought of the time she had seen him at the auction house acting as a sort of bodyguard.

She walked towards them and they looked at her and smiled.

'You know Bill, I believe?' said Sonia.

'Yes, hello.'

'Hello,' he said, nodding curtly.

The wind is getting up, shall we go inside?' Sonia led them indoors again and the gathering had grown. Laura recognised several tradesmen, a solicitor and a bank manager. Behind the heads of some grey-haired men she spotted Anna and Charles. She went towards them gratefully.

'Hello Laura! What are you doing here?' said Charles.

'Don't be so rude, darling,' his wife said. 'Laura doesn't only know us.'

'Did you know that young Thomas has gone to London for a break, before he goes back to university?' said Charles.

'No, I didn't know,' said Laura, with a pang of familiar guilt. Why did she spend all her time feeling guilty these days? 'I suppose he wasn't too unhappy about me and him?'

'No, of course not, Laura, he's just a boy, he'll get over it. Don't worry. Lucky lad, I say.' Charles squeezed her arm, looking furtively over his shoulder at his wife, who was embroiled in a discussion with the mayor's wife about the new traffic system.

Laura found herself being pushed from one group to another, being introduced to people she should have known, but didn't. There was a heavy artistic contingent: men in silk waistcoats and colourful bow ties, women in flowing skirts with their long grey hair tied up in untidy knots, and wearing no make-up. Very seventies.

Bill Montpelier was suddenly pressed up against her.

Her back was jammed against a white grand piano, which was played by a musician hired for the occasion.

'Where's Aaron, tonight?' she said, for lack of any other subject of mutual interest.

'Why, isn't he with you?' said Bill, a large pungent cigar between his strong teeth.

'I didn't ask him,' she said, unsmiling.

'No, he'll be here later, though, my lover.'

'Oh, that will be . . . nice.' She was at a loss. The diver was antagonistic towards her, but she didn't know why. He pushed his large, heavily lined face into hers and she smelt whisky on his breath.

'You muck up Aaron and you'll have me to reckon with, my bird.'

'I beg your pardon?' She was shocked at the hostility in his voice. Had she really got herself a reputation for ruining young men? Perhaps she had. Ah well, life in a small town!

'I think Aaron is old enough to know his own mind, and doesn't need you nursing him,' she said, bristling.

'He's my nephew, and my business, and I don't want him messed up by any London tart.'

'How dare you!' she cried, slapping his face hard. He laughed mirthlessly and walked away. She thought she heard him say, 'Like mother, like daughter.' One or two people turned around and stared, not having seen the incident, then turned back and whispered together.

Sonia appeared, having seen the fracas, took Laura's shaking arm and gave her another drink.

'Come with me, I want to show you my home.'

She put her long arm through Laura's and together they walked up the blond wood staircase to the upper floor, which was as light and airy as the ground floor, with coloured glass panels and white-painted wood.

'This is the main bedroom,' announced Sonia, and swept into the square room with pleasure, eager to show off her design expertise.

The bed was large and low, built on a blond wood base, and covered in white and cream cotton. A canopy of white muslin was draped over it like a mosquito net. The furniture was simple and expensive: antique chests of drawers in dark oak, banded with chestnut; a sofa of brown leather, battered and creased with age; long gilt-framed mirrors and a chandelier of Venetian glass.

'Unusual style. Lovely!' pronounced Laura, impressed with the eclecticism of the furnishings. This room showed more of the architect's personality than the rather austere modernism of the downstairs.

Sonia flung herself on the bed and lay back, her bare arms behind her head. Her flame-coloured hair blazed. Her long legs stretched and her red toenails gleamed like fireflies.

'Oh dear, Laura, why doesn't Bill like you?'

'I cannot imagine,' said Laura. She sat tentatively on the edge of the bed and gazed admiringly at the long, lean body of the highly attractive woman before her. 'Except that I'm sleeping with his nephew, Aaron, and he seems to think the man is an innocent virgin who needs to be protected from a London harpy.'

Sonia laughed and stroked Laura's still shaking hand. 'Don't worry about Bill, I can handle him.'

'How come you know him?' said Laura, aware of the long fingers caressing hers.

'Oh, we do business together, sometimes. Anyway, everyone knows everyone in this place. You are absolutely gorgeous, do you know that?' she said casually, and raising herself, she leant forward and kissed Laura full on the mouth. Laura was stunned. But her lips answered Sonia's, and she gave herself up to the embrace, thinking that this was the first time she had ever been attracted to a woman. It was as if she was kissing herself: the full lips, the soft cheek, the curved neck. The caresses became more frantic and suddenly they were both clutching each other desperately, tearing at each other's clothes. Sonia's chiffon overdress was pulled over her head with the silk slip and her long, fair-skinned body was revealed to an amazed Laura. The full breasts were pressed against her own; their nipples met. Their bellies warm against each other, they caressed, Laura tentatively, the older woman more more ardently. Laura found herself under the beautiful body of the architect, whose full breasts hung down to be taken into her mouth.

Sonia writhed above Laura, grinding her pubis against the smaller body, touching her in the most intimate places. She took Laura's nervous fingers and placed them between her legs and led her into the secret folds of her moist flesh. Laura was hypnotised by the nipple in her mouth, the scent of female flesh, the musk and perfume of sex. They answered each other's call for release in the most knowing way, as if they were masturbating, aware of the most pleasurable sensations and how to give back, to answer the other's sensuality. Laura's breathing jerked, her breasts heaved and her mouth opened wide as the climax came. She grasped Sonia's thighs and held her close, and her fingers went down to the swollen sex.

Sonia trembled and sank, at peace, on to the moist warm body of Laura. 'Wow! You are lovely!' She rose, without another word and disappeared through a flush door into the bathroom.

Laura lay under the white muslin, drowsing, unthinking, listening to the sounds of the shower through the open door. Sonia reappeared wrapped in a large white towel and flung another at Laura. 'Here, take this, go and shower quickly before they send a search party for us.' She grinned. Her hair was damp and she rubbed the curls with the end of the towel.

Laura rose slowly, hesitating to lose the languorous feelings that enveloped her, the mood of timelessness that a vivid orgasm had achieved.

'Thanks,' she said. 'Sonia, did you really watch me through the telescope?'

'I certainly did, and very entertaining it was, too.' She blew her a kiss and walked out of the door followed by a blushing Laura.

The guests were getting on without the hostess. Aaron had arrived and was chatting with Bill, who looked less belligerent now, but more inebriated. Laura and Sonia entered the sitting room together, arm in arm.

'I am starved,' laughed Sonia.' Do you want something to eat?'

She led the way to an adjacent room, where a long table had been set with seafood of all descriptions. There were plates of half lobsters, red as Sonia's hair. Giant prawns bristled on a huge silver platter with crab claws, oysters on ice, smoked mackerel and gleaming white scallop shells, their orange coral and juicy white flesh exposed like a woman's sex. The waiters, local lads in long aprons and black waistcoats, served the waiting guests, whose mouths watered at the wonderful harvest of the sea.

Of course, this is the business that Sonia has with Bill Montpelier, Laura thought. He has supplied the shellfish. What was it he had meant as he had walked away? Like mother, like daughter? Had he known her mother? He must be in his early forties. That would have made him about eighteen at the time of her mother's death. Her mother had been only twenty-three and her father twenty-eight when they died. He probably had known them both. There was a mystery here, she thought. She determined to make him tell her what he meant, but not now. Another time.

She saw the diver and Sonia talking together, laughing conspiratorially and they eventually went off together into another part of the house.

Laura chatted to Aaron over her plate of crab claws and lobster tail meat.

'Is this seafood all your doing? Your uncle's I mean?'

'I suppose,' he said.

'He doesn't approve of you seeing me, you know.'

'Oh, don't mind 'e, he's just jealous,' he laughed. 'Thinks I'm still a youngster, he does.'

Laura's senses had been fired by her second sexual experience with another woman, but now she needed a man to thrust inside her. 'Come home with me now, Aaron,' she said.

'I'll come d'rec'ly my flower,' he said. 'I have some business first.'

'What business?'

'Oh, just a few strings that have to be tied up, you know. I won't be long.' He patted her on the bottom and she felt as if she had been dismissed.

'OK. I'll see you later.' She could not find Sonia to say goodbye. Presumably she was with the missing diving boss. Probably paying him for the shellfish, she thought.

She said goodnight to Anna and Charles, who were having a wonderful time, chatting with their Tory Member of Parliament.

She walked home down the hill, leaving the lights of the house behind her, and enjoying the sight of the harbour lights below. Her eighteenth-century granite house looked boring in comparison with the understated luxury of Sonia's modern design, and she felt herself cheap, unclean.

I suppose I should stop acting like a cat on heat, she thought, and do something constructive with my life. I'm just drifting, going with the flow, and it's not right. I must make changes. After this summer, I'll think about it more clearly. The sun and sex has turned my head, weakened my morals.

Meanwhile she had to make herself desirable for Aaron.

She dressed in a black suspender belt of satin, with split-crotch panties of black silk, and a strappy bra that she had bought in Paris, last year. The bra left her nipples and areolae exposed. The straps that surrounded her breasts made her feel wickedly naked. This outfit always made her feel desirable. She pulled up the fine black stockings and attached them to the suspenders.

She brushed her hair until it gleamed, remembering the red hair of her woman lover, its lights and shimmers, its soft silkiness in her face and on her belly.

Laura turned the lights down low and lay on her bed, touching herself lightly, feeling herself as if she were Sonia, appraising the fineness of her skin, the delicacy of her muscle tone, the firmness of her buttocks and breasts. Yes, she was satisfied that the older woman had not been disappointed with her flesh. She arched her back and lifted her pudenda to her fingers. Where was Aaron? She desired his strength, his big hands holding her down, his thick rod inside her, pumping at her.

She heard the door click open and closed and he entered the bedroom silently. The white of his eyes flashed in the dim light. He fell on her without a word, his hands between her thighs, on her exposed nipples, under the tight satin ribbons of the suspenders, scraping her smooth flesh. She shuddered with delight as he thrust into her, not waiting to remove all his clothes, just getting out his swollen cock and pushing it into her. His orgasm was sudden and violent and she had wanted it to last, wanted the thrusts to hurt, to rasp at her heated flesh.

She fell back in disappointment. But he was drunk and had only needed release.

He slept, still dressed, and she got up in disgust and washed herself. She took off her gorgeous undergarments, the trappings of desire, and fell back into bed, pushing him over to the far side. She touched herself again, needing the continuing pressure of flesh on flesh. She rubbed herself against him, trying not to wake him.

She took his hand and put his thick thumb inside her, clasped her legs together and writhed on it. It was better than nothing, and she came on to his hand, pulsating on his sleeping thumb.

When she woke it was nine o'clock and he had gone. She felt wretched, decadent; her make-up was smeared over her face, and her mouth felt dry and sour. Then she remembered her previous night's unlikely experience in the bed of the woman architect.

'Red Sonia!' she thought, smiling to herself. Then she had another thought: her mother, May – had she been unfaithful to Laura's father? Her imagination was vivid enough without it being fuelled by flames of suggestion. Was this what Bill Montpelier had meant? Was she promiscuous, like her mother? Was she causing mayhem in the little town?

Chapter Fifteen
Sunken Treasure

*T*he outlines for the articles that Laura had started to write had lain forgotten on her desk for two weeks or more. She had arranged with James to write about a garden that a famous Cornish novelist had made, and his house. But when she telephoned to make an appointment for an interview, and to look at the garden, the novelist's secretary said that he was very ill and they would have to cancel the feature.

Damn, what was the other article she was supposed to write? She looked through her notes, couldn't find it, and telephoned the offices of *Young Living*.

'Hi, it's Laura! James, how's things? Oh, it's lovely here, no rain for a week. What? Pouring there? You poor thing!'

She suggested to the editor that she had found a different house feature they could do instead of the sick novelist's: Sonia Stallone's seaside home.

'All right, do it. I'll send a photographer next week.'

'Hang on, I'll just make sure it's OK with Sonia and get back to you. I'll speak to you very soon. Oh, and James, what was the other piece we decided I could do, here? I can't find my notes.'

'We were discussing that today, in a meeting. It was an investigation into the Cornish tradition of smuggling and wrecking. But I know it isn't your sort of thing, so don't worry if you don't get anything. Stick to the houses and gardens, my sweet. I'll find a proper journalist to do the investigative stuff.'

'How dare you!' she laughed. 'I'll do it, don't worry.'

'Only joking. Send me some Cornish cream, you lucky bastard,' said her editor, laughing, 'And a young, blond surfer – no, two! And I'm coming to see you soon. I won't wait for an invitation.'

Laura, dressed in jeans and white T-shirt and sneakers that had seen better days, knocked at Sonia's door. A cleaning woman opened the door. The debris of the party was no more; the house was pristine white, not a crumb in sight.

'Is Miss Stallone in, please?'

'No, my 'andsome, she's at her office.'

'Oh, of course, how silly of me.'

She walked down the steep hill, through cobbled lanes with wild valerian and escallonia cascading from tall granite walls. A canary in a hanging cage above an open cottage door sang prettily to itself. A fat tabby cat preened on a step and stared down haughtily at her.

She walked around the harbour, into the main part of town, pushing through the throngs of tourists with their plastic sandals and their red-faced children, ubiquitous buckets and spades clutched in sandy hands.

She found the architects' office, housed in an old Wesleyan chapel, which had been altered to fit the offices of the three partners. Outside was a sign on an upturned boat: ERNEST, STALLONE AND STEWART, ARCHITECTS.

She opened the heavy oak door and went inside. She walked up steps and into the reception area.

'Can I help you?' asked a plump, pretty girl, smirking at Laura.

'I'm looking for Miss Stallone.'

'Have you an appointment, please, madam?'

'No.'

'You're Laura Mackay, aren't you?' the girl asked.

'Yes,' said Laura, surprised.

'I'm Aaron's sister, Becky.' The girl looked at Laura with interest.

'Oh, hello, pleased to meet you, Becky.' Laura thought of all the nights they had shared the same roof without meeting. She wondered if Becky was wearing her white cotton Marks and Spencer panties or the black lace ones. She wondered if Becky had heard her moans. She was bound to have heard every sound in the small cottage.

Becky dialled a telephone number and announced Laura. 'You can go in. It's the second door on the right, the one with a blue handle.'

Laura knocked lightly and went into the room. It had high ceilings and brightly coloured metal beams. The windows were too high to see out of, which was frustrating, as the view must have been fascinating – old fishing lofts and cottages, and roofs and chimneys where herring gulls nested. She could hear their raucous gossiping.

Sonia stood, her arms held out to Laura. 'Come here.' The older woman wore a grey silk-and-linen suit, softly draped and with wide trousers. Her red curls were loose about her shoulders.

Laura found herself instantly under the spell of the tall redhead. She was probably around forty, thought Laura, aware in the daylight of the woman's stretched skin around her very green eyes.

They embraced lightly and Sonia bade Laura sit on one of the metal-and-leather chairs that dotted the spacious room, where a tilted table stood and a high stool, and a large old plan chest.

'How did you like my party?' she asked.

'I liked it. How would you like to be featured in a magazine?'

'What, "Yoof" magazine?'

'Yes, *Young Living*. They do include sensible articles, you know. It's not all sex and male pin-ups.'

'Why not, darling? I could do with the publicity. Any PR is better than nothing.'

'We'd feature the house of course, and mention any prize-winning buildings you have done, and I would interview you,' enthused Laura. 'There's no money in it, but the coverage you'd get would be enormous.'

'You don't have to sell yourself, darling, I'll do it.'

'Great! I'll tell the editor and we'll get a photographer down here next week, probably, if that is all right?'

'Fine, I'll just look in my diary. When do you want to interview me?'

'When you like,' said Laura, silently applauding herself. She remembered the minder's words: 'Miss Stallone doesn't give interviews.' Huh!

Laura found herself in the older woman's arms, Sonia's hands up inside her T-shirt, over her breasts. They kissed. Laura felt a surge of desire in her loins. Her nipples stiffened.

'Come to my place tonight,' Sonia ordered. 'I'll make us something to eat.'

Later, after Laura had bought extra tapes for her recording machine, and washed her hair for the second time that day, she dressed carefully. A loose-fitting, short dress that skimmed her hips, in electric blue, with a bright-pink pansy design – a Japanese designer item bought on location in Hong Kong. It was an easy dress to wear and remove. Her tanned legs shone with oil, and her toes were freshly lacquered.

She carried her tape recorder in her old leather backpack, a bottle of white wine, and a bunch of sweet peas from the garden.

'You're all flowery,' said the delighted Sonia, taking

the wine and flowers and kissing Laura on the mouth. 'Come and sit on the deck. It's out of the wind and still warm. In fact I think it's at its best at this time of day.'

Laura sat in one of the faded silver-grey cedar chairs on a cream-coloured cushion, and gazed at the sun setting over the beach. It was delightful here, certainly. She wished she had brought her sun-glasses. Would Sonia notice her laughter lines?

Sonia, wearing a grey marl sweatshirt and jeans, and with her hair tied back in a ponytail, looked younger than she had earlier. She wore no make-up apart from a little mascara, and her fair-skinned face was wide and unblemished. Her high cheek-bones were almost oriental, thought Laura, examining her closely. How she would like to paint her!

They clinked their glasses and drank.

'Do you want to get the interview over with before we eat?'

'Good idea,' said Laura. She took out the tape recorder and set in on the table between them.

'How long have you been in the town?' asked Laura.

'Oh, only two years. I was in Morocco before that, for a short time, and before that I was in Russia.'

'Russia? What were you doing in Russia?'

'Er, this and that. Buying and selling art work mostly. A bit of interior design, you know.'

It sounded rather vague to Laura, but she did not push it. If Sonia had secrets, so be it. 'And what made you want to move to Cornwall?'

'Ah, the ambience of this place: the light, the artistic community, the mild climate, the people. The feeling of artistic integrity that pervades an area that has been a centre of excellence for centuries, and a place where creativity is encouraged.'

Oh yes, a good quote, that. The Cornish tourist board would be pleased with that one. 'And this house – did the local people mind having such an unusual building in their town?'

'There was some opposition, but the planners passed it after one or two changes to the design,' said Sonia. She poured more wine and stood to fetch some smoked salmon-wrapped asparagus spears.

'Yum!' said Laura, popping one into her mouth.

'You sound about twelve when you come out with expressions like that,' said Sonia with a smile, leaning over and stroking Laura's hair.

'Tell me what other buildings you have been involved with designing and building,' said Laura, ignoring the stir of desire in her belly.

Later, they went indoors to eat a wonderful soup made from the leftovers of the party fare – a thick, fiery fish soup made of prawns and crabmeat, with a hot red rouille and croutons. It was delicious. Laura felt satiated, full, and excited at the thought of the woman's embrace. They sat on a wide white sofa, before a large fire that looked like coal but was in fact gas, and drank malt whisky.

Laura sat, barefoot, her dress up over her knees, her legs tucked under her. The room darkened and Sonia did not switch on the lights. The fire's authentic flickering glow turned their skin to molten gold. In Sonia's hair lights leapt and flashed, so it was like a river of fire. She removed her sweatshirt and sat with her breasts free, the nipples large and dark. Laura was suddenly shy and did not move to touch her, but Sonia stood and slipped out of her jeans and knelt at Laura's feet. She slipped her hands under the short-skirted dress and slid them up towards Laura's thighs. Laura sighed and allowed the caresses to continue. She felt the fingers find their way around to her buttocks and stroke the fleshy globes. She lay back, her legs stretched out now, to allow the hands to explore.

Her dress was lifted over her head and off. She sat in

total abandon, her loose-legged black silk panties twisted and pulled aside. The woman knelt and stroked and then put her lips to Laura's thighs and gently kissed the thin taut skin of the inner leg. Laura's breasts were sore with longing. She stroked the head that was between her legs, clutching the fine silky threads of golden chestnut flame. Her legs were weak, she felt faint, and desire sang in her veins. Her mouth opened as she gasped for breath. Her toes curled as the woman's tongue infiltrated her secret folds and found the swollen bud. Laura clutched Sonia's head more firmly, encouraging each delicate caress, pressing her intently, wanting the tongue to penetrate completely, to overwhelm her. She felt the first flutterings of her orgasm overtake her. She sank on to Sonia's ardent mouth, wanting to be consumed, bitten, swallowed alive.

Sonia lay on the wide white leather sofa naked, next to the sobbing Laura. They were in each other's arms.

'Why are you crying? What is it, love?' whispered Sonia, stroking Laura's cheek.

'I'm sorry, it was just so fantastic. I don't know why I'm crying,' said Laura. She tried hard not to think of Jerry – his angular body pressing her to him.

Laura kissed Sonia's mouth gently, feeling the nuances of desire return to the older woman's movements. Laura caressed the squarish shoulders, stroked the length of the long arms to the slender fingers. She kissed her not as if this was some bizarre experiment, which she had felt the night before, but with indecent lust. Sonia's bodily scents were musky; her pubic hair was thick between her legs. Laura wanted to explore this beautiful body, which felt so strange yet so familiar. It was a sort of self-love, she thought, making love to someone of the same sex as oneself. The echoes of skin, elegance of movements, subtle differences of womanly flesh, the soft hair, the fleshy breasts. Sonia's breasts were so much bigger and rounder than Laura's, she was fascinated by them, their weightiness, their curves. She sucked at the dark nipples and took the puckered areolae into her mouth, licking and tasting the fragrant skin.

Sonia sighed contentedly, and held Laura in her arms. Their bellies curved into each other's shape, their legs entwined. Suddenly Sonia lifted the smaller woman on to her, sitting her over her thighs, her legs wide. Laura sat upright, her dark wedge of hair over her face, her small swinging breasts pressed to the eager hands, her sex open and wanting the contact of flesh. She felt the firm belly beneath her, the thighs soft. She slipped her fingers behind her and felt for Sonia's moistness. Laura's round bottom pressed the soft belly. Her fingers fluttered like butterflies over and around the other's sex, tantalising, teasing, giving pleasure, withholding the final joy, touching now gently, now harshly. She knew how to please herself, so she knew what would also please Sonia. Sonia writhed on the subtle embrace and shouted out her ultimate satisfaction.

Later, still naked, still with the fire's glow warming them, tired after love-making, they talked.

'Wouldn't you like to live here?' Sonia asked.

'Yes, and no. I love London and my life there. I enjoy the theatres and concerts and restaurants and friends.'

'Of course. But life here is like being on holiday all the time, you know? I have a ball here.'

'You must earn plenty from architecture.' Laura had not thought about it, but the leather sofa, the antiques upstairs: perhaps they were inherited?

'I don't make enough money in this small town to afford a place like this, if that is what you mean. You must have realised?'

'No, what do you mean?' asked Laura, perplexed.

'I deal in antiques and antiquities. Rather unique antiquities – I have many antique dealer contacts in

Russia and Italy and Morocco. They are looking for unusual objects for very rich men, who want trophies that no one else can buy to put in their palaces and gloat over.'

'And where do you buy the antiques?'

'Oh, here and there, you know,' she laughed, lightly. 'Other dealers, house sales, auctions.'

'I saw you, about a month or so ago, in London, at an auction at Phillips.'

'Did you? What were you doing there?'

'I was with a photographer working for *Young Living*.'

The redhead flicked her hair back, raised an arched eyebrow, but did not pursue the matter.

'You must work very hard, with the architecture, too?' said Laura.

'Well, I want the best in life, Laura, only the very best. If I don't get it for myself, I won't ever have it, I reckon.'

Laura was full of admiration for this strong woman, who worked at two jobs so that she could achieve what she wanted from life. What did she, Laura, want? She had been delighted to be working for a magazine like *Young Living*. The work was varied and she met all sorts of people. At this thought her mind strayed to Jerry, and she sighed. What did she want from life, except Jerry? A pang of sorrow and longing pierced her like a knife, which went in sharply and twisted in her guts. She half heard Sonia's next words.

'He sometimes has the odd item for me.'

'Who? Bill Montpelier?'

'Yes, he has connections.' Sonia sipped her drink and smiled.

Chapter Sixteen

Corresponding

A postcard from James:

Dear Laura,

I'll come for the weekend, may I? Phone me! What's your mobile number?

PS Is there room for two of us – I've persuaded Guido I'm not too old for him after all.

Love, James.

A letter from Thomas:

Dear Laura,

I miss you. I did not think I would, but I do. I have to tell you that our affair was the most important thing to happen to me in my entire life. I have such precious memories of the idyllic time we shared. Thank you, Laura.

Your loving Thomas.

PS I have met a very pretty girl, Dorina, and I am teaching her all the things you taught me.

Laura laughed delightedly.

A letter from Jerry, forwarded to her from *Health and You*.

Dearest Laura,

I think of you constantly. I cannot tell you what has been going through my mind since we parted. My wife and I are no longer together. I have told her that I am in love with you. She has gone for good – home to her family in Scotland for now. I wish I had had the guts to tell you I loved you, and now I fear I have lost you.

Laura, I am so sorry for being weak and stupid. I do love you, darling, and want to be with you. If you can forgive me, write, please,

Always yours,

Jerry.

Laura put aside James' demand for a free weekend's love-nest, and read Jerry's letter again. She didn't know what to do about Jerry. Her instinct was to telephone him immediately and fall into his arms at the first opportunity, but her head told her to go gently, carefully. He was still married, after all. Nothing had really changed except that his wife had gone to Scotland and he was lonely. She hardened her heart against the possibility of being hurt by him a second time. He didn't have her address in Cornwall. He wouldn't be able to reach her easily. She had time to think.

Chapter Seventeen

Laura Turns Detective

'Mrs Poldhu, it's me, Laura.' She opened the back door and went inside the small dark kitchen. Her neighbour was hoovering the front room and Laura had to walk into the room before she became aware of her.

'I'm just finishing, my cheel, I won't be a moment.'

Laura perched on the edge of a chair while she watched the elderly woman unplug the machine and wind the lead and tuck it away. She pushed the old carpet cleaner into the hall and put it in a cupboard.

'There, that's done. Do you want a tea or coffee?'

It had become a daily ritual, the coffee or tea, the chat, and then Laura reading aloud for about an hour. They were well into *Frenchman's Creek*.

'Do you know that your grandmother and I used to go bowling together?' Mrs Poldhu asked, triumphantly.

'Did you? No, I didn't know Gran did any bowling. Was she good at it?'

'Oh, yes, we both were. My 'usband used to play too. We took her with us after your grandfather died.'

'Wouldn't you like to play still?'

'No, cheel, I'm too old for that, now. My knees won't

bend. Anyway, I wouldn't be able to see the ball.' She laughed.

'How long were you married?' asked Laura, gently.

'Fifty years.'

'Fifty? Goodness, what a long time!' Laura could not imagine it, all that time with one man.

'And was it a happy marriage?' she asked, daringly.

'Oh, yes, as happy and as unhappy as anyone's marriage, I suppose. We had no children, of course. That probably helped.'

'Helped?'

'Oh, yes. We just had each other. And so we concentrated on that. Made the most of each other, you know.'

Did she know? Did Laura know anything about love, loyalty, faithfulness? She felt humbled by the old woman's wisdom and lack of rancour or bitterness at what life had given her and taken away.

'We always looked after each other, you know,' Mrs Poldhu continued. Then she sobbed suddenly and put her head in her hands.

'Oh, dear, I am sorry. I shouldn't have asked you about him. I've upset you.'

'No, no, I like talking about him. I want to talk about him. Most people don't want to mention his name but I want to. I see him every day, there in his chair. I do talk to him.' She blew her nose and patted Laura on the hand. 'Come on, where's the Daphne du Maurier?'

Later, Laura phoned James.

'James, I need your help.'

'Hello, Laura! It's great to hear from you. How are you, pet?'

'I'm fine, James, how are you?'

'Oh, you know young boys. Guido's giving me a hard time. Playing hard to get. Did I tell you he's a singer in a choir?'

'You love it, James, you don't fool me.'

'Are you going to invite me down there?'

176

'Maybe. Not yet. I need some help, James.'

'What help do you need?'

'I need some background info about a shipwreck, for this piece I'm doing.'

'Shoot,' he said. He was an experienced journalist and could get hold of information easily.

'The *Elizabetta*, a Spanish barque, I think. And anything you can find on treasure trove. Is finding keeping?'

'I'll get on to it tomorrow and get back to you as soon as I can.'

'Thanks, James, you're a star.'

'Perhaps you'll invite me down to your ancestral pile?'

'Not with a virgin choirboy,' she said, smiling at the phone. 'When can you send the photographer for the house shoot?'

'The day after tomorrow, if that's all right. Can you put him up? Or find a hotel? There's an assistant, too, of course.'

'I'll sort something out and get back to you later today.'

Laura went out into the town and asked at the tourist information office for a list of rooms available. The town was full; there was not a bed to be had. Well, she was glad the tourist industry was thriving. There was nothing for it – she would have to put them up herself. She went back to the house and found sheets and pillow cases. There were four bedrooms in the house. The beds were not the firmest she had known but she was sure the photographer and his assistant would be fairly comfortable. She noticed that the rugs on the floor were rather tired looking so she shook them out of a window and let them air for a while. There were wash basins in the bedrooms and she cleaned them. It would keep the pressure off the bathroom, she thought. Then she found some blankets and old-fashioned eiderdowns in a cupboard. She threw out the thin blankets and shook the pretty feather-filled eiderdowns.

It was hard to stop, once she had started changing things. She picked some nasturtiums and marigolds from the garden and found pots for them to go in. The bedroom curtains were dowdy. Old chintz that needed washing. She took them down and left the cream holland roller blinds at the sash windows. The rooms looked lighter, brighter, cleaner, somehow, without the dull, dark curtains. She removed some of the old photographs from the walls, but they left patches on the wallpaper, so she put them back. She remembered the stripy rose-patterned paper from when she had slept here as a child. She had lain awake listening to her grandfather play hymns on the piano. Her grandparents had also sung together the old songs from their youth.

She picked up a pile of sheet music and nearly threw it out, but then, over-ruled by her heart, put it by the piano. She had learnt to play as a child and had not enjoyed it one bit, but that didn't mean to say that she wouldn't now. She pressed a key, experimentally. It sounded clear, clean, a note from her childhood, when all had been so simple.

Had her grandparents had a simple life? She had not known them intimately. She had been a beloved only grandchild, spoilt, loved, protected from the awfulness of life, like the deaths at sea that happened regularly. The sea took its toll of young men each year, plucking them from rocks where they fished, or lifting them from fishing boats. Death by drowning was part of life in a fishing community. Her grandfather had been a lay preacher at one of the many chapels. She had been kept from the funeral services as she had been protected from the reality of her parents' relationship – maybe their marriage had been wrecked on the rocks of passion and infidelity. What had happened to them? She had never known the truth of what had happened in their lives.

There was an oak-framed photograph of them on their wedding day, propped on the mantelpiece. It showed a brown-haired young man in policeman's uniform and a slender, dark-haired girl in an understated muslin dress that came down to her slim ankles. On her feet she wore white satin shoes with a strap that encircled the ankles. On her head was a muslin veil, caught with fresh flowers at each side, over her ears. She had a tentative smile, while he looked rather solemn. Laura had looked at this picture many times, trying hard to remember the strangers shown. Her last memory of her mother and father was when Laura was just three. She had been put to bed but had come down again, sat on the stairs and watched her parents through the banisters. She remembered her mother shouting, screaming words Laura could not catch and her father saying nothing, but she could still see his hurt eyes, the expression like an injured dog. Laura sighed.

The photographer arrived next day and his assistant unloaded the metal cases of cameras, the tripod and the lights from the car.

'Hello, you must be Laura. I'm Rick. This is Steve.' The photographer was a tall redheaded twenty-five-year-old, with brown eyes and an olive skin. His hair was all extravagant curls, long and thick. Most women would have died for it. His assistant, Steve, was even taller, with long dark hair tied in a ponytail. He was about twenty. They looked like rock musicians, or Celtic heroes from the Rob Roy movie.

'Come in and let me show you your rooms,' she said. 'I'm afraid you'll have to slum it with me, as the town is full.'

'Sounds good to me,' said Steve. 'Where shall I leave all this stuff?'

'Oh, where it is will have to do, for now.' She led

them up the stairs and showed them the newly cleaned rooms. 'Right, when you are ready come outside and have a drink.'

'Great! Thanks!'

In five minutes they had come downstairs.

'What a lovely view you have!' Rick sat at the outside table and stretched his long legs.

'Tea, coffee, or beer?'

'Tea, thanks.'

'Yeah, tea would be good,' said Steve. He wandered around the deck taking in the view of the harbour, the blue sky, the gulls wheeling overhead. 'Wow! This is something!' His accent was south London. He had a voluptuous mouth and a broken nose. A bit of a lad, thought Laura. Rick, on the other hand, was a serious Scot.

'Is that the house, on the hill?' Rick pointed to Red Sonia's 'bunker.'

Laura put the tray of tea on the table and sat with them. 'Yes, that's it. Unusual, isn't it? It looks better inside, actually. Lots of white and light. Good for "pics", I should think.'

'Great views, too, I should imagine,' said Rick. 'And worth a pretty penny,' he added.

'I've arranged for you to go first thing in the morning, about eight thirty, is that all right?'

'The earlier the better. Get the low morning light,' said Rick. 'It does face east doesn't it?'

'Yes, that's east, and the sun sets over there, as you can see. There's a deck facing west. I've arranged for us to eat out tonight with the owner of the house. I hope that's all right with you two? Just a pub on the harbour, but the food is good. You don't have to go if you don't want to.'

'Fine, whatever you say,' said the photographer, shaking his golden locks and pushing them behind his shoulders with both hands. His arms were muscular in the navy T-shirt and she caught a whiff of his sharp sweat as he raised his arms.

'I'll show you where the bathroom is. There's only one, and a separate lavatory. We eat at eight. I'll see you here at seven, if you like, or at the pub at seven forty-five. You can't miss it, it's on the harbour: the Galleon. The restaurant is upstairs.' She left them to their own devices and went back to her writing. She had not finished Sonia's house article yet. It was difficult, not knowing enough of Sonia's background to flesh out the story. She must ask her for more detail, she thought. She tapped at the laptop. She thought of the antique dealing part of Sonia's background. She must ask her more about that.

Sonia knocked on the door at half past seven. She wore a short navy-blue linen dress and a matching jacket. Her long legs were bare. She wore low-heeled strappy brown sandals. The skirt just showed below the jacket. She really was in good shape for a woman her age, thought Laura.

Sonia leant forward and kissed Laura on the lips. 'How are you, Laura, my sweet?'

Laura blushed. 'I'm fine. If the boys aren't here in a minute, we're seeing them at the Galleon just before eight, I think.'

'Are they dishy, darling?' Sonia raised a beautifully curved dark eyebrow.

'Yes, they both are, actually, veritable gods. One's a redhead like you.'

'Goodee! We can have a little flirtation, perhaps? Which one's mine?'

Laura looked shocked. 'But I thought you were . . .'

'A lesbian, darling? Only sometimes. I think it's stupid to shut oneself off from life's many interesting opportunities, don't you? I like to keep an open mind about these things.' She linked her arm with Laura's and they walked down the hill together to the pub.

'This is good!' Rick ate his lobster with gusto, tearing the tail from the body, scraping out the flesh from the shell and sucking the meat from the hollow legs.

'You've got garlic butter running down your chin,' remarked Sonia, her fork delicately lifting the oyster from its shell and tipping it into her mouth, her head tilted back to show the arc of her white throat.

'Where are you from?' he asked her.

'Me, I'm from nowhere and everywhere,' she said enigmatically.

'Bullshit, where were you born?'

Laura listened avidly. Here was Rick asking questions that she should have asked.

'Rome, in fact. But I have lived all over, never in one place for too long. I like to move on. I am an international mongrel.' She laughed at her own cleverness.

Laura could see that Rick was interested in Sonia. They could have been siblings, with their fiery locks. She sank into a fantasy of imagining their bodies intertwined, the red pubic hair, curly and fiercely wiry, the long legs. They were like red-furred animals, perhaps wolves, their teeth sucking at the fishy flesh, the juices running down their chins.

'How's your crab meat, Laura?' said Steve.

'Yummy!' declared Laura. 'Do you want to try it?'

'No, ta. This steak is a bit of all right,' said Steve.

'Have you always been Rick's assistant?' she asked him, aware that the other two were flirting outrageously with each other.

'Yeah, since I left art school. I'm getting my own portfolio together now, and Rick's helping me with that. Let's me use the studio equipment. He's a good bloke to work for.'

Laura had had several glasses of wine and her body began to buzz with a mild desire. Her desire was not aimed at Steve or Rick or Sonia in particular, but rather at all of them: their skin and hair, their glistening teeth, their wet mouths, their physical presence. She noticed a table of girls giggling together behind her. She glanced at them and saw Becky, Aaron's sister, and Kat, the hairdresser, and another girl, very young. They were whispering behind hands and looking at her table. She supposed that if she stayed in Porthzelah long enough she would get to recognise everybody eventually. Could she really be bothered with flirtation with a bisexual woman and these two young men? She felt guilt suddenly at what she was becoming. Her grandfather would have called her a loose woman, and rightly. She was too easy with her affections and gave her body too readily. Why should anyone want to cherish her if she did not feel precious to herself?

'Hello, Laura, hello Sonia.' It was Aaron standing in front of them. 'Aren't you going to introduce me to your new friends?'

'Hi, Aaron, have you eaten? Join us,' said Sonia, holding out her hands to him. 'This is Rick and his assistant, Steve. They've come to photograph my house.'

'I've eaten, thanks,' he said. 'Just came to make sure my little sister gets home safely. Are you free later?' he asked Laura, looking at her directly.

'Yes. In about an hour. I'll be home.'

'No, come to my place,' he said and left, before she had a chance to comment.

'Masterful! I like that in a man,' said Sonia.

'I like that in a woman,' laughed Rick.

The four left soon after. Rick paid the bill, saying it would go on expenses and then suggested he saw Sonia home on the pretext of having a preview of the house he was to photograph in the morning. Steve went off to 'suss out the night life of Porthzelah.' Laura declined the invitation to go with him and went out into the night air, breathing in the cold wind and wrapping herself in her cashmere shawl. Should she go home first and change her clothes or go to Aaron as she was? She was sure he had some rubber games in mind, so it would not matter what she wore now. He would remove it and cover her in baby oil and surround her with black latex.

She walked along the harbour. Holiday-makers still strolled along, but most of them were inside pubs or tucked up in their hotels and guesthouses. She saw a very young girl, about fourteen, being kissed by an adolescent youth in a doorway. Their mouths devoured each other, inexpertly. The tide was a long way out. The wind blew and stretched her hair. Laura hurried to Love Lane and knocked on Aaron's door. No one answered.

She opened the unlocked door and walked in. She called his name but the cottage was empty. The exposed granite wall of the cramped sitting room looked cold. One wall had shelves of ornaments – his parents', she supposed, or his sisters' – porcelain dolls, horse brasses, photographs, a clock and a good oil painting of a seascape. She sank into a deep scruffy armchair. This had been his father's house, he had told her. His father and mother had died several years ago, she thought. Just then Aaron and Becky came in. Becky was crying and had a red face.

'Go to your room,' he said to her. 'Go on, little slut you're turning out. I'll give you the back of my hand.' He raised his hand at the girl, who fled upstairs without a word.

'What was all that about?'

'She's no good. She'll end up pregnant if I don't keep an eye on her.'

'She's only young, Aaron, and wants to be with her friends,' Laura said.

'Is that right, my bird? Well, then what was she doing with a couple of middle-aged Brummy bastards in the pub last night? They were hanging around again tonight downstairs in the Galleon. I won't have it. She's only sixteen.'

'Come here and give us a kiss,' said Laura, bored with his domestic concerns. 'I have been a naughty girl too, having dinner with strange men. Aren't you going to punish me?'

He grabbed her fiercely around the waist and pulled her to him. His bristling beard, which was short and thick, hurt her face. He pushed his tongue into her mouth and lifted her silk shirt above her breasts. She wore no bra and her nipples were hard little beads. He squeezed her breasts in his large hands.

'That hurts too much,' she whispered. 'I was thinking of a spanking, perhaps?'

He pushed her before him up the narrow stairs to his room.

'I ain't letting you go home to those two randy photographers, that's for sure. I'm tying you up and keeping you here all night,' he whispered, as she lay on his bed and he stripped her of her clothes. He removed his own clothes and she saw his sturdy erection pointed to his stomach. She writhed naked on the rubber sheet. He took two long leather belts and tied her hands to the top and bottom of the brass bedstead. She was face down across the bed, her bottom raised and her feet on the ground. Her breasts rubbed on the cool black rubber. He had been reluctant to tie her when she had first asked him, but now he was only too keen to have her powerless.

'I forgot the mask,' he said, and tied a piece of rubber across her eyes and behind her ears so it rendered her deaf, also. This had been her idea, to cut off a piece from a sheet to make into a mask. Now she was blind, deaf and tied up, and her pubis pressed against the rubber-covered bed. She wriggled her bottom. He pressed his tumescent cock on her buttocks and rubbed it to and fro. Then he used it like a hammer on her flesh, raising it and dropping the heavy weight on her thighs.

He rubbed himself over her back and bottom and she could feel him harden further.

Then he started spanking her. His hand raised and fell and he touched her between her legs with the other hand. The fondling and the punishment were simultaneous and she writhed on his fingers, desperate for a more searching, deeper caress. He pressed his cock between her buttocks and rubbed himself on her. She pressed into the rubber sheet and breathed its erotic scent. He lifted her buttocks and put his hand under her to stroke her belly and pubis. She was helpless, tied, unable to fight off the caresses. Only by squeezing her thighs together could she control the love-making.

He pretended to be angry that she would not open her legs voluntarily and forced them open, spanking her as he did do. He penetrated her from behind, and she felt his shaft go deep inside her, fill her, flood her with sensation. Her body felt as if it was flying in the clouds. She was drunk with sex. He pounded into her, pressing her hard into the rubber. Her mask added to her sensory deprivation, but gave her more than she lost. Her body was full of cock, her nose full of the perfume of latex. Her thighs melted and became a thousand skylarks singing. As he thrust into her for the umpteenth time, her groans were muffled and stifled by the rubber on the bed.

Chapter Eighteen

Red Sonia's Bunker

*L*aura had woken in her own house, having left
Aaron's cottage at two in the morning. Steve and
she shared breakfast alone.

'Well, Rick's well in there, I'd say,' said Steve.

'Yes, it seems he is. More coffee?'

'Ta! Nice bacon and eggs!'

'How did you get on last night? Did you find the
night life?'

'Yeah, The Nite Spot! Great! Lots of girls on their tod.
Had a great time, ta! Went with one, Rowena she was
called, to this older bird's house – French, she was. Into
rubber. Quite an eye-opener. Know what I mean?'

The phone rang. It was Rick.

'Tell Steve to get on up here *toute suite*. I've started
work without him,' he said.

Laura left them to get on with the photography and
made her way to Sonia's house at about ten o'clock. She
would go and see Mrs Poldhu later, she promised
herself.

'Is that where you store your antiques?' Laura asked
Sonia about a locked room.

'Yes, that's it. Can't leave them lying around, can I?'

Sonia looked her age this morning, thought Laura, disloyally. Her eyes looked smaller and her nose was pink and pinched, as if she had a cold coming. She asked herself if she was jealous. Of course not.

'May I interview you further, Sonia? I need more background, really,' said Laura.

'Oh, if you must, darling. Let's pour some wine, now they've nearly finished, and sit on the deck, shall we?' She led Laura out on to the verandah with a tray of drinks in her long hands, calling to Rick and Steve to come out when they wanted a drink. There were pistachios and olives on little silver dishes.

'These dishes are pretty,' said Laura. 'How old are they?'

'Sixteenth-century. Spanish,' said Sonia and popped an olive in her red mouth.

'Wow! That old!'

'Probably.' Sonia slid the stone out into her hand and threw it over the balcony.

'Shall I get another dish to put the stones in?' asked Laura, rising.

'If you like. They're in the top cupboard on the left in the kitchen.'

Laura stood, the cupboard door open. She could not believe the hoard of silver that was stacked on the shelves. There were candle-sticks, dishes, platters, beakers, engraved and plain, a glistening treasure trove of silver and gilt. Pewter too: a stack of dishes and plates.

She chose a small bowl of exquisite design, oval, decorated with a raised pattern of grapes and cherubs. 'Will this one do?' she asked, showing it to Sonia.

'Of course, any one will do.'

'You have some lovely things,' said Laura.

'Yes, I have,' said the architect, smugly. 'I do like pretty things.'

'Did you obtain them through your family or your antique contacts?' asked Laura, tentatively.

'Is this for the article or for private consumption?'

'Whatever you like,' said Laura, 'but I would like to know more about your past, for the article, I mean.'

'The antiques in the house are ... presents from satisfied customers, mostly. Satisfied antique collectors. This is not for public use, this information, Laura, all right, darling?'

'Ah, all right, whatever you say.' Laura did not persist. Sonia obviously had something to hide and she was not about to reveal all to Laura. Laura wondered what it was exactly that Sonia was ashamed of. Was she hiding something in the locked room, or was it just as she said – a store for unsold antiques?

The photographer and assistant had packed up and left Porthzelah to make the long trip back to London and Laura had finished the article to go with the pictures. She would show it to Sonia before she posted it to make sure she had got the names right of the awards she had won. She made herself a coffee and looked out at the grey sky. It was a chilly day, quite unlike the previous hot one. She went upstairs and took off the sheets and pillow cases that Steve had used. Rick's bed was untouched. She picked up the dirty towels and took them downstairs to the washing machine. She'd had it installed as soon as she had arrived for the summer. Her grandmother had lived without such luxuries. It was Laura who'd had a telephone put in, too. She phoned James to tell him that all had gone well with the shoot, and then Sally, for a chat.

'How are you, Laura?' said Sally, sounding as if she really was interested.

'Fine, Sal, fine. Much better.'

'Did you get the letter that I forwarded to you?'

'Yes, it was from my doctor friend.'

'I thought it might be. What did he say?'

189

'He says he loves me and his wife has left him. He told her about me.'

There was a brief silence.

'Do you believe him?'

'I . . . don't know.'

'What are you going to do?'

'Nothing at the moment. Work, paint, clear up a few things about my past – or rather my parents' history.' She had not seriously thought about that until Sally had challenged her. Now, she was determined.

'Good luck, darl', and send us the odd postcard.' The phone clicked dead.

Laura took up the framed photograph of her parents and stared at it as if she might find the answers she sought in the faded image. She picked up *Frenchman's Creek* and went to her elderly neighbour's house.

'Mrs Poldhu?' she said as she closed the book on its last page. 'Did you know my mother well?'

'Little May? Of course I did, my cheel. Pretty as a picture she was. She did used to be a model sometimes at the school of painting on the harbour. There were portraits of her in galleries.'

'Really? I didn't know that.'

'Yes, real doll-like she were. Dark curls, dark eyes, yes. She were trouble to your grandmother, though.'

'How do you mean?'

'Well, I don't like to speak ill of the dead, but . . .'

'Go on, please. I need to know.'

'Oh, she were always after the boys, May was. Your grandmother had a terrible time of it keeping her out of trouble. Round 'er like flies, they was. Glad I never had a daughter.' She cackled like a herring gull.

'She was very young when she married my father, wasn't she?'

'Oh, yes, only just eighteen. Didn't know who she'd choose to marry, though. They all wanted her.'

190

'My father, he was a policeman.' Laura sounded tentative.

'She married a policeman, yes,' Mrs Poldhu said, pointedly, and Laura suddenly realised that she did not know for sure that Arthur Mackay had been her father. Is that what Mrs Poldhu was hinting?

'Who else was interested in marrying her, then?'

'One of the Montpelier boys was.'

'Not Bill Montpelier?' Laura was horrified.

'No, not Bill, he was but a boy. His older brother, Harold. Good-looking man he were, yes, big man, with dark thick hair. Car mechanic. He was right 'mazed by your mother, he was.'

'Was? Is he dead?'

'No, not dead. He's in prison. Bad lot, that family, all in all. Not that they found any proof that the rest of them were involved. But Andrew Montpelier – he what works for Bill sometimes – he's just as bad. Been in and out of prison a few times. He was car mechanic with Harold when your parents died.'

'I didn't realise he was in the family, too,' said Laura.

'Oh, yes. Cousin, 'e is. He never got on with anybody, didn't Andrew, not even as a boy.'

'I'm not surprised. And were there stories about how my parents died – why they crashed the car over the cliff?'

'Well, you know, cheel, in a town like this, there's always gossip, not all made up from nothing, neither.'

'So, what did people say?'

'Are you sure you want to know, cheel?' Mrs Poldhu peered at her through red, watery eyes.

'I think knowing is better than not knowing,' said Laura.

'They did say that you were not the daughter of Arthur Mackay, but that Harold Montpelier was your father, and May wanted to leave Arthur and go to her lover, Harold.'

Laura swallowed hard.

'Your grandmother told me that May had had a blood test done on you and wanted to prove that Harold was your father. She were mad on him, one time. She made Arthur have a blood test too.'

'What happened then? Did the tests prove anything?'

'That I don't know, my cheel. They did say that May and Arthur had argued about it and he killed her and himself rather than lose her to another man.'

'Oh, how awful!' Laura sobbed and ran out of the house.

Laura ran back to her house and closed the door behind her. She went upstairs and sat at the dormer window staring out at the leaden sky.

If what Mrs Poldhu had said was true, perhaps her father had not been her father at all. Perhaps she was related to Bill Montpelier. Oh my God! Perhaps she was related closely to Aaron. Could she be his cousin? No! His sister! She felt a shock run though her body. She had been having sex with her half brother! She had to know for sure.

At least Laura didn't have to face the moral dilemma of deciding whether to carry on having sex with Aaron for the moment. He'd left a message for Laura at Ethan's shop to say that he'd had to go to the Scillies again for a few days. She breathed a sigh of relief when she read the note.

She got on with her painting and drawing. She had persuaded Mrs Poldhu to sit for her. Instead of reading to her she asked her neighbour to sit in her favourite armchair and talk to her while she did several charcoal sketches of her before starting on a painting. Mrs Poldhu was flattered to be asked, though she put up a convincing display of reluctance.

'You don't want to paint a picture of an old body like me,' she laughed. 'I'm all wrinkles and creases.'

'You're beautiful,' said Laura, 'and I want to make a portrait of you.'

She finished the work after four days, taking it back with her to her attic and working on it after each sitting. She didn't want to tire the old lady. Mrs Poldhu talked of Laura's grandmother. She told of the good times they all had had together, when both couples went dancing at the Palais de Dance, and bowling on the green down by Zelah Cove.

'I didn't mean to upset you the other day, my cheel,' she said. 'Your mother probably was married to your real father. I was only telling you what the gossip was at the time they died. That's not saying it was true. There was other gossip too, telling a different yarn.'

'I know, Mrs Poldhu, thank you for trying to comfort me. I should let sleeping dogs lie, I suppose.'

'I would, cheel, I would,' said Mrs Poldhu, nodding her grey head.

Ethan was involved with running the new shop with Eugene, and Laura did not feel she could intrude on their closeness. She desperately wanted to talk to someone, though, about Jerry, what to do about Jerry, and about her parentage. Who to talk to? Anna had become rather distant with her, since Laura's affair with her son, and she could not talk intimately with her. Sonia? Sonia was an unknown quantity – sexy, desirable, exciting, but obviously not serious, and Laura did not want to become emotionally involved with a bisexual. Life was problematic enough. And anyway, Laura had bad feelings about Sonia; there was something not right, something ruthless about her. She felt she would use her and throw her away – suck her in and spit her out, much as some would say Laura had done with young Thomas. She felt ashamed.

Who could she really rely on for help? Sally was a real mate and knew about Jerry, but she was three hundred miles away. James was not really a close friend. Laura poured herself a whisky and sat on her deck out of the wind and watched the boats bob in the harbour in the dark. One had just docked at the pier and was unloading into a van. Sounds travelled up the surrounding hills from the harbour: waves crashing on the foreshore, men's voices. She thought of the story she had heard about pottery Staffordshire dogs. When your sailor husband was away at sea, you put the dogs in the window to watch for his home-coming. When he was home, you turned the dogs around to face inward.

The wind was chill and she wrapped her cashmere shawl around her shoulders. She wished she could have a cigarette, but she had given up smoking years ago. She could really enjoy a deep inhalation of nicotine. Her thoughts went to Jerry: his dark, sensuous hands, like hairy spiders; his gentle doctor's touch on her skin. She shivered. She sat for ages in a reverie, watching the stars. It was August, the time of the Perseids, and shooting stars fell in showers. She thought she was dreaming. The herring gulls, excited by the high wind, rose on thermals overhead, while their still gawky adolescent offspring jumped on the rooftop, flapping their wings, lifted a little into the swirling wind in an attempt to join their angel-like parents and then fell back on to the roof.

Could she live here? She thought about it. But this was a rest-cure, she remembered, a break from real life. London is where I should be, working at my real job, not pretending to be an artist.

She was cold and stood to go indoors. She saw out of the corner of her eye a vehicle move up the hill towards Sonia's house. The car showed no lights but the chrome of its bumpers glinted as the moon appeared from behind a cloud. It was two in the morning. Who could be calling on Sonia at that hour and trying not to be seen? Laura had been sitting in darkness, and her eyes were attuned to the lack of light. She saw the vehicle stop and heard two muffled slams. It was a small, dark-coloured van, and she had seen it before. It was Bill Montpelier's. Of course: it had been his boat at the pier a moment ago. She watched as two shadowy figures opened the back door of the vehicle and started unloading something heavy. The door of the house was open, and Sonia stood, her tall straight form unmistakable in the sudden moonlight.

Whispers, hushed grunts and shifting of boxes. The door closed on the mystery. Two minutes later the men emerged and got back into the van and it drove slowly, in neutral gear, down the hill, past Laura's back door. There were still no lights showing.

It wasn't burglars, thought Laura. They had been delivering something, not taking things away. Should she call the police? No, what could she say? She had seen a car being driven with no lights, that's all. It could have been sheer carelessness. Or it could have been part of something more sinister. Her vivid imagination saw pirate treasure being unloaded into the locked room at Sonia's house.

That was it! She had hit upon the truth! Bill Montpelier and his merry men, including Aaron, she supposed, were involved in some shady dealings with antiques, which Sonia was getting rid of. But she had no proof. Could she find out? She went to bed, excited at the prospect of playing detective, and perhaps writing a real scoop. She put out of her mind the uncomfortable suspicion that it was possibly her kinsmen who might be involved in criminal activity.

Chapter Nineteen

Red Sonia, the Pirate Queen

*A*fter a night of sleeplessness punctuated by vivid dreams Laura went into the health food shop – Full of Beans, as Ethan and Eugene had called it – and saw that Ethan was on his own.

'Hello gorgeous,' said her friend. He wore white chinos and an Hawaiian shirt in primary colours. He looked like an oversized rag doll.

'Hello, Ethan, how's business?'

'A lull in the storm,' said Ethan, smiling. 'It's been very busy up until a few minutes ago. Have you got time for a cup of tea? Peppermint?'

'Mmm, thanks. I could do with one,' said Laura and perched on a bentwood chair that the old biddies who came in for a piece of carrot cake or a banana slice sat on while they chatted. Two such women came in the door, causing the bell to sound. They looked at Laura and nodded their old heads. Sisters, they always went everywhere together. Laura thought they were like donkeys with large, long heads and sad, big mouths. They looked sourly at her.

'Good morning,' she said brightly and stood up. They both looked like they might collapse on to the chair.

They sniffed simultaneously.

'What can I get you ladies?' said Ethan, solicitously.

'A pint of soya milk,' brayed the older donkey.

She paid silently and off they trotted.

Laura laughed.

Ethan shook a finger at her. 'Don't you laugh at Dorcas and Lettie,' he said. 'Ninety-five Dorcas is, and her sister is ninety-two. They are my favourite customers.' He made the tea, served a few more customers and then sat on the chair behind the counter while they drank.

'When are you going back to London?' he said. 'You seem very settled here.'

'Ethan . . .' She did not know how to broach the subject.

'What is it? Are you pregnant or something? You look troubled, darling.'

'No, nothing like that. It's an ethical problem, I suppose you could call it.'

'Another young man bites the dust?'

'No, Ethan, it's not sex. Well, not really. I have found out about something and I'm not sure what to do. I think I've uncovered something illegal.'

'Are you serious? What do you mean?'

'Oh, dear, come and have a drink with me after work and I'll tell you about it. I need to talk to you. Please!'

A group of tourists walked in at that moment and Ethan had to serve them. Laura left, and Ethan waved and said, 'I'll come after I've shut up shop.'

'Thanks Ethan, you're a doll.'

Laura did the rest of her shopping, picking up hot granary bread and fresh fish from the fish market.

She walked past the architects' offices, then turned, went back to the door and walked in. Becky was at reception.

'Hello, Becky, is Sonia in? Can I have a word with her, please?'

'Do you want to leave your shopping here?' asked Becky.

'Oh, yes, what a good idea. I don't want to get her office all fishy, do I?' she said, smiling at the dark-haired young girl.

'Come in, darling, come in. What can I do for you?' Sonia looked sophisticated and well groomed, as usual. Her red hair was piled up on her head. Her black silk trouser suit fitted her beautifully, showing her narrow waist and flared hips and large breasts.

Laura gulped. She must not let this woman manipulate her. Stay away from her, she told herself. Do not get close.

'Sit down, darling.'

'No thanks.'

'I haven't seen you for ages. What have you been doing with yourself?'

'I saw you last night. I saw Bill Montpelier at your house, unloading something.'

'Well?' Sonia simply looked amused.

'I want to know if you are up to something illegal,' said Laura sternly.

'What for? Are you going to turn me in?'

'Tell me, Sonia.'

'Darling, don't look so tragic. Yes, of course I am!' she said triumphantly.

'You are?'

'I thought you knew. I thought that Aaron must have mentioned our business arrangements.'

'No!'

'Oh, well, it's nothing much. Bill unloads some stuff on to me and I sell it, and we share the proceeds.'

'What stuff?'

'Darling, I hope you can keep your pretty mouth closed about all this information, can you?' Sonia drew close to Laura and touched her lips with her long fingernails. Laura felt hot and blushed. 'Yes, I'm sure you know when to keep your mouth closed.'

'Is it from the wreck in the Scillies? The *Elizabetta*?'

'Yes, of course it is. Bill shows the boring stuff to the authorities and we keep the exciting stuff to dispose of abroad. No point letting the government know our little secret, is there? I deal in treasure trove, darling, and you are a treasure I would love to have.' She lowered her head and kissed Laura on the lips. Laura was angry that Sonia was expecting her to be complicit, but she allowed the caress. Encouraged by her acquiescence, Sonia drew Laura to her and pressed her breasts against the smaller woman. She put her hands under Laura's T-shirt and stroked her nipples.

'God! You are desirable, you know.' She quickly locked the solid pine door and pressed a button. 'I don't want to be disturbed, Becky.'

Sonia tore off her jacket and white silk shirt and stood in only her trousers. Her breasts swung on the narrow rib cage. Her shoulders looked strong and square. She took off her trousers, too, and laid them carefully over a chair.

'Take off your clothes, darling. Don't be shy,' she said.

Laura slowly removed her T-shirt and shoes and then her jeans, telling herself that this was necessary if she was to gain the woman's confidence. She stood in her black lace panties, her arms folded over her breasts. Sonia had red silk French knickers on, loose-legged. They were obviously expensive, with black lace edging – exquisite. She took Laura into her arms and kissed her, pressing her pelvis close. Laura breathed heavily. The older woman propelled Laura to the polished steel desk and placed her against it, so she was leaning back on the metal, her buttocks on the edge. Sonia held her arms away from her body and began kissing her breasts and belly. She slid down Laura's body and pulled the elasticated legs of her panties aside and licked the tender skin on her inner thighs. Laura panted. Sonia kissed her pubic mound, biting lightly the fine dark regrowth of pubic hair. Laura's arms were free, but instead of pushing the woman away she found herself pushing down on the red head that nuzzled her belly, urging even more tender embraces. Sonia sucked at Laura's swollen sex-lips and nibbled at the pink bud. Sonia wrenched at the lace panties and they tore. Laura felt the fluttering of her thighs, and her belly shook; her breasts were hot hard mounds. She threw back her head, her buttocks pressed the metal desk, her mouth was open. She came in a sudden rush of explosive sensations that left her shaking and weak.

'My turn now,' said Sonia. She kissed Laura hard on the mouth, and drew her hands on to her breasts. Laura caressed the heavy softness of the fleshy globes. She pressed the nipples between her fingers. Sonia sank on to the leather swivel chair and threw back her head. Her red-gold hair had come undone from its cage of pins and combs and fell in glorious disarray over her white shoulders. Its tendrils kissed her nipples. Laura took the hair up and held it away from her neck. She kissed the white column of curved throat. My God! she thought, Sonia is like some magnificent pirate queen. She kissed the curve of breast and belly. She kissed the milky thighs. She sat on Sonia's lap, contriving to place her own legs over the arms of the chair. Sonia braced herself, her legs against the desk. Laura writhed on Sonia's belly, her buttocks gyrating on the older woman's lap. Laura's hands went down between Sonia's silky thighs. She pulled the loose silk and lace away from the secret folds of flesh to explore the ginger fur of her sex. She parted the pink lips and caressed inside and over the mound. Sonia moaned and writhed beneath her touch. They kissed passionately as they both reached orgasm, their knickers wet, torn, their hair tangled and damp.

Sonia dressed unhurriedly and giggled as Laura removed her torn panties and put them in the pocket of her jeans.

'I can trust you not to tell anyone of my little secret, can't I, Laura? And you can trust me not to tell anyone what we do together. You really can, darling.'

Laura stepped out of the architects' offices into the bright sunshine. Holiday-makers thronged on the harbour beach, old-aged pensioners sat in deckchairs soaking up the sun, children ran in and out of the gently lapping water, and Laura slunk through the narrow alley like a guilty thief.

She thought of Aaron. She could not think how to get out of the situation she had got herself into. She assumed that Sonia, at least, expected that Laura would not let out the information of her receiving stolen property to the police. The threat was there, that she would make public their lesbian activities. What about Aaron? Could he be persuaded to give Laura information that would embroil him in the dirty business? Surely, he could not be unaware of what was going on? She didn't know how to handle this. Could she sleep with someone who she knew was a thief? Should she just step away from it and ignore the information she'd been given? Wouldn't that make her an accessory? She didn't know what to do. Then she remembered her backpack. She looked inside. Yes, as she had planned, the tape recorder had been playing all the time she had been in Sonia's office.

She was, in spite of her recent promiscuity, a thoroughly old-fashioned girl, a chip off the old block. Her Aunt Celia and Uncle John had brought her up well. She had attended a convent high school. Her father, if he had indeed been her father, had been an ordinary beat policeman and Aunt Celia had taught at Sunday school. Laura could remember the hymn singing, the tissue-thin pages of the bible with its pressed flowers, like hidden treasure, between the leaves.

Hidden treasure! What was she to do?

Back in her house she turned on the tape recorder to listen to what Sonia had said: 'I deal in treasure trove, darling.' She had the proof already, or at least a statement of duplicity from Sonia. She removed the tape from the machine. Then she thought she had better make a copy. Her machine had the facility. The procedure took less than half an hour. She put one tape in a padded envelope and placed it in a drawer of the table. The other she placed in another padded envelope and addressed it to James. She put it in her backpack. She completed the article about Sonia's new house with ease, high on adrenalin, full of thoughts of glory. But then she thought: should I make money out of this? Then she thought, well, it is my job. Aaron, too, would have to be confronted.

The doorbell sounded. She assumed it was Ethan and went to open it.

It was Stan.

'Hello, Stan, how nice to see you, come in.'

'Hello, my dear, I hope you don't mind me coming to your house? I need to talk to you about something and . . .'

'Sit down, Stan, let me pour you a drink – whisky?'

'Thanks, yes, wonderful.' He sat at the kitchen table, which was still strewn with her magazine work.

'What is it, Stan, you look concerned. Is it your daughter?'

'No, not this time,' he laughed. 'I know I fuss like a mother hen about her, but she is very precious to me.'

'She is a lovely child.'

'Yes, and since her mother died she's been everything to me.' His voice cracked and he took a sip of whisky.

'I didn't know your wife had died. How long ago was that?'

'She died in childbirth. Seventeen years ago.'

'Oh, how awful for you.'

'Yes, it was awful. But I have not come here for your kind sympathy, my dear, I have come to warn you.'

'Warn me?'

'Yes! I believe you know the Montpelier family rather well?'

'Well, I suppose you could say I know one of them fairly well, yes.' She blushed.

'Aaron, yes?'

'Yes.'

'Well, send me away if you don't want to hear this, but I feel someone should tell you.'

'Tell me what?'

'The family is rotten, rotten through and through. Bill is the worst, now his brother Harold is out of harm's way. He's in prison. Did you know? He's been in and out of gaol most of his adult life. Harold used to be a car mechanic with his cousin Andrew – dealt in stolen vehicles as a side-line, then went on to the harder stuff: extortion, GBH.'

'Go on,' Laura urged him.

'Becky is Harold's daughter, and Aaron is his son.'

'Yes.'

'Their mother died several years ago. At least she had a civilising effect on her children. Rowena goes to school with Becky. I begged her not to be friends with the girl, but she's wilful.'

'But Becky's not a criminal.'

'Not yet, maybe, but she's always looking for trouble. Hangs around with much older men and I don't want Rowena involved with her. There are stories about her dubious relationship with her uncle Bill, too.'

'Stan, I'm sorry, but I don't know what this has got to do with me.'

'So sorry Laura, I'm rambling again. Where was I? Oh yes. It's just that the whole town knows that Bill,

203

Andrew and Aaron are involved in some sort of villainy.'

'What sort of villainy would that be?'

'Theft, handling stolen property, smuggling, probably. Under the guise of diving, of course.'

'I had suspected as much myself.'

'Had you?'

'Yes, I intend to tell the police if it's true.'

'Be careful, Laura, they're not playing games, these men. Bill and Andrew can be ruthless.'

'Stan, I need to know something else.'

'What is it?'

'You seem to know everything about the town and its people. Did you know my parents?'

Stan tugged at his ponytail. 'Yes, I knew May and Arthur. Painted May several times. Lovely model.'

'Did you? Tell me about them. I don't really have a clear picture of them in my mind, just vague memories.' She poured them both another drink.

'Well, they seemed very happy . . .'

The door bell rang, and Laura stood to answer it. It was Ethan.

'Ethan, I forgot you were coming, come in, darl', I've got another visitor.'

Stanley stood politely as Ethan blustered in. His hair was awry and he wore a Barbour jacket.

'Goodness, it's getting windy,' he said, 'Hello. You're the artist, aren't you? Loved the portraits in your exhibition.'

Laura poured him a drink and they sat at the kitchen table.

Stan finished his drink and stood to go, embarrassed to continue the conversation with Ethan there.

'Remember what I said, won't you dear? Be careful whom you call your friends.' He went out into the dark, windy night.

'What did *he* want?' said Ethan. 'I hope he didn't mean me!'

'Ethan, it's time for you to know things.'

'What things?'

'Ethan, I'm in too deep, and I need a good friend on my side.'

'Tell me all about it, hon'.'

'First of all, I have heard that my father may not have been my father after all, and that my real father might be one of the Montpelier family: Harold, who's in prison for handling stolen goods or something.'

Ethan gasped and poured himself another drink.

'I've been sleeping with Aaron, who's probably my half-brother, and Sonia, who's involved in some shady dealings with Bill and Andrew, and, to cap it all, Ethan, I'm in love with a married man.' She burst out crying and Ethan hugged her and patted her head.

'Now, now, hon', don't cry. What married man?'

'You don't know him. He's a doctor in London and I met him before I came down here this summer. He's called Jerry. Oh, shit, shit, shit, what a mess!' She sobbed some more and Ethan soothed her.

'Look hon', there's nothing you could have done about the incest if you didn't know you were related – and anyway, you only suspect you might be. Why do you think he is your brother, anyway?'

'Mrs Poldhu said it was well known at the time my parents died that my mother was having an affair with Harold,' explained Laura.

'But that was probably only gossip. It's all gossip here, you know. What they don't know they make up. They think you're gay because you're friends with Eugene and me.'

Laura burst into tears again. 'I'm also being blackmailed by Red Sonia who says she will tell the world I've slept with her if I mention her illegal involvement with Bill.'

'Oh dear, oh dear. You have got yourself into a mess, haven't you!'

'What can I do, Ethan?'

'I don't know, hon'. You could tell the police what you know, and damn Miss Stallone.'

'It's only conjecture really. No it isn't! I have a tape recording of Sonia admitting to selling treasure trove and sharing the proceeds with Bill,' Laura said, jubilantly.

'What about the married man you're in love with?'

'I only slept with Aaron and Thomas and Sonia to help me forget him,' Laura said through more sobs.

'Men are bastards, darling, I know that and you know that. Stick to women.'

'Sonia is blackmailing me,' said Laura.

'Look,' said Ethan, 'Eugene was cooking when I left. Do you want to join us? It's a vegetarian pasta dish and salad, I think.'

'Thank you, Ethan, that would be great. Give me ten minutes to clean up, and I'll be with you.'

'See you later, then. Don't be long.'

'Bye!' Laura closed the door and leant against it. It was time she grew up and stopped acting like a randy schoolgirl, she thought. I've got myself into this mess and only I can get myself out of it. She would go to the police in the morning. Her parentage would have to remain a mystery. After all, who knew for sure who their father was? She would not, however, sleep with Aaron again, just in case.

As she changed into clean jeans and T-shirt and chose a bottle of wine to take to Ethan and Eugene's flat, the doorbell went again.

It was Becky, Aaron's sister.

'Hello, Laura.' She sounded almost too familiar.

'Oh, Becky, I was just going out. Come in.'

'I've come with a message.'

'From Aaron?'

'No, from Uncle Bill.'

Laura bristled with anger, and nervous trepidation. 'What is it?'

'He says you are to come to the harbour straight away – the little pier. He wants to see you now.'

'You can tell Bill Montpelier he can go to hell,' Laura said, more calmly than she felt, and walked back to the door and opened it. Becky swayed her hips in the tight skirt and smiled slyly at Laura over her shoulder as she walked out.

'You can't beat him, you know, he always gets what he wants, does my Uncle Bill.'

Laura slammed the door and stood staring at it, as if it held the answers to her questions. What could he do to her anyway? He didn't know that she knew of his smuggling activities. She put on a denim jacket over her T-shirt and jeans and determinedly walked out the door. Then she returned and picked up the pocket tape recorder and a new tape, which she slipped into her canvas backpack and slung over her shoulder. She had meant to post the duplicate tape to James, for safe-keeping, but she had no stamp and the post office was closed. The padded envelope containing the damning evidence burnt a hole in her bag.

She strode purposefully to the wharf, the cool breeze shifting her hair from her forehead and making her nose run. Evening had brought a cool breeze and clouds covered the sky. It was colder than she had thought. The tide was high and the waves splashed over the railings on to the road. Huddles of tourists screeched with glee as a large wave covered an unsuspecting couple and they ran away from its icy fingers. She should have worn something warmer. Cornish summer evenings were never warm, and when the wind came from the southwest, rain would surely follow. She saw Aaron first, in waders and waterproof, then behind him, taller and bulky, Bill Montpelier, his peaked cap over his eyes, his beady eyes watching her approach.

The diver's craft, a forty-foot fishing boat, rocked at the pier, straining at its lines. Aaron and the older crew member, Andrew, stood close by on the pier.

'What do you want?' said Laura, ignoring Aaron and speaking directly to his uncle.

'Ah, you've come, have you? I'm surprised. I thought you'd be more difficult than this,' he said with menace in his tone.

'I'm not frightened of you, Bill Montpelier. What is this all about?' She glanced at Aaron.

Bill Montpelier laughed. 'Don't you get so uppity, miss clever clogs. I only wanted to make friends with Aaron's ladyfriend, make amends for my bad manners, so to speak. Didn't I, Aaron?' He grabbed Aaron's broad shoulder and squeezed it. Aaron looked shamefaced and would not meet her eye.

'Come aboard,' said Andrew Montpelier and suddenly grabbed Laura's arm. She cried out in alarm and pain, but her cries were lost on the gusting wind, like a herring gull's cry. Not one of the many tourists thronging the windswept and wave-soaked pier noticed a bedraggled young woman being manhandled down the metal steps on to the rocking boat.

'How dare you!' Laura was furious, not frightened. She wrenched away from the claw-like grip and swept her wet hair from her eyes. His breath was foul and she saw his rotting teeth as he smiled at her. She looked around her. In the small cabin a map lay on the table. She heard the engine being started and felt the boat slip away from the pier and surge speedily across the relative calm of the harbour, round the large pier, and hit the large waves of the bay. She immediately felt nauseous, furious with herself at her weakness, and sat down, her head between her hands on the table.

Andrew Montpelier said nothing, but left her, went

up the narrow companionway and shut the door behind him. She shivered and hugged herself. My God, I've been abducted, she thought. The seasickness hit her anew, and she moaned.

Chapter Twenty
Kidnapped

*A*aron stood, smiling at her, a mug of tea in his hand.
'Here, drink this, my flower, it'll make you feel
better.'

She sat up from the prone position she'd adopted as
the only way to cope with the motion sickness, and
banged her head on a cupboard above her.

'Oh, Aaron, I feel terrible. Where are we going? Why?'
She sipped the hot drink as he knelt and held the mug
for her. He was right, it did make her feel better. But
the boat was still lifting and dropping sickeningly into
the deep troughs of the waves. She could see through
the porthole that it was almost dark, and there were no
stars. The wind sobbed in the rigging. She heard a faint
voice on a radio phone – the ship-to-shore device that
all fishing craft had these days.

'Don't you worry none, my cock,' he said, reassuringly. 'Bill only wants to entertain you for a while, show
you a thing or two.'

'This is abduction, Aaron,' she whispered urgently.
'Do you do realise that? A criminal offence, like
kidnapping.'

He laughed. 'You do like a bit of drama, don't you!

Nah, he's giving you a ride, that's all, a trip around the lighthouse – tourists pay good money for a trip like this, you know.'

'Aaron, he means me harm. He knows I know something.'

'What do you mean, my queen?'

'Sonia told me about the treasure trove.'

'Oh, I see.' Sudden realisation dawned on him. 'So what?'

'She must have guessed I disapprove and might tell the police.'

'Why would you want to do that, Laura, my lovely?'

She felt nauseous again and lay down, trying to keep the threatening sensation from engulfing her.

'Aaron, you've got to help me. You can't let him get away with abduction.'

Her backpack, which had been on the bunk with her, rolled off at a sudden lurch of the boat, and the contents were spilled. At that moment Bill Montpelier came down into the cabin and picked up the bag. He pulled the tape out of the machine and pocketed it.

'You don't want to be bothering with no work on this trip, my 'andsome,' he said, glowering, and kicked at her possessions, including her comb, a notebook and pen, her purse and the envelope containing the damning tape. He then stood on her things with his heavy boots. She gasped and looked at his feet.

'What's this, then?' He picked up the envelope, the address smudged and damp, muddy from his feet, and shook it. To her dismay he took out the tape and smiled. Then he placed it in the tape recorder and switched it on.

'I deal in treasure trove, darling,' came Sonia's voice.

'She's not too bright, that one,' Bill snarled. He looked like an old-fashioned pirate, his dark eyebrows meeting over his cold eyes. 'You won't be needing this any more, will you?' He took the tape, envelope and tape machine and walked out of the cabin with them.

'Oh, Laura, you've done it now. He was only trying to frighten you. He thought you were too close to Sonia for comfort. She talks too much, she does.' Aaron shook his head and left her.

Laura lay back on the bunk and started to cry.

The boat pitched and tossed and Laura was sick. Where was Bill Montpelier taking her? Why? What did he mean to do to her? She groaned and heaved again, unsuccessfully, her throat parched, her eyes watering.

She must have slept because a grey dawn hazily lightened the porthole. She dragged herself off the bunk and looked out. A hump of darker grey-green showed on the horizon: an island. It was the Scillies, of course. She should have guessed. But why were they here?

Aaron brought her a bowl of porridge and a hot milky tea, which she consumed hungrily, needing something in her empty stomach. She desperately wanted to shower and wash her hair, which had matted and clung to her head in her feverish sickness. It was getting lighter every minute, and a faint sun shone hazily through the foggy gloom. The mist shifted, revealing bright-yellow gorse and a reddish bracken on the low hill that loomed ahead. It looked uninhabited and her ideas of escape became more remote. But now she had food inside her she felt better and made herself think how she was to begin to gain control of her situation.

Aaron let her go to the tiny bathroom and gave her a towel. She cleaned herself as best she could, the cramped space reminding her of airplane ablutions. She felt so much better when she had washed her hair, even though she had to use washing up liquid. She had at least remembered to bring her comb. Her pride reasserted itself and her determination not to be intimidated by the bully Bill Montpelier or the other nasty piece of work – Andrew Montpelier. He was in his sixties but a wiry, fit-looking man, except that he smoked heavily and had a cough. He seemed to be the worst of the bunch, the unreasonable, aggressive one. He and Bill appeared and sat to drink a mug of tea.

'Enjoying our little cruise, are you, my flower?' Bill asked.

Laura had put on a man's checked shirt that she had found in the cabin. It was huge on her, and made her look smaller than she was and even more vulnerable. She rubbed at her damp hair with a towel.

'Which island are we at?' she asked, without rancour. She knew what she had to do. She had decided to play along with the smuggler and pretend to be won over by the glamour of the operation.

'Samson, of course, don't you recognise it?' said Bill.

'No, I've never been to the Scillies, would you believe,' she said pleasantly. He looked bewildered.

'So, why do you think we've brought you here?' he said, his eyes narrowing under his black brows.

'To show me the wreck, I suppose?'

'That's right, my 'andsome, to show you the *Elizabetta.*'

'Wonderful, I can't wait. Seeing as I am probably related to you, rather closely, I had better be let in on the secret.' She beamed at him and allowed a bare thigh to flash from under the long-tailed shirt. He leered at her.

'Look, Bill,' she said conspiratorially,' I don't know what Sonia has told you about me, but I am a magazine journalist. I would love to hear about the wreck and your work on it. The bronze cannons and stuff you have found. I can get the story published and you would get good publicity. Naturally I won't mention the other stuff that you and Sonia deal in.' She smiled seductively at the beefily handsome Cornishman. 'I don't ask for much – just a weekly lobster or two, that's all. Of course, I'd like to know if we really are related. I wouldn't want

213

to be screwing my own uncle, would I?' She barely touched his crotch with one hand and her own with the other.

His eyes narrowed. His jeans stretched over his bulging cock. He showed a gold-toothed grin through his red lips.

He still looked suspicious. 'You mean to say you'd tell the story the way I tell it, not turn us in?'

'If you make it worth my while, yes.' She was taking a big chance. Not wanting it to look like blackmail, but making him think that she was dishonest enough to take money for keeping quiet.

'Don't listen to 'er, William, she's not to be trusted,' Andrew hissed.

Bill Montpelier rubbed his heavy chin, thoughtfully. His bulk filled the small cabin. She carried on with her unsubtle caress.

'Perhaps you'll make it worth my while to let you in on things?' His lips parted and a thick, fleshy tongue licked them. His white teeth, punctuated with gold, were wet and glistening. Laura slid closer, her thigh uncovered. He slid his fingers into the gap where the cloth gaped. 'Suits you, wearing my shirt.' His mouth opened and he laughed loud.

Bill and Andrew went back on deck and Aaron came down into the cabin.

'Aaron, do you happen to know what your father's blood group is?'

'Eh? Why do you want to know that?'

'I need to know, to clear up the problem of who my father is,' she said. 'You must have heard the gossip about my mother and your father?'

'Can't say as I have, my flower. But I can tell you what his blood group is. He's an unusual blood group. He's AB, he is. I know that because he needed a transfusion five or six year ago. He cut his wrist badly. Put his hand through a glass storm door and cut the main

214

artery. He were in a temper with me and I ran away and he tried to grab me. Had to go in the air ambulance to the Plymouth hospital. Touch and go it was.'

Bill called down the companionway to Aaron. The man rose. She followed him up.

The boat was docking at a small stone pier. Her eyes smarted in the bright light. The mist had dissipated with the sun's rising, and the wind had dropped. Land was a beautiful sight. A grey seal looked up at the boat and slid into the turquoise water from a black rock. She went back down below to put on her jeans and sneakers and get her jacket and bag. She remembered Bill had removed the tapes and recorder. She smiled at the scowling Andrew and said a bright, 'Hi!' and took Bill's offered hand as he helped her ashore.

Chapter Twenty-One

Treasure

Samson was small, and the nearest other island, Bry-her, appeared close enough to swim to, if Laura had been a good enough swimmer.

'Surely, the *Elizabetta* isn't wrecked here, is it?' she asked Bill Montpelier.

'I'm not showing you the shipwreck, just what we've taken off her, so far, that is.'

His enthusiasm for his trade was obvious. He was like a small boy showing a chum his secret den. The cave was well hidden under a wing of gorse and the entrance was from above, between granite boulders. Aaron tied a rope around a sharp rock and lowered himself down first. He called up, his voice faint and echoing. Laura went down next, frightened and excited. She had entered fully into the game of smugglers with the men. She didn't need to pretend curiosity. As Aaron's strong arms lifted her the last few feet on to the dank rock floor of the cave, she felt the rope taut above her hands and felt the heavy weight of Bill Montpelier descending.

There, in the gloom of the sea cave, where light filtered from the distant sky and the boom of sea was like thunder claps all around them, she saw a pile of something covered by hessian sacks. Bill Montpelier slipped to her side. His torch beam illuminated the mysterious heap.

'Look here,' he said, and with a magician-like flourish, he whisked off the top sacks to reveal the dull glint of silver and pewter, bejewelled carved wood, a tall cross of gold. There were candlesticks of silver and tall candelabras. Laura could not help gasping at the astonishing sight. It really did look like treasure from a child's picture book – *Rupert Bear in Sandy Cove* perhaps, or Enid Blyton's *Island of Adventure*.

'Wow!' she exclaimed. 'Wowee!'

Bill Montpelier laughed in delight. 'We couldn't let Her Majesty's customs officers know anything about this little lot, could we? Waste it would be, wouldn't it? I hands it over to Sonia and she disposes of it elsewhere – no questions asked, and us all benefit, don't us, Aaron?'

'Aye, Uncle, us do.'

Laura picked up a particularly heavy pewter salver, which was engraved with birds and flowers and figures. 'This is beautiful. How did it come to be on the *Elizabetta*?'

'A pirate ship, she were, a Spanish barque, captured by Black Jack, and happened to be carrying these ill-gotten gains when she struck the rocks off 'ere, or nearby. We just happen not to mention all what we haul up from her. Only mention the cannons and brass work and such, and the coin.' He smiled a satisfied, smug grin at his own cleverness.

Laura was impressed. She was also cold and had begun to shiver.

'Well, I think it's brilliant, and you are so clever,' said Laura. She smiled at Bill Montpelier and put the salver back on the heap.

'We'll take a few things back with us.' He and Aaron

began to tie various candlesticks into hessian, which they fashioned into slings and placed around their necks. They sent up two sacks of silver on a rope to Andrew who had waited above.

Aaron climbed first, and then helped Laura up to the fresh springy turf and yellow, lichen-splashed rocks. Bees buzzed in the purple heath bells and herring gulls screamed. Laura looked around her, casually, trying to imprint the scene on her brain, so she could remember where to find the cave. They walked back to the moored boat, which was bobbing in the sparkling blue-green shallows. The seal had resumed its place on the rock and looked at them mournfully. However, this time it did not bother to move away from the strange creatures with long flippers. Laura was trying to remember the way to the cave from the stone pier. The island was not large, but the rocks and horizons all looked similar to an untutored eye. She snuggled close to Bill Montpelier and looked up into his cold eyes, admiringly.

'Thank you, Bill, that was the most exciting thing I've ever done. You can trust me to write exactly what you want me to write about your diving operations. The magazine will love it. I'll do an interview with you when we get back, shall I?'

He seemed to be completely taken in by her apparent change of attitude. She hoped she had shown him that she, like all his cronies, could be bought off, bribed into dishonesty. She also knew that that his male ego was proud, and that he wanted the trophy of his young and virile nephew's mistress. Maybe the idea that she was possibly his niece added to the attraction he felt for her. She had wondered about Becky's relationship with Bill. What had she said? Her Uncle Bill always got what he wanted? She could see that Aaron seemed to accept his fate as a powerful man's puppet. Laura was disappointed in Aaron but not surprised. He was dependent on his uncle for his livelihood, and obviously could not escape Bill's overbearing personality. Andrew was the one to watch. He was vicious. All she had to do, she felt, was pretend to go along with the smuggler's demands, even Bill's sexual demands if need be, just for a while, just until she had all the proof she needed to tell the police of the smuggling ring. First, of course, she would hint to the national press that she had a story worth telling.

She felt excited about this, her first real journalistic assignment in years. She had been playing at journalism with stories of protective sportsgear, garden features, sob stories from the suburbs, titillating sex stories, all sorts of filler stories for the not-too-bright readers of *Young Living* and magazines like it. At last she had her teeth into something big!

It was an unfortunately timely metaphor. The boat had chugged off towards Land's End, leaving the shallow blue calm, and Aaron was on deck steering. Down below, Bill Montpelier had undone his belt, slipped his jeans down to his knees and had his cock in his hands. 'Like to get your mouth around this?'

Laura laughed and said, 'Wow, so much treasure all in one day!' She moved towards him. A large wave took the craft up and let it fall into a deep trough, and she held herself steady by clutching a table. 'Oh dear, I'm going to be sick,' she said, and went past the half-naked man to the small bathroom. She made great efforts to be noisy in her coughs and retching, although she was not sick at all, yet. When, half an hour later, she emerged, her would-be lover was gone. She sighed in relief.

If she had to prostitute herself in order to survive, then obviously she would, but she did not really want to have sex with Bill Montpelier. She had also gone off Aaron. He had shown himself to be weak and easily led, and anyway, he was as big a scoundrel as his uncle. And she had not forgotten the fact that he could be her half-brother.

When she heard footsteps descending, she rushed back into the bathroom and kept up the pretense that she was sick again. The outward voyage had been much worse than this, and she found that she was not at all nauseated, in fact.

Before they came in sight of the mainland she searched for the treasure in the cabin. She couldn't see it.

She crept up the companionway and, without letting them see her, she listened to their conversation.

'What do you think, then Aaron? Will she keep quiet?' said Bill.

'I reckon I can keep her happy, Uncle, keep her sweet on me. She won't want to give me up.'

Laura's mouth fell open in amazement at this outrageous example of male arrogance.

'That's not good enough, Aaron. I reckon she's brighter than she pretends to be. She'll not be satisfied with the odd lobster and your body, my 'andsome. She'll get greedy – want a proper cut of the action. Maybe even find out about her parents. We can't have that.'

'She won't stay here,' said Andrew. 'She'll try and leave town, you'll see. She's a journalist. You know what that means. She'll put her nose in where it's not wanted and find out more than we want her to. I'll fix her, Bill, like I fixed her slut of a mother.'

He moved off astern.

Laura went cold. She could not take in the enormity of what she had overheard.

'What did he mean, Uncle?' said Aaron.

'Never you worry, Aaron. He's all mouth. I'll sort this one out.'

'But what was that about her mother? I thought she died in an accident. Both her parents did.'

'Ah, Aaron, you were bound to find out one day. Andrew couldn't bear to see Harold miserable over her.

220

She led him on and then pushed him away. Slut she were. She asked for it.'

'Asked for what, Uncle?'

'Don't ask, Aaron. What you don't know can't hurt you. Your father was lucky to have Andrew to do his dirty work for him. Andrew went to prison for him before. Now it's Harold's turn. You just keep her 'appy in bed.'

'I can do that, Uncle Bill.'

'What's she like in bed, anyway?'

Laura could not stand any more and she made a loud clatter with the hatchway and went up on deck.

The two men were laughing together, seemingly unaffected by the violence of their behaviour or the enormity of the act that Andrew Montpelier was contemplating. She had forgotten the treasure in the light of this new development. It was going to be an effort to keep up the pretence that she was unaware of the smugglers' intentions.

She smiled at them both. 'I'll make some tea,' she said. 'I want to be a useful member of the crew.'

'Thankee, my flower,' said Aaron.

Bill took the proffered mug with a smile. 'I'll show you how to be useful, later,' he threatened, his eyes on her crotch.

She put an arm round each of the men and jokingly said, 'I've never had an uncle and brother at once, how does it sound to you?'

Bill looked astonished, then shocked. 'No, I don't think I do fancy that.' Aaron laughed, unrestrainedly, until he cried. Laura laughed too, at the sudden Methodist morality that had shown itself in the villain's makeup.

'I was only joking,' she said.

It was late morning when she got back to her house and she suddenly remembered Ethan and last night's dinner invitation. She bathed and washed and dried her hair. She telephoned James.

'James, I think I'm on to something big. Maybe too big for *Young Living*.'

'What are you rabbiting on about Laura? Come on, the sun has got to your brain.'

'No, seriously, I'm not joking. Something is going on here. Lots of locals involved in a smuggling deal: treasure from wrecks, selling it abroad, no tax paid, totally illegal deals. There might be worse.' She was suddenly frightened. The reality of the threats hit her.

'Have you been reading old Enid Blyton stories? Are there caves? Smugglers in black masks?' James laughed, a tinny sound on the phone, and Laura's heart beat fast as she realised that she really was in the middle of a serious crime, involved with two of the perpetrators, and that they must not know that she was going to turn them in. She had heard the implied threat to her life and she was hardly able to believe the other thing that Andrew Montpelier had hinted at – that he'd had a hand in the sudden deaths of her parents.

Why didn't she simply tell the police? But she had no proof. However, she had the bit between her teeth now and wanted to write the full story.

'By the way, Laura, I've posted the information you wanted.'

'Oh, thanks! I'll speak to you again soon, keep you in touch,' she said and put down the phone.

She ran down the hill and called in at the Full of Beans health food shop.

Eugene stood in denim dungarees and bright orange T-shirt serving a customer with wholemeal flour from a tub.

'Oh! Here you are!' he said, as Laura pushed open the door. 'Ethan's frantic with worry about you. And dinner was ruined.' He sounded angry.

Laura had to think up a cover story for her virtual disappearance for the last twenty-four hours.

'Oh, dear!' She said, apologetically. 'Where is he? I can explain.'

The customer paid for several packages and left.

'He's upstairs, go on up.' Eugene opened the door that led to the small flat and Laura brushed past him, aware of the disapproval in his stance.

Upstairs, the flat the two men now shared was light and airy, with an interesting view over chimney stacks and slate roofs. Ethan stood as Laura emerged from the open stairwell.

'Laura, where the hell have you been? I was about to call the police.' He pecked Laura on the cheek and hugged her briefly.

Before Laura spoke she looked out of the sash window down on to the cobbled street and saw Andrew Montpelier climbing the hill.

What was he doing, there? He lived in the old part of town where Aaron lived. She remembered his words – 'I'll fix her, like I fixed her mother.' Laura had not really had a chance to think about her adventure and suddenly she was very scared, and shock set in. She trembled and sat down heavily, almost swooning, into a cane-backed armchair with a large feather cushion on the seat.

'Oh, Ethan!' She suddenly found that she was crying and could not stop.

'Oh, Laura! What is it? What's happened to you? Where were you?' He poured a stiff brandy and held the glass to Laura's trembling lips.

'Darling, I can't tell you without including you in the danger,' she sobbed.

'What danger, Laura? You're not making sense.'

She calmed down after a large gulp of brandy, the heat in her throat and gullet taking took away the violent emotion of fear. 'Sorry, Ethan. I'm overwrought. I can't say any more. I've said too much already. Forget

I said anything, please, darling. I'll be all right in a minute.' Laura wiped her eyes and blew her nose with the tissues that Ethan gave her, and sniffed hard. 'That's better!'

'You can't expect me to not ask you where you've been,' said Ethan, sniffing in hurt pride.

'Believe me, Ethan, you don't want to know. I've been working on a story.'

'The shipwreck story?'

'Well, yes.'

'So, it's the story that has you in this state?' said Ethan.

'No, no, of course not.' Laura threw back the glass and finished the drink.

'Want another?' said Ethan glumly.

'No, thanks, darling. Look, I'm sorry about that little outburst. I . . . I'm just having a moral dilemma, that's all. Ethan, forget what I said last night. I was wrong. I shouldn't have jumped to conclusions. I've got a suspicious mind, that's all. Forget it.'

'Laura, Sonia hasn't hurt you, has she?'

'No, no!' The tangled web of misconceptions tightened around Laura. 'It's nothing like that, Ethan. I must go and finish some work. I'm sorry if I worried you. I'm sorry about dinner.' She stood and hugged her plump friend lightly and before Ethan could ask any more embarrassing questions she went down the stairs, through the shop, aiming a quick goodbye at Eugene, and out into the bright sunlight.

She ran up the narrow lane to her house on the hill and found that the postman had delivered a pile of mail. She picked it off the tiled floor and flopped into the kitchen chair at the table where she worked. There was a postcard from Thomas: how far away that little affair seemed. She barely glanced at it before tearing open the London-postmarked A4 envelope with her name printed on it. It was the Xeroxed copies of tear sheets about the *Elizabetta*.

Good old James, she thought, and riffled through them. There was a small item explaining treasure trove and who owned it, the finder or the crown. It was quite complicated but clearly put, for laymen to understand. She understood that the treasure that Bill Montpelier and Sonia Stallone were selling was not the finders' at all, but belonged to the state, or crown. She sighed and picked up her phone. Then she remembered the tape: the copy of the tape she had made at Sonia's office, the statement of involvement with selling stolen antiquities – the treasure brought up from the *Elizabetta*. It was there, in the deal table drawer. She left it there, not knowing what to do for the best.

She could probably lead police to the spot where the hidden cave was, but what if she couldn't find it? There was no real proof, just a woman bragging. She couldn't procrastinate too long. She phoned James.

'James, Laura. Hi! Yes, I got it, thanks. Listen, I'm on to something big. Can I send the story to you in case anything should happen to me, here?'

'What do you mean, happen to you? What have you got yourself into, for God's sake?'

'I'll send you a tape, James. And a map. Look after it with your life.' She drew a sketch of the island and where she thought the boat had moored and where the cave was, placed the drawing with the tape in the padded envelope and put it in her backpack. She found her purse, a sweatshirt and baseball cap and went out into the bright day. She deliberately averted her eyes from the gleaming white edifice on the hill above her house, and the telescope that pointed accusingly at her from the terrace.

She posted the tape and felt immediately safer. This was ridiculous. Why should she be worried? She would go home, escape to London, back to work and away from the moral dilemmas and dangers that faced her here.

The town's narrow pavements were full of cheerful holiday-makers buying bread for beach picnics and clotted cream to send home to envious friends. Children ate ice-cream, dads pushed baby buggies in which sun-hatted infants slept or screamed. It was a typical summer scene in the little holiday town.

Laura went into Full of Beans.

Eugene was there on his own.

'Is Ethan here, Eugene?'

'Yes, upstairs, having a cup of tea. Go on up.'

Laura ran up the stairs. 'Ethan, I've got to go back to London, right away. I can't explain now. I just wanted to say goodbye, and I'll phone you.' She hugged her large friend, who kissed her on both cheeks.

'Laura, what is it? Why the rush? Is it Sonia? Or the doctor? What are you doing?'

'I'm not sure, Ethan, but I have to go back and sort things out. Then I can tell you.'

'I shall expect a full explanation for this strange behaviour.' He kissed her fondly. 'Bye, gorgeous. Look after yourself.'

'Bye Eugene,' called Laura as she opened the shop door.

She went back to her grandmother's house, only stopping for a moment at Mrs Poldhu's house.

'I have to go back to London,' she said. 'I didn't want to worry you. I might not be back right away.'

'Don't you worry about me, my dear, I'll see you when I see you. And another thing: my first cataract operation might be soon. I saw Doctor Blaine today and he said it were ripe enough.' The old woman was cheerful and Laura smiled at her hope.

'You look after yourself, Mrs Poldhu,' she said.

'And you, cheel. Don't be a stranger.'

She hurriedly packed, locked up and threw her luggage into the car.

As Mrs Poldhu stood and waved at the departing Beetle, she remembered what she had meant to tell Laura: that a little while ago Andrew Montpelier had been looking at Laura's car in her drive. She had passed him on the path or she would not have seen him. She had been suspicious of him being there and asked him what he was up to.

'Miss Mackay asked me to check her car for her,' he'd said.

Laura drove out of the busy town, and headed for the main road to London. All she could think of was escaping the death threat that she'd overheard. There had been a crash at a roundabout – a large truck had overturned, and no vehicles were being let on to the London road. A traffic jam was building up. She decided to take a longish detour, on the winding road that followed the coast. That way she could get back on to the main road after about ten miles.

She let out the new clutch and changed into top gear and the Beetle sped along the narrow, stone-hedged lane, where willow herb and heathers bobbed in the wind.

She was doing forty miles an hour, sailing down a long hill, when she put her foot on the brake. Nothing happened. She pressed down hard. The car went faster. She changed gear, moving down to third, but the engine roared and she hit the bend going much too fast. She yanked the wheel over to get the car around, terrified by now. She kept calm, breathed deeply and noted other cars passing her the other way, their drivers and passengers looking angrily at her. She saw the sign in the road: Doom Rock Point, 1 mile. That was where her parents had died together. She sobbed in terror. Was she going to die like them, hurled in a car over the high, steep cliff, to plunge to the white waves and black rocks below?

She managed to change down to second, the gears screeching and rasping under her hand. The road was flat at this point, but she tried to steer clear of the edge, where she could see the cliffs and the water far below. Another bend and she'd make it, but she couldn't slow down any further.

On the right of the road she saw the narrow entrance to a dirt track. She swung over, just behind a truck coming the other way, and negotiated the turning successfully, her wheels screaming across the hot tarmac. The car rattled and shook over the bumpy track and she hung on grimly. In front she could see another bend with a granite barn on one side and a large heap of compost on the right. Several Rhode Island Reds ran desperately in front of the out-of-control car. She yanked on the handbrake as hard as she could. The car skidded. She aimed the car at the compost heap. She was aware of the crash, but it sounded far away.

She awoke in a hospital bed, her arm bandaged, her head bandaged and her ribs taped.

'You're a lucky young woman,' the doctor said.

'How long have I been here?' She wanted to say, where am I? but felt it was too trite.

'Only a few hours. We were beginning to get worried about you, but you seem to have had a miraculous escape. Concussion, of course, and bruised ribs, a badly bruised arm, and multiple abrasions. We'll have to keep you in for a few days, to make sure you're all right.'

She gazed up at the handsome young doctor and burst into tears.

He called a nurse to deal with her and left, hurriedly.

'Nurse, is my mobile phone in my bag? Could you look, please?'

'Your bag was brought in by the farmer who found you. What were you doing going so fast in a farm lane?'

'There was something wrong with my car – the brakes failed. I think it could have been done deliberately.'

'What? What are you saying, my dear? Are you still feeling groggy? Here. Here's your phone.'

'Thank you! Will you leave me, please, nurse? I have some important calls to make.'

999 was the first number she dialled.

After two policeman had come and interviewed her for an hour, Laura slept.

She phoned Ethan and her aunt and uncle, who said they would come straight away. Next she spoke to Sally and then James in London.

'I'll come down, with Guido. We'll stay at your house in Porthzelah, shall we, and visit you?' said James.

'Fine,' said Laura. As long as she didn't have to cook for the choirboy she didn't care. 'There is a key with my next-door neighbour, Mrs Poldhu, and another at the health food shop – Full of Beans. There's plenty of linen, and . . . please James, no parties.'

'Parties? *Moi*? You must be joking, Laura. I'm past all that, my dear.'

Chapter Twenty-Two

London Again

'*A*re you quite recovered?' asked the editor of *Health and You*.

'I'm fine.'

'Well, you look wonderful, anyway,' said Sally, admiring Laura's tan and slender body in the short brown linen dress. 'Even your feet are brown, for heaven's sake. I went to Rome for a week and it rained.'

'Sally, it's wonderful to be back,' said Laura.

'Did the pirates or smugglers or whatever really tinker with your brakes to try and kill you? Have you heard what's going to happen to them?'

'They're being held pending trial. My car brakes had been deliberately damaged. Apparently, my neighbour actually saw one of them tampering with the car. The police are on to their smuggling activities too. I've got to give evidence, of course, when their trial comes up.'

'Well, what a dreadful adventure! What about your car?' Sally knew how fond Laura was of her silver convertible Beetle.

'Write-off, I'm afraid. But I should get insurance, eventually. My laptop is damaged beyond repair, too.'

'Laura, we have a position going – only temporary,

but you might like to take it. My assistant editor has had her baby and is on leave. You remember Joanna?'

'Yes, of course, is she all right? What did she have?'

'A boy. Yes, she's fine. But the bloke who was going to take her place has let me down. What do you say, Laura? Loads of money, of course. Start on Monday, OK?'

'Well, yes, all right, why not? Thanks.' She kissed Sally on both cheeks.

'Problem is, darl', you might have to go back to Cornwall, soon. I want someone to do a story on rubber fetish clubs and I've heard there is one down there somewhere.'

'Oh, really?' Laura gulped.

'Yes, we are doing a series on fetishes – their contribution or otherwise to sexual health, of course.'

'Of course!'

Laura was first and foremost concerned with finding out about her parentage.

She went home. The tastefully decorated dove-grey and white space was all her own. She looked out on to an autumnal Primrose Hill, the tall limes and sycamores losing their brown leaves in a strong wind that blew from the east. Crows cawed loudly. She picked up the phone and toyed with the idea of contacting Jerry, but stopped herself. She phoned her doctor instead and made an appointment to see her the following day. She phoned James and left a message that she was back in London.

She didn't know if Sonia had been arrested with the smugglers. She had told the police all she knew about the gang.

'Laura, you are recovering well,' said her doctor, after her examination. 'You were lucky not to suffer any whiplash injury.'

'Thanks. Actually, there was something else I wanted

to ask you. I want to find out if my father really was my father or if it was another man. How do I do that?'

'Well, that's fairly simple, Laura.' She looked at the notes she had in front of her. 'We'll take a blood sample from you for starters.' She did the test there and then and told Laura to telephone for the results the next day.

'Laura, you are group O. Do you know what group your mother's husband was?'

'I believe that the man I suspect might have been my father is group AB, according to his son, who says he had to have a transfusion in Plymouth, I think, about six years ago. My mother's husband – I have no idea. They died when I was three. My grandmother might have known, but she died last year.'

'I am going to get someone else to look into this for you – it's not beyond my powers, but to be sure I'll put you in touch with a genetic specialist. You'll have to pay – the National Health Service won't do this for free. Is that all right?'

'Of course, thank you,' said Laura and put down the phone feeling that at least she had made a beginning.

James was taking Laura out to dinner to meet his fiancée. Laura dressed in a pale-grey wool trouser suit, with a white silk shirt open at the neck. The girl was only eighteen, and looked even younger. She was in red suede nineties-styled hotpants and black tights with a tight black mohair jumper, which carved her tiny breasts and revealed a skinny white midriff with a gold belly-button ring. James acted like he had made her, created her out of fluffy stuff and red lipstick, silky nylon and long blonde hair. She looked like a Barbie Doll. Laura wondered what had happened to Guido.

Daisy was a hairdresser – a styliste, she called herself. Poor child! thought Laura. He'll tire of her in a few months. She has an empty head, no brain. But James was proud of his youthful paramour and preened himself like a peacock, in his green velvet shirt and red flared trousers. He looks like an aging pop star, thought Laura. Poor James.

James had the tape with him and gave it to Laura.

'I did listen to it,' he said. 'Hot stuff, Laura!'

She had forgotten the background sounds that went before the denouement of Red Sonia. The obvious sex that had taken place. She blushed.

'Yes, well, all in the line of duty,' she said, smiling.

'Who would have thought it, though?' he said.

'Look James, I didn't come here for you to make snide remarks about me.'

'No, I didn't mean that, you idiot. I mean the criminal shenanigans in Porthzelah.'

'Oh, right. James, thanks for the help with the research on the shipwrecks and treasure trove. It was a great help.'

'I really enjoyed my visit to your village, Laura. Lovely friends and neighbours you have. Loved the old lady. She likes a good gossip, doesn't she?'

Barbie Doll chose this moment to go and powder her turned-up nose.

'James, I don't think I can write the article about smuggling, after all. It's too close to home.'

'Leave it to me, Laura. Let me sort it out for you,' James said.

Barbie Doll came back, her red mouth pursed for a kiss for James.

The evening went by and Laura left James and Barbie Doll, who were off to a club, to drive home alone. She felt terribly alone in her smart flat. Perhaps she should get a cat? Or a husband? She put thoughts of Jerry out of her mind. He had left messages at work for her, asking her to contact him. He said he had moved house, having given his wife half the proceeds of the sale of the marital home. She had his new telephone number off by heart. But she didn't phone him. She knew he didn't know her whereabouts, having been told by

Health and You that she didn't want to let anyone know where she'd gone. As far as he knew, she was still in Cornwall somewhere, nursing a broken heart.

She took herself off to her big, cold bed, a mug of Horlicks and a hot-water bottle for company. God, was she going to grow old on her own? She suddenly thought of poor Mrs Poldhu, with her cataracts and her dead husband and no children. At least she'd had a loving relationship for most of her life. She thought of her grandparents: Granddad playing the piano, Grandma singing. She cried herself to sleep.

Next day, a Saturday, she telephoned her aunt and uncle.

'Hi there, how's things?' she said brightly.

They had visited her once in the Cornish hospital and had phoned many times, trying to persuade her to recuperate with them in Exeter, but she had refused. She had gone back to London as soon as she was able.

'Laura, how are you, dear?'

'I'm better, thank you, Aunt. Much better. Almost good as new.' She took a deep breath. 'Aunt Celia, I need to know something and maybe you can help. Did you happen to know what my father's blood group was, by any chance?'

'Oh, dear, Laura, is it those rumours that have got to you at last? Don't listen, dear, people in small towns always gossip; it's all some of them have got – dirt on other people's lives.'

'So you know the story?'

'That your mother was in love with another man and wanted to leave your father? Yes.'

'Aunt Celia, I want to know if he really was my father. I have to know.'

'Sorry, dear, I can't really help you. But I do seem to remember that he used to be a blood donor.'

'Thanks, Aunt. That might be the breakthrough I need.'

'Laura, that man, Harold Montpelier. He was a bad lot. He pestered your mother for years after she broke up with him and married your father. He hated being beaten, that was it. Couldn't take the rejection.'

'Didn't my mother want to be with Harold?'

'I don't think so, no. She was a terrible flirt, but she loved Arthur.'

'I see.' Laura was even more confused.

'Are you coming for Christmas, dear?' Aunt Celia usually made the assault on her diary in November. It was only September, for goodness' sake.

'Can't say, yet, Aunt, sorry. I'll let you know in good time, don't worry.'

Saturdays in London were spent doing the washing, mending, cleaning the flat, and shopping. Laura loved the weekends, usually, but this, her first weekend in London, she felt sad. She remembered Jerry's lopsided smile, his banana-shaped penis. His head between her thighs.

She went to Camden Lock market and spent too much money on an antique silk-and-lace blouse: retail therapy. It didn't work. She met two old friends for lunch and told them about her adventures in Cornwall, leaving out her brief lesbian experience. She did brag about Thomas and Aaron, though, and hinted at rubber fetishism.

Her friends were impressed, but she felt no joy or pride in her conquests. She wanted Jerry, she realised, with a hunger, not lust exactly, but with an underlying deep need, a hurt that would not go away. She had tried to purge herself of his memory, and it hadn't worked.

Two weeks later she walked into the private rooms of a genetic expert in Wimpole Street.

She had the information with her about her own blood group and Harold Montpelier's probable blood group, and the information that Arthur Mackay had given blood many years ago. She told the doctor of her need to know who her father was. She also told him of the little town's gossip.

'Well, Miss Mackay. If Harold Montpelier is in prison, as you say he is, his doctor there might give it to us. It's hardly patient privacy. I'll need to follow that up. It's an unusual name. I should be able to discover which prison he's in. But if he really is group AB and you, as we know, are group O, there is no way that he could be your father. AB is rare, and A or B has to be passed on to offspring. And I'll try to find out Arthur Mackay's blood group as well. May I suggest that you get the results from a genetic counsellor? I'll recommend one at your local hospital.'

Laura went home to await his report. She should have found out which prison Harold was in. She hadn't thought about it. Maybe they would refuse to give out that sort of information on a prisoner. However, she had done all she could for now.

'Laura, have you phoned your doctor friend?' Sally was troubled that Laura had not bounced back into work, as she had hoped she would. They were drinking in a tapas bar near the office after work one day.

'Do you mean Jerry?'

'Who else would I mean?'

'No, I haven't.'

'Why haven't you?'

'Oh, come on, Sal, you were the one that said all men are bastards. Why should I phone him? He let me down, badly. I can't risk that again.'

'Do you love him?'

'I . . . yes,' she whispered.

'Then you're a fool. Phone him. Bugger pride.'

Laura knew Sally's story. She was a no-nonsense woman with a partner she lived with but refused to marry. She had always reckoned that once she gave in to his demands to make him an honest man, he would lose interest. He was Italian, very good-looking and jealous, but he cooked 'divinely' and did his share of the housework, as well as bringing in his share of the money. He was desperate to have six bambinos, but only if Sally married him. She was still holding out.

'I'll think about it, Sally.'

She cried herself to sleep yet again.

Chapter Twenty-Three

The Festive Season

*L*aura was going back to Cornwall for some of the Christmas break. She had left her Cornish address with the GP in case any news came through from the geneticist, though she was warned it could take several weeks. She drove down through snow and hail, rain and wind, and got to her aunt's house on Christmas Eve. She had wanted to be in Cornwall for the Christmas Eve carol singing, but Aunt Celia would have been disappointed if she had not put in an appearance. Christmas day was spent playing cards and Monopoly, watching television and eating too much, as usual.

'Have you met Mr Right, yet, dear?' Laura knew that her aunt was desperate that she did not become an old maid. She knew that she loved her as if she had been her own child, even though she wasn't a very affectionate woman.

'For goodness' sake, Aunt Celia,' she said, embarrassed. 'No, I haven't.' She always felt like an errant child with these kindly elderly people, who had nothing in common with her. She was fond of them, grateful for their care and for making sure she'd had enough of everything when she was growing up. They had even given in to her demands to go to art college, when they had wanted her to go to teacher training college: 'There's always a need for good teachers, Laura. Who needs artists? There's no future in it, dear.'

She drove the rest of the way to Porthzelah, through gale-battered landscapes of rusty gorse and windswept moorland. Real and artificial Christmas trees decorated house windows and their coloured lights lit up the gloom.

She arrived at lunchtime and parked the car she had borrowed from Sally. Nothing had happened about her insurance yet, and she couldn't afford to replace the Beetle. Celia had given her a leg and breast of turkey and stuffing, ham, mince-pies, Christmas pudding and cake. She was set up for the rest of the week. The sun had come out and she opened the sitting-room window to let in the fresh air. She turned on the hot water system. Gulls hovered in the blue sky, battered bamboos sang and swayed. She phoned Ethan to say that she had arrived and then had a bath and changed into a short black woollen dress and thick black tights and flat shoes. Ethan was having a Boxing Day lunch party.

As she left the house, a black cat mewed at her from the wall. She stroked him. It looked like Sonia's cat. It had a red collar. She glanced up at the house. The cat curled itself around her arm and she took it indoors and gave it some scraps of ham and a dish of milky water. It lapped eagerly. She left a window open so it could get out. How lovely that she could leave the window open here, she thought. She'd never think of doing such a thing in London.

She ran down the hill to the flat.

She was early and could tell Ethan and Eugene all about her new job and show them her scars. They'd visited each day when she'd been in hospital. They'd particularly enjoyed the fact that she'd been airlifted by air ambulance to the hospital.

'Tell us about the pilot – what was he wearing? Lots of straps and belts and zips?' Ethan had asked and Eugene had punched him playfully.

Anna and Charles arrived with Thomas, who looked more mature than the last time she had seen him, handsome as ever and cheerful. He had his girlfriend with him, a pretty, dark, sturdy Cornish beauty. Laura kissed cheeks with him and shook the girl's hand. Laura was pleased to see how happy he looked. Had he told his girlfriend about 'the older woman'? She couldn't tell, but the girl, Dorina, was looking at her with admiration, anyway.

'Laura, how sophisticated you look, *ma petite.*' It was Odile, dressed outrageously in a long black rubber cloak, high black boots and fishnet stockings with a corset worn over a silk short dress. They kissed, French style, on both cheeks. Rory was with her, wearing a studded leather dog collar with a leash fastened to it. Odile held the chain leash tightly and he smiled brightly at Laura. His long lean body was encased in a rubber outfit that showed every bulge of his groin, and the muscles of his buttocks.

'Like our outfits? We're rehearsing for New Year's Eve. What are you wearing?'

'I hadn't thought,' said Laura. It was a tradition in the town to go out in fancy dress on New Year's Eve. Years ago 'guisers' had the run of the houses in town for the twelve days of Christmas. Disguised and masked, the young men had run in and out of cottages playing tricks on the townsfolk. Nowadays, it was an excuse to dress outrageously and drink too much. It had become a large street party.

Ethan and Eugene had a mainly gay circle of friends, but lots of straight friends too. Laura was quick to remember that she too had briefly been one of the gay fraternity. Why on earth should she have been ashamed of it? It was only the embarrassment that people might have the wrong idea about her. But why should she care? In this town, people believed what they wanted to believe. Her own mother had probably suffered at the hands of gossips.

She liked Ethan's friends: they were tough and funny, bright and amusing. Lunch was for both vegetarians and meat eaters, with sausage rolls and vegetable samosas, smoked salmon and turkey and vegetable curries. It was a feast. The little flat vibrated with the sound of laughing people.

Later, when most of the guests had gone and Laura was helping load the dish-washer, she asked about Sonia.

'Oh, she upped and went, right after your accident, it was. Gone to pastures new – Morocco I think. Her house is up for sale, didn't you see? The police took all sorts of stuff away.'

'What about Becky? Is she still around?'

'I think she is. Her auntie is with her. She'll be taking her away, I hear. She was tarred with the same brush as the rest of her family after they were all arrested.'

'What about Stan? Have you seen anything of Stan, the painter?' said Laura.

'Stan and his pretty daughter have gone away for the winter. He's having an exhibition in London sometime, I think.'

Laura went back to her house.

The cat was asleep on top of the Rayburn. Laura gently removed it and found a cardboard box and an old towel for it to sleep on. It purred.

'What can I call you?' she asked it. 'I know: Pirate.'

'Mrs Poldhu, it's me, Laura. I've brought you a present.' Laura called through the house and went in. The elderly woman stood and held out both her hands to Laura.

'I see you clear as day – with my one good eye – and

you are the image of your mother when she was a girl. Such a pretty little thing she was.'

'Happy Christmas, Mrs Poldhu. Did you have your operation?'

'I did, cheel, and I have the best Christmas present in the world: my sight back. They'll do the other eye in a few months, when it's ripe – whatever that means.'

'I have something for you,' Laura repeated, and gave the woman the large canvas wrapped in festive paper.

'Is it my portrait? It is!' She cackled loudly at the painted portrait of herself. 'Is that me? That old biddy? Hee, hee! I look old.'

'Do you like it?'

'I suppose I do, yes, cheel. Thankee.' Laura found herself crying on the old woman's shoulder, for reasons she could not fathom.

'I wasn't expecting you, or I should have had a present for you, too.'

'I don't need anything, Mrs Poldhu, thank you all the same.'

'But you've been kind to me, you know, reading to me and getting my shopping. Ooh! I've remembered something. Someone left you a package. Yes, I'll get it. You stay there.' Laura's neighbour went out of the sitting room, which was warm with the fire on, and sun coming through the large sash windows. She came back in a moment with a large package under her arm. It was wrapped in brown paper and tied with string.

'Go on, open it.'

She cut the string with a pair of scissors that Mrs Poldhu found for her, and unwrapped the paper.

'Is it my mother?'

'It is, my cheel. Painted by that artist you know, that Stan with the grey ponytail. He came up here looking for you to give it to you. He knew you was my friend, he said.'

The oil painting was in dark rich colours, reds and

browns, with her mother's dark brown eyes gleaming, and her mouth smiling. She had been a very pretty young woman. Laura started crying again and the old lady comforted her awkwardly.

'It's a sad thing to lose your mother, my maid, a sad thing.'

'Yes,' said Laura, 'it is.'

'And your father, too,' said Mrs Poldhu. 'I met your friends who were here when you was in hospital. Very friendly they were. I hope you don't mind. I told them about that mechanic, Andrew Montpelier, with his head under your car. I told the police too, you know, as soon as I heard about your accident. I had a feeling about that Andrew. Always had a bad feeling about him.'

'No, of course I don't mind, Mrs Poldhu. Thank you for all you have done.'

'Do you know who that black cat belongs to?' Laura asked, as Pirate suddenly appeared on the window sill.

'It's a stray, I think. Been feeding it, I have.'

'Do you want to adopt it?' she asked Mrs Poldhu.

'No, my maid, I haven't time for cats. You have him if you want.'

Two days later, in the lull between Christmas and the celebrations of New Year there was mail. Laura opened the letter in trepidation. It was from the geneticist. 'Harold Montpelier died in prison, on the 20th December 1998, from natural causes. His blood group was AB as you thought. I have found the records of Arthur Mackay. He was group O, like you. Harold Montpelier could not have been your father.'

There was a bill attached.

Cheap at twice the price, thought Laura.

Laura had taken the picture of her mother back to her grandmother's house – her house – and propped the portrait against a wall in the sitting room, where she could stand back and see it properly. Yes, Stan was a good painter. The paint was thick and glossy, spread on with a palette knife in places. It was done with verve and passion, like the pictures of his wife, she thought. She went up to her attic room and got out the large folder of work that she had left there. She took out the charcoal drawings she had done of Thomas – they were quite powerful, she thought, very erotic: the tied wrists, the twisted torso, the muscles highlighted in white. His solid buttocks. She looked at the other work she had produced that summer. A summer of smugglers and sun and sex. Yes, there were one or two really quite good pieces of work. Perhaps she wasn't too old to make it as a painter?

She got out her paints and the palette and put one of the prepared stretched canvases that she had not started work on before she had left in such a hurry, on to the easel. She stared out of the window. She started to paint straight on to the canvas – no pencil marks, no charcoal, but thick gobs of paint in bold strokes. She painted the town, the church tower, the bamboos, which were like a curtain. She painted the gulls wheeling and swerving and the boats bobbing in the harbour. She painted until the dark crept up over the little village, and the moon rose in the purple sky. Tonight no gulls cried.

She shivered and cleaned her brushes and left them neatly on a cloth. She tore herself away from the dormer window and went down to light a fire. She was alone tonight. No festivities for once. There seemed to be parties every day in this little village. She needed her sleep. She heated up the remains of her turkey soup and had a bath. The black cat mewed and rubbed up against her leg. She pulled the towelling robe tighter.

'It's just me and you, puss – Pirate Puss.' She stroked its chin and the cat rolled over in ecstasy and let her rub its tummy. 'No Thomas, no Aaron, no Red Sonia. What am I to do with myself? Shall we settle down to a quiet middle age, you and me? No more adventures, eh? You were a pirate queen's cat, and now you are simply a writer's cat. Shall I take you back with me to London, puss? I'll have to buy a cat basket to carry you in.' The black cat purred encouragingly as she rubbed its fur.

The soup smelled marvellous and she sat at the kitchen table and sipped the hot broth, dipping thick granary bread into the bowl. The cat sat quietly by the Rayburn, on a brightly coloured rag rug that her grandfather had made. She placed a small bowl of the soup by its side and it lapped delicately.

The grace of cats! Laura reached for her sketchbook and an HB3 pencil and began to draw the cat.

The next day she felt refreshed. The day dawned bright and blue-skied. There had been rain in the night but now it was dry and sunny. She remembered how, when she had been a child, the Breton fishermen had come to the terrace to gather snails from the gardens and dry-stone hedge. She had often woken to the sound of their wooden clogs on the path.

Laura bathed and fed the cat with leftovers. She must do some shopping today: buy a cat basket and food. She was a responsible pet owner now. She waved to Mrs Poldhu, who was hanging out her washing. 'Lovely day for it!'

'Yes, dear, 'ansome!'

All the shops were open. There were lots of visitors wandering around.

'Hello, my bird, did you 'ave a good Christmas?'

'Bert! Yes, thank you. And you?'

'Oh yes! I 'eard about the Montpeliers. Not sorry to see the back of that lot in the town. Is it true Bill Montpelier tried to kill you? Bad as 'is brother, Harold, he is. It was said at the time, you know, that Harold was jealous of May and Arthur. He wanted May to go with him – 'mazed by her, he was. And she wouldn't go with him. She loved your father, she did, but Harold wouldn't let it go. He hated to be crossed, Harold did.

And his cousin, Andrew, he were always a bad'un. He was vicious even as a boy. Killed seagulls he did. Loved killing things. He was laughing when they brought the news of your parents' car crash to the pub. He said "Good riddance." Never forgot that, I didn't.'

Laura was trying hard not to show her emotions to the old man.

'Anyway, well done, my bird! You did well to get the Montpeliers put away. Shame about the lad, though. He isn't as bad as the rest of the family, Aaron isn't.

'Well, I'm off to the Sailor's Mission. There's a snooker competition today.'

'Good luck, Bert.'

'Oh, I don't play any more, my flower. Not with these legs. I do love to watch, though. How's your neighbour – Mrs Poldhu?'

'Oh, not bad, you know. She's had one of her cataracts done.'

'I knew her man. Good bowler he was.'

'Did you, Bert? She's lonely without him, I think.'

'Yes, I expect she is, my bird. If I had better legs I'd run up and pay her a visit.'

'I'll take you in the car if you really mean it.'

'Would you, my bird? Well, give me time to think about it.' The old man laughed and waved his stick at her. 'I might not want to come down again once I'm up there.'

'Let me know, Bert. It's no trouble.'

'See you New Year's Eve in the Galleon?'

'Oh, yes, I suppose so, Bert. I haven't thought about what to wear, yet.'

'I'll be there, seeing all the maids dressed in next to nothing.' He laughed a rich, meaty laugh.

Laura did her shopping, stopping every few minutes to speak to local people. It was always like this, she thought, a few items to buy and it took forever to get round the shops, because everyone wanted to say hello and pass the time of day. Now, of course, everyone wanted to hear about the smugglers and her escape from certain death.

The town was lovely. A cold crisp day, with the blue water lapping the sand in the harbour. The Christmas visitors were not like the summer holiday-makers. They were more subdued, less rowdy and more appreciative of the town and what it had to offer out of season. People gazed in the gallery windows.

'Laura!' It was Anna. 'You're looking peaky, still. How's your forehead? Oh, yes, much better. I expect you'll have a scar though. You haven't come to see us, yet. We're having a party Thursday lunchtime, if you can make it. Thomas is announcing his engagement.' Anna, wrapped in a scarlet cloak with a white fur hood, looked like an aging Red Riding Hood.

'Anna! Thank you. I'll be there. No, I won't. I have to be back in London. Oh, what a shame. Give him my love and congratulations. She seems a lovely girl.'

'Yes, a lovely *young* girl, just right for him,' Anna smiled smugly and kissed Laura on both cheeks. 'But you might see them at New Year.'

New Year! What would she wear? She wandered into the charity shops, which were very busy, to see if she could find inspiration. Nothing but psychedelic prints and crushed velvet. No thank you, she thought. She wanted to look glamorous, not embarrassingly stuck in her own history. Then she thought of her grandmother's clothes. Perhaps she could wear something that had belonged to her. She climbed the hill.

'Pirate! Puss, puss, puss, puss!'

The black cat came running to her. It looked like Laura was stuck with the stray cat. Sonia's cat. It must be the same one. It was very sleek. Perhaps it had some Burmese in it, thought Laura. It was slender and shiny. It purred as she opened the tin of cat food.

'There you are, Pirate. You and me are going to be good mates. I know we are.' It suddenly occurred to her to look at the little barrel-shaped metal container on the cat's collar. Why hadn't she thought of it before? She unscrewed the tiny holder. There was a piece of paper coiled inside.

The word 'Stallone' and a telephone number were written on it. It was not a local number, but a London one.

'Well, well, well! I have Red Sonia's town number, Puss. Your mummy's number! Better keep it in case we need it, hadn't I?'

The black cat purred and cleaned its paws carefully. It was giving away no secrets.

Next day it was raining heavily and cold. The Easterly was fierce and strong and she stayed indoors all day, painting and reading. The wind rattled the sash windows and she put folded newspaper in the gaps. Maybe it would snow. In the evening she built up the fire and sat huddled by it with the cat on her lap. She ate tinned sardines on toast and shared her supper with the cat. She watched something mindless on the television and went to bed, happy for once and satisfied with what she had achieved during the day's work. She woke once, the wind howling, the cat on her feet. It felt cosy. It felt like home.

Laura painted throughout the last day of the year. She found it very satisfying. She couldn't wait to start on life drawing classes again. Her new temporary job at *Health and You* meant that she would have to wait until Easter or even later before she could return to the village again, but she knew she would return, with Pirate Puss. The light was blinding in the attic room, even at this time of the year. She would have to put up blinds if she worked here permanently. She hadn't phoned anyone in London since she'd been here. She ought to phone

Aunt Celia, but she would wait until New Year's Day for that.

Laura dialled the number on Pirate's collar. Nothing. A dead line.

Perhaps the gossip was right, for once. Perhaps Sonia had debunked to Morocco. She had connections there, Laura remembered. The architect had actually lived there.

She suddenly knew that Sonia would not return. Her house was for sale. She had abandoned the cat. Laura had no need to fear her. Even if she did come back she would be arrested on suspicion of handling treasure trove.

She had a long bath and got into the clothes she had decided to wear for the fancy dress evening celebrations. There was no pattern to the festivities. People simply dressed up and went out on the streets and in the pubs and restaurants, as usual, but disguised. There were no prizes for the best costume. It was a street party.

She had arranged to meet Ethan and Eugene in the Galleon at ten o'clock. They had arranged to eat at a restaurant at eleven thirty, so they could be together for the midnight chimes.

She didn't really want to make the effort. She had a good book – Katherine Mansfield's short stories – which she was rereading. She could get into her pajamas and cuddle up with a blanket and the cat in front of the fire. But no, she must go out.

She bathed, dressed and wrapped herself in the black velvet cloak. She felt cold as she ran down the hill and through the windy streets, which were clogged with already inebriated people. She did not recognise anyone.

A Cornish male voice called out, 'Hello my bird,' and laughed.

She forced her way through the rowdy crowd outside the pub and pushed open the door. She took an age to get to the bar and she wished she had brought a flask of whisky with her. But her costume had no pockets. She put her cloak on a hook and looked around to see if she could recognise anyone. It was nine forty-five. She adjusted her mask.

'Is that you, Laura? My God! You look stunning, darl',' cried Ethan.

'Yes, hello, you look great!'

Ethan wore a clown's costume of loud checks, with baggy trousers, red braces, a top hat and a red false nose. His huge false feet were a terrible liability. Customers kept treading on them. 'I'll have to go outside, Laura. Eugene is there, anyway. Are you coming?'

'I suppose so, it's a bit chilly though. I'll just have a couple of scotches. Ethan, how did you know it was me?'

'Your perfume, darling. See you later . . .' The clown backed out like a snorkeler backing into water with flippers on his feet.

Laura felt sexually powerful in her outfit. It was a bit like something she had seen Odile wearing at the rubber club sessions. But she wore less than the skinny Frenchwoman and looked better in it. Knee-high leather boots covered her legs and black stockings held up by a black lace suspender belt. A rubber skirt just about covered her hips and thighs. Her belly button was bare. Her black rubber top was slashed so that the curve of her breasts bulged enticingly through the gaps cut in the cloth. She wore a blonde wig – her only purchase that morning. She had made the skirt and top from a part of the rubber sheet that Aaron had given her. She felt very naughty. Men and women stared at her. Her black mask hid her features except for her mouth – painted scarlet – and the long blonde wig hid her real identity. Her homemade rubber skirt slid up her legs and exposed her stocking tops.

She saw Becky dressed as a mermaid, her bobbing

breasts barely hidden by scallop shells. She was surrounded by young men in surf baggies.

'I heard you had moved, Becky,' Laura said in passing.

'Not until after the celebrations. And Laura, I always liked you. I thought it was evil what my uncles did to your car.'

'Did you know about it?'

'Well, yes, I told the policeman. I heard them argue with Aaron about it. Aaron thought he'd persuaded Uncle Bill and Uncle Andrew not to do anything so drastic, but obviously they did it anyway. I'm pleased to have Uncle Bill out of my hair, anyway.'

'What do you mean?'

'You know what I mean, Laura.'

'Have you told the police about that, too, Becky?'

'I'm still thinking about it.'

Kat, the hairdresser, was in the middle of the group, dressed as Tank Girl. Her hair was a mess.

There were groups of Teletubbies. At least they were warm. There were several Star-Trek crews. There were teams of fat men dressed in black-and-gold striped Cornish rugby kit, ears pinned back with head bands. There were the three bears and Goldilocks. Laura counted at least six sets of Spice Girls.

Through the little window she could see the crowds of partygoers outside, their clothes blown sideways by the gale-force wind. An amazing human *SS Titanic* complete with funnels sank into the pub patio. A policeman with a feather in his helmet and a flower in his button-hole smiled at a drunk who was staggering around dressed as a semi-naked woman.

Charles forced his way to the bar and ordered a double whisky with ice for Laura. He wore false breasts under a floral dress open to his cleavage and high-heeled shoes. Lots of men were dressed in women's clothes. Laura waved frantically at Anna, who fought her way to where Laura sat by the window and pushed in next to her.

'My God, you look rather outré, Laura. Everyone's staring at you. Who are you supposed to be, anyway?'

'A rubber fetishist, actually.'

'Have you seen Odile? She was going to wear something similar. She said to tell you to call on her later – for a nightcap.'

'No, haven't seen her yet.' They had to practically shout to hear themselves speak. The crowds were packed like pilchards in a salting barrel in the small low-ceilinged pub. It was like a bad day on the Japanese underground. The noise and excitement reached fever pitch. Everyone was pretending to be someone else.

Anna was dressed as a man in top hat and tails and looked much more attractive than she did usually. She smoked a foul-smelling cigar and Laura flapped her hands in horror at the smoke.

'Have you seen the *Titanic* outside? It's amazing! Very clever costume. How did they do it?'

'Oh! Here comes the happy couple.'

'Hello, Thomas, no room to sit, sorry.' Anna stood up and let his fiancée take her place, where Anna cooed over her like a pet cat. Laura was thrust against the young man, who was dressed as a cavalier.

'You look interesting,' he said, and she felt the hardness of him through his velvet trousers.

'You look very dashing, Thomas. Are you happy?'

'I can't hear you.'

'I said, are you happy?' she shouted in his ear as he bent towards her.

'I am. We are. Thanks to you, mostly.'

'How do you mean?'

'You taught me how to please a woman. It was an excellent education.'

'I'm glad you appreciated it.' She smiled smugly and allowed him to press up against her and she felt his large callused hand sliding up her thigh to the damp triangle between her legs. No one could see. He pressed fingers on her sex. She moved on to him. Her hands squeezed his eager cock through the thin velvet. He had the natural enthusiasm of youth.

'Remember when I made you come in the restaurant?' he whispered in her ear.

'How could I forget?'

'I did the same thing with Dorina. She liked it.'

'Well, have fun and be happy.' She kissed him lightly on the cheek and removed his hand from its interesting position. She felt suddenly overcome with the heat and crush of bodies and had to go outside. It took her several minutes to cut a swathe through the crowd.

Outside, she joined Ethan and Eugene with their gay friends, who were all having a wonderfully raucous time. She felt slightly out of true – like a little girl at a party she hadn't been invited to. But the whisky helped her lose herself and incidentally warmed her. She had stupidly left her cloak in the pub. The thought of fighting her way back inside was not attractive.

Eugene thrust a small silver flask at Laura and she drank the burning spirit. She watched as her gay friends kissed and laughed together. They knew who they were. They had chosen to work together in their own business and live together. It seemed to be working, for them. In spite of their homosexuality – or because of it – they were accepted here, even though they were outsiders. She noticed several of the people she had met at the art classes. A tall, very thin character with a curling moustache who always dressed like Sherlock Holmes hadn't changed his costume tonight. He fitted in very well. He waved his curly pipe at her and smiled.

'How's the painting, Laura? It is Laura, isn't it?'

'Yes, Oliver, how did you recognise me?'

'I've seen you and painted you in the nude, my dear. I'd know those beautiful breasts anywhere.'

'Really?' She had seen his poor efforts at painting. He sat always at the front of class, his eyes glued to the private parts of the model. He had particularly liked looking at the young Rowena. Stan had watched him carefully. But he was a harmless old man – a voyeur, that's all. She suddenly remembered the time at Odile's cottage when she had hidden behind the curtain and had caught the pungent scent of pipe tobacco. Had he also been a voyeur like her? Did Odile offer this service to favoured guests to her private club? She coloured at the thought that this old roué had played with himself while watching her and the young surfer.

'See you later, Oliver. Must go.' She wandered off into the crowded streets, staggering slightly on her high-heeled boots on the cobbles. The wind blustered and whined and the Christmas trees hanging up outside the shops shook their dying needles over the hysterical crowds below. She found herself headed towards Odile's cottage. A pink glow haloed the window. She slipped into the front yard and hesitated before knocking at the door. No one answered. She tried the door handle and the door opened. There was a heavy blanket at the door to keep out the draught. She pushed it to one side and saw the dominatrix in full costume: rubber corset, fishnet stockings, high-heeled rubber thigh-boots, and split-crotched rubber bikini pants. She was standing with one foot on the naked back of her slave – the blond surfer, Rory, who was on all fours. He wore a mask and couldn't see. He had a studded collar around his neck and Odile tugged at a lead attached to his groin area. When Laura had seen the two rubberists at Ethan's party a few days earlier Rory had been wearing a rubber thong that exposed his firm buttocks but hid his genitals. Now he was fully exposed. His elongated penis was pierced at the hood and a gold ring hung from the skin. A fine chain was attached to this ring and the chain was attached to the leather lead that Odile tugged.

His cock twitched appreciatively. The rubber straps around his chest drew attention to his pierced nipples.

Laura's thighs felt warm. Odile put a long-nailed finger to her lips. Laura watched as the blond surfer writhed under the dominatrix's administrations. She flicked at his buttocks with a small whip, and he raised his hips to meet the blow. Laura wanted to join in. She sat close to the boy on the fur rug, and felt the warmth of the fire heat her limbs and face. Odile smiled slightly and indicated to Laura that she should handle the boy's private parts. Laura did so, in a dream, a drunken haze of eroticism. She stroked his smooth cock and touched the hairless balls. He breathed heavily. She suddenly saw the ring that enclosed his cock at the root. It was stopping his orgasm. The dominatrix could taunt and tempt him to come but he could not. He was kept in permanent erection. Laura caressed him tenderly and Odile tugged at his bonds. She tied the lead to a ring on the wall and left Rory helpless.

Odile silently kissed Laura on the lips. Laura's wig was tangled and her facemask pinched her nose.

'Who are you, beautiful woman?' whispered Odile. 'Who sent you to me?'

She surely knew it was Laura, but Laura felt safe in the fantasy that she was disguised and unknown to the dominatrix.

Odile placed her rubber-clad hand on Laura's half-exposed breast and pressed. Her hands explored beneath the strappy top, caressing her hard nipples. The Frenchwoman kissed her hard all the while, and Laura almost swooned. The fire's heat made her languid. She slid to the floor and Odile moved on top of her. The dominatrix was naked above her corset and below it. Her hard little breasts dug into the softness of Laura's. Her firm thighs pressed close and Laura felt her pelvis grind against her. Rubber-encased fingers slipped inside Laura's wetness, the kisses came faster and her tongue invaded Laura's pliant mouth. Laura closed her eyes and gave in to the voluptuousness and the warmth of the other's embraces. She felt her sense of reality slipping away. She was a stranger in a wig and mask. Her body needed sex. Her thighs melted.

When she left she felt cold and only wanted her bed.

It began to rain and she ran along the cobbled street, crying, she knew not why. She passed a man lying in a doorway, drunk.

'Are you all right? You'll freeze,' she said to him. He was dressed as a banana in pyjamas. There was something completely pathetic in the idea of an inebriated banana in pyjamas.

She helped him up and he leant against the door and threw up. 'That's better! I'll go back to the pub now,' he slurred. She abandoned him and went up the hill. Mrs Poldhu's lights were off.

Her erotic costume felt silly in the cosy kitchen. She had wrapped a woollen tartan dressing gown around herself and put the kettle on the hot Rayburn to make a Horlicks drink. Pirate pressed against her boots, purring.

She should go to the restaurant soon. Could she bear any more pretense at being cheerful? Ethan wouldn't miss her. She went upstairs and took off her finery, had a long hot bath and put on warm pyjamas and her dressing gown. The kettle was boiling on the Rayburn and Pirate purred at her. She still felt a little giddy from all the alcohol she had consumed. She went up to the attic and, as she sat down at the window, the church bells began to chime midnight. The end of an eventful year and the beginning of another. Tears ran down her scrubbed face. She felt very alone.

Laura went to her large bed. She clutched a hot-water bottle to her tummy. The cat settled on her feet.

* * *

'Day one of the rest of my life!' she told the black cat, next morning, as she cooked toast on the Rayburn. A large cafetière of strong coffee soon revived her. She dressed in old 505s and two layers of sweatshirts and climbed to her attic studio. The grey light glowed silver on the heaving sea and the gulls chatted to each other in flight. A lone ship rolled in the bay. The wind was fierce and the telegraph wires sang. She began to paint, taking the view from the window as her subject. Her palms bent and sighed in the wind, and the tall bamboos curved and whispered.

She painted for an hour or more and then looked down at the path in disbelief.

She ran down the stairs and tore open the front door.

'Laura!'

'Jerry!'

They fell into each other's arms and found lips with lips, kissed ears and necks and clutched at each other in relief. He picked her up and carried her up the stairs to her bedroom. She was sobbing and laughing. 'How did you find me?'

'It was your editor, Sally. I kept phoning her and begging her to give me your address. She's a tough cookie, sounded like she was your mother. Wanted to know what my intentions were. She gave in to my charm eventually.' He stroked the red slash of a scar on her forehead.

'Oh, Jerry!'

'Laura, I love you and want you to marry me.'

'But you're married already.'

'The divorce is through. Here are the papers. I'm free. Do you want me?'

'Hang on, Jerry. Slow down.'

'Laura, darling.' He was lying over her on her grand-mother's bed. His brown flecked grey-green eyes held hers. He began to remove her sweatshirt. Her breasts emerged like soft peaches. He kissed them reverently, silently. She lay back, her hands up and behind her in submission. He slipped off her suede loafers and kissed the instep of each foot. She shivered. He undid her jeans and slid them over her hips and off her feet. Her thighs tingled at the suspense of his tongue delicately tracing the long bones, the muscles, behind her knees, her muscled calves.

'Oh, Laura, I've missed you so much,' he whispered. He bent his head to her belly and kissed her. She took his head in her paint-spattered hands and pressed his mouth to her belly. He kissed and licked her, quietly, slowly. She was in an agony of desire. Her thighs and belly rose from the bed to meet his caresses. He placed his hands under her buttocks and kneaded the fleshy globes. He pushed his long tarantula-like fingers under the silk. He nuzzled her pubic hair. He snuffled like a dog and licked with a long penetrating tongue. His hands were in her, invading her wetness. She groaned and sighed and lifted his head away, eager to make this last.

'Let me wash the paint off, at least,' she said.

'Why? You smell wonderful, your salty sex with the turps or whatever it is.'

She laughed and gave in.

Many hours later, they were still in bed.

'What's this? Have you taken up fly-fishing?' He pointed at her rubber waders standing in the corner.

'Something like that,' she murmured. 'I'll show you, later. Jerry?'

'Yes?'

'Do you like cats?'

'Yes.'

'Good!'

The sun had set, and the curtains remained drawn back. From the glowing sky a shooting star fell into the sea.

BLACK LACE NEW BOOKS

Published in April

HAUNTED
Laura Thornton
£5.99

A modern-day Gothic story set in both England and New York. Sasha
Hayward is an American woman whose erotic obsession with a long-
dead pair of lovers leads her on a steamy and evocative search. Seeking
out descendants of the enigmatic pair, Sasha consummates her obsession in a series of sexy encounters related to this haunting mystery.

ISBN 0 352 33341 3

STAND AND DELIVER
Helena Ravenscroft
£5.99

In 18th century England, Lydia Fitzgerald finds herself helplessly
drawn to Drummond, a handsome highwayman. This occurs despite
the fact that she is the ward of his brother, Valerian, who controls the
Hawkesworth estate. There, Valerian and his beautiful mistress initiate
Lydia's seduction and, although she is in love with Drummond, Lydia
is unable to resist the experimentation they offer.

ISBN 0 352 33340 5

Published in May

INSOMNIA
Zoe le Verdier
£5.99

A wide range of sexual experience is explored in this collection of
short stories by one of the best-liked authors in the series. Zoe le
Verdier's work is an ideal reflection of the fresh, upbeat stories now
being published under the Black Lace imprint. Many popular female
fantasies are covered, from sex with a stranger and talking dirty, to
secret fetishes, lost virginity and love. There's something for everyone.

ISBN: 0 352 33345 6

VILLAGE OF SECRETS
Mercedes Kelly
£5.99

Every small town has something to hide, and this rural Cornish village is no exception. Its twee exterior hides some shocking scandals and nothing is quite what it seems. Laura, a London journalist, becomes embroiled with the locals – one of whom might be her long-lost brother – when she inherits property in the village. Against a backdrop of curious goings-on, she learns to indulge her taste for kinky sex and rubber fetishism.

IBSN: 0 352 33344 8

Special announcement!
THE BLACK LACE BOOK OF WOMEN'S SEXUAL FANTASIES
Edited and Compiled by Kerri Sharp
£5.99

At last, Black Lace brings you the definitive Book of Women's Sexual Fantasies. This special collection has taken over one and a half years of in-depth research to put together, and has been compiled through correspondence with women from all over the English-speaking world. The result is an astounding anthology of detailed sexual fantasies, including shocking and at times bizarre revelations.

ISBN 0 352 33346 4

To be published in June

PACKING HEAT
Karina Moore
£5.99

When Californian Nadine has her allowance stopped by her rich uncle, she becomes desperate to maintain her expensive lifestyle. She joins forces with her lover, Mark, and together they steal a vast sum of money from a flashy businessman. But the sexual stakes rise when Nadine and Mark try to put the blame on someone they shouldn't. Their getaway doesn't go entirely to plan, and they're pursued across the desert and into the casinos of Las Vegas. Full of sexual intrigue, this action-packed erotic novel is reminiscent of a *film noir*.

ISBN 0 352 33356 1

TAKING LIBERTIES
Susie Raymond
£5.99

When attractive thirty-something Beth Bradley takes a job as PA to the arrogant Simon Henderson, she is well aware of his reputation as a philanderer. She is determined to turn the tables on his fortune through erotic manipulation. But she keeps getting side-tracked by her libido, and craving sex with the dominant man she wants to teach a lesson.

ISBN 0 352 33357 X

If you would like a complete list of plot summaries of Black Lace titles, or would like to receive information on other publications available, please send a stamped addressed envelope to:

Black Lace, Thames Wharf Studios,
Rainville Road, London W6 9HT

BLACK LACE BOOKLIST

All books are priced £4.99 unless another price is given.

Black Lace books with a contemporary setting

ODALISQUE	Fleur Reynolds ISBN 0 352 32887 8	☐
WICKED WORK	Pamela Kyle ISBN 0 352 32958 0	☐
UNFINISHED BUSINESS	Sarah Hope-Walker ISBN 0 352 32983 1	☐
HEALING PASSION	Sylvie Ouellette ISBN 0 352 32998 X	☐
PALAZZO	Jan Smith ISBN 0 352 33156 9	☐
THE GALLERY	Fredrica Alleyn ISBN 0 352 33148 8	☐
AVENGING ANGELS	Roxanne Carr ISBN 0 352 33147 X	☐
COUNTRY MATTERS	Tesni Morgan ISBN 0 352 33174 7	☐
GINGER ROOT	Robyn Russell ISBN 0 352 33152 6	☐
DANGEROUS CONSEQUENCES	Pamela Rochford ISBN 0 352 33185 2	☐
THE NAME OF AN ANGEL £6.99	Laura Thornton ISBN 0 352 33205 0	☐
SILENT SEDUCTION	Tanya Bishop ISBN 0 352 33193 3	☐
BONDED	Fleur Reynolds ISBN 0 352 33192 5	☐
THE STRANGER	Portia Da Costa ISBN 0 352 33211 5	☐
CONTEST OF WILLS £5.99	Louisa Francis ISBN 0 352 33223 9	☐
BY ANY MEANS £5.99	Cheryl Mildenhall ISBN 0 352 33221 2	☐
MÉNAGE £5.99	Emma Holly ISBN 0 352 33231 X	☐

THE SUCCUBUS £5.99	Zoe le Verdier ISBN 0 352 33230 1	☐
FEMININE WILES £7.99	Karina Moore ISBN 0 352 33235 2	☐
AN ACT OF LOVE £5.99	Ella Broussard ISBN 0 352 33240 9	☐
THE SEVEN-YEAR LIST £5.99	Zoe le Verdier ISBN 0 352 33254 9	☐
MASQUE OF PASSION £5.99	Tesni Morgan ISBN 0 352 33259 X	☐
DRAWN TOGETHER £5.99	Robyn Russell ISBN 0 352 33269 7	☐
DRAMATIC AFFAIRS £5.99	Fredrica Alleyn ISBN 0 352 33289 1	☐
RISKY BUSINESS £5.99	Lisette Allen ISBN 0 352 33280 8	☐
DARK OBSESSION £7.99	Fredrica Alleyn ISBN 0 352 33281 6	☐
SEARCHING FOR VENUS £5.99	Ella Broussard ISBN 0 352 33284 0	☐
UNDERCOVER SECRETS £5.99	Zoe le Verdier ISBN 0 352 33285 9	☐
FORBIDDEN FRUIT £5.99	Susie Raymond ISBN 0 352 33306 5	☐
A PRIVATE VIEW £5.99	Crystalle Valentino ISBN 0 352 33308 1	☐
A SECRET PLACE £5.99	Ella Broussard ISBN 0 352 33307 3	☐
THE TRANSFORMATION £5.99	Natasha Rostova ISBN 0 352 33311 1	☐
SHADOWPLAY £5.99	Portia Da Costa ISBN 0 352 33313 8	☐
MIXED DOUBLES £5.99	Zoe le Verdier ISBN 0 352 33312 X	☐

Black Lace books with an historical setting

THE SENSES BEJEWELLED	Cleo Cordell ISBN 0 352 32904 1	☐
HANDMAIDEN OF PALMYRA	Fleur Reynolds ISBN 0 352 32919 X	☐
JULIET RISING	Cleo Cordell ISBN 0 352 32938 6	☐
THE INTIMATE EYE	Georgia Angelis ISBN 0 352 33004 X	☐
CONQUERED	Fleur Reynolds ISBN 0 352 33025 2	☐

Black Lace anthologies

PAST PASSIONS £6.99	ISBN 0 352 33159 3	☐
PANDORA'S BOX 2 £4.99	ISBN 0 352 33151 8	☐
PANDORA'S BOX 3 £5.99	ISBN 0 352 33274 3	☐
SUGAR AND SPICE £7.99	ISBN 0 352 33227 1	☐
SUGAR AND SPICE 2 £6.99	ISBN 0 352 33309 X	☐

Black Lace non-fiction

WOMEN, SEX AND ASTROLOGY £5.99	Sarah Bartlett ISBN 0 352 33262 X	☐

------------✂------------------------

Please send me the books I have ticked above.

Name ....

Address ....

....

....

.... Post Code ....

Send to: Cash Sales, Black Lace Books, Thames Wharf Studios, Rainville Road, London W6 9HT.

US customers: for prices and details of how to order books for delivery by mail, call 1-800-805-1083.

Please enclose a cheque or postal order, made payable to **Virgin Publishing Ltd**, to the value of the books you have ordered plus postage and packing costs as follows:

UK and BFPO – £1.00 for the first book, 50p for each subsequent book.

Overseas (including Republic of Ireland) – £2.00 for the first book, £1.00 for each subsequent book.

If you would prefer to pay by VISA or ACCESS/MASTERCARD, please write your card number and expiry date here:

....

Please allow up to 28 days for delivery.

Signature ....

------------✂------------------------